ULRIK

By Wendy L. Anderson

ISBN Paperback: 978-1-64456-252-9
ISBN Mobi: 978-1-64456-253-6
ISBN ePub: 978-1-64456-254-3

Library of Congress Control Number: 2021930482

Indies United Publishing House, LLC
P.O. Box 3071
Quincy, Illinois 62305-3071
www.indiesunited.net

This book is dedicated to Eric, my best friend, my love, my everything.

Table of Contents

Prologue – Before

It was her 85th birthday, or rather the end of her 85th birthday. Sitting at her small vanity table she looked at her wrinkled face in the dusty mirror and contemplated the events of the long day. There had been a dry, yellow cake, plastered with too sweet, yellow icing made with lard and an abundance of powdered sugar. To drink was overly sweet lemonade made artificially sour-tasting because of the icing.

How she hated yellow cake, she thought, *"yellow cake and yellow frosting."* Lemonade gave her a stomachache. At least her nephew had made the effort to come to the home and visit her on this momentous occasion.

She looked at the bright yellow sweater he had given her. It lay halfway folded and sticking out of the white tissue paper like a large canary that had collapsed dead in the gift box. It was a sad reminder of her age and how little she seemed to matter. She recalled how she had fussed happily over the thing. Truly, she hated the color yellow. How little her family actually knew about her.

Flashes of memory clicked by in her mind, like an old ticking movie reel of how she had been forced to take yellow medicine when she was very young. The taste was so horrible she would throw it up, but her mother would force her to take it again and again until she kept it down. She could not even recall what she had to take the medicine for, but the association with the horrid taste had formed a severe dislike of the color yellow for the rest of her life. Looking at the sweater she just shook her head and wondered what she would do with it.

"Oh well," she sighed and tried to smile.

"It was nice of him to remember me." She repeated the phrase over and over in her mind, trying to quell the grumpiness that swamped her.

She reached up and undid the hair clip from the back of her head and placed it on her vanity table. Thin tendrils of white hair fell to her shoulders. As was her habit, she reached for her brush and smoothed the wisps around her head slowly down one side and then the other. The only noise in the room was the soft swish of the brush pulling through the thin strands. Putting the brush back in its proper place, she stared into the vanity mirror.

"Eighty-five!" she lamented to herself once again. "Dear God, how had the time flown by so quickly?"

She smoothed her age-spotted hands over her wrinkled face, her bloodshot eyes welled with tears as her mind reverberated with clichés of old age.

"Oh my! Time has not been good to you." "You look older than dirt!" "Your face has more lines on it than a road map."

On and on old age sayings echoed unbidden through her mind.

Other recollections of her past continued to flit through her thoughts, memories of her long, uneventful, and lonely life. She never married, nor had children of her own. She had been through numerous careers, but she had not stuck with any one thing, and she had not accomplished much during her time on Earth. Life had been one long, lonely, dreary event of work and the struggle to make a living. Regardless, she had made enough money to retire to the assisted living home where she now resided. She would have enough left to leave a small sum to her nephew when she finally went to meet her Maker.

"I never made it to Ireland." She lamented, suddenly remembering, and then, "No children of my own."

She turned and stared back at the box with the yellow sweater partially hiding in the tissue paper as it rested on the single chair in her room an unwanted visitor.

"At least my nephew remembered my birthday."

Another realization suddenly hit her.

"Oh, my good Lord, I'm wallowing in self-pity!" She tried to smile again. "Well, enough of that!" she reprimanded herself.

Slowly she stood and shuffled haltingly. Bent body aching and shooting with pain, she eventually reached the head of her single bed in the small room. She rubbed at some tingling in her left arm and scoffed at old age aches and irritations. Removing her pink synthetic satin robe, she carefully folded it and placed it over the chair where the box with the yellow sweater lay. She shuffled back a couple of steps, slipped out of her worn, matted, fuzzy pink slippers, and eased down into the bed. The plastic mattress cover, which was a requirement of the cleaning crew at the assisted living home, crinkled loudly under the sheets and she made a scowling face at the ceiling. Drawing her legs beneath the covers, she settled in.

As was her nightly ritual, she pulled the sheet up over her face, then reached for the thin blanket over the sheet pulling it up, then reached for the quilt and pulled it up. Grasping the edges of the three together, she neatly folded the covers down over her chest and straightened the two sides. She never could sleep without organized covers.

Letting out another deep sigh, intending to invite sleep to come, she fixed a smile on her lips. If she died in her sleep, she did not want the Lord to see her coming with a frown on her face. The coldness of the room crept into her bones, she tried to take a deep breath, and smelled the antiseptic and mothballs scent of the home. She folded her hands and said her nightly prayers.

Bone aching weariness descended, and she fell asleep. Dreaming, her entire life flashed before her closed eyes in the moments before falling into a deeper slumber. It flitted by in surreal solemnity. A subconscious record paraded her uneventful life before her dreaming eyes and reflected how fiercely unsatisfied she was on this, her 85th birthday. All the things she had not done and had not accomplished in her lifetime ached like a sore tooth. A last feverish thought burned through her mind and heart, and an aching wish consumed her entire mind, body, and soul.

"How I wish I had a second chance!" The words echoed in her subconscious. With her next breath, a wrenching pain stabbed through her chest. She gasped, eyes flying wide open, and her sight went dark. Then with a few last painful breaths released slowly and shakily, she breathed no more.

Chapter One – Ulrik

Ulrik sat on the bank of a cool stream that ran down the mountain where he usually hunted. He watched as the water trickled over smooth rocks and sprayed the moss-lined bank. Down the mountainside, the stream narrowed and was eventually joined by another river, widening to become a rushing, roaring froth of cold, crystal blue water flowing swiftly over rapids. His gaze followed the stream as it meandered off into the distance and gently widened into a deep slow-moving river. He listened to the different sounds the water made. The roar, as it cascaded down the waterfall further uphill, to the trickle of the stream over moss-covered rocks, and finally the faint pounding of distant rapids. The forest was raucous with sound and full of breath-taking sights.

The forest's majesty was lost on him today. Ulrik was bored. He reached for a stone and tossed it into the stream then stood, grabbed his spear, and walked up the hill toward the lake at the bottom of the waterfall. He decided he had better find something for his supper and thought fish sounded as good as anything else.

Memories swamped him as he recalled all the times he had fished with his brothers as a young man. Those thoughts led him to contemplate, for the hundred thousandth time, his current solitary situation. By his count, it had been around two years that he lived alone in these mountains in this strange place. Being banished by the Gods he knew, enraged him and his loneliness made him feel like less of a man. Two years without speaking to another soul or without seeing another human's face made him angry. He cursed, kicking at a stone in his path. The stone shot forward, struck a tree, and fell uselessly to the ground.

"By Odin and all the gods! I wish I had a woman!"

He cursed out loud and continued stomping up the path until he came to his usual fishing spot at the lakeside. He hefted his spear and waded into the lake, not even bothering to remove his boots.

The warm spring wind blew across his face. As he had a hundred times before, Ulrik stood still, slowed his breathing, and searched the deep emerald depths for the flicker of a silvery tail. Quick as lightning he stabbed down and, wrenching his arm back, pulled an impaled fish out of the water. He grasped the wriggling tail, pulled it from the spear blade, and threw it to the bank of the lake where it flopped, struggling to breathe as its life leached away.

Turning back, Ulrik resumed his fishing. He waited and watched, as still as a held breath. Just as he began to despair that he would only have one fish for dinner, a ripple caught his eye further out on the lake's watery surface. The water pushed up from underneath and began to froth and bubble until something large slowly arose from the depths of the lake. Ulrik froze poised to strike. His eyes grew wide with wonder and curiosity slowly creased his forehead and narrowed his eyes as he stared at what was heaving up from the depths of the lake. A huge bubble surrounding something within gave a pop and sprayed water upwards which swiftly rained back down. Abruptly, Ulrik flung his spear to the bank and dove out into the lake waters. A few strong strokes brought him to the middle. Stopping and treading water, he stared with his mouth open at what he found drifting on the water's surface before him.

A beautiful, sleeping maiden floated on top of the water. Long, golden blonde hair swirled about her head, and a flowing gown the color of a pink flower billowed out from her slim figure. She appeared to be sound asleep.

Ulrik reached out and gently grasped one of her small hands folded over her breast. At his touch, her eyes flew open and she gasped, breathing in water as she came fully awake and began to sink. Suddenly, she was flailing and kicking, coughing up water only to gulp more into her mouth in her panic. She looked around wildly, and then she slipped beneath, sinking into the deep water.

Ulrik lunged forward and grasped the girl as she went down. She continued to struggle and cough, gulping air as he pulled her up to the surface. Reaching around her slim body, he held her head out of the water where she continued to sputter and spit trying to fill her lungs with air. Then, with one arm, he towed her to the safety of the lake edge, fear taking hold of his heart as her movements slowed and stilled. As he neared the shore, he picked her up, one arm under her legs and the other behind her back, cradling her against his chest. Her head fell against his shoulder as his heart pounded with excitement over discovering her and he fretted about how cold she felt.

Even as Ulrik carried the lake maiden to dry land, his brain reeled with superstition and tales of watery spirits who snatched young men from the safety of the shore, only to drag them down into the depths and a watery grave with a deadly kiss. He also felt a momentary shock that the gods had heard and answered his prayers for a woman, but he quickly tossed that thought aside. The gods were responsible for stranding him here alone and his prayers fell on their deaf ears.

Ulrik gently lowered the girl to the grass, but kept an arm around her, holding her close so that the heat of his body could at least begin to warm her. The girl coughed a few more times and turned to the side to spit up lake water. She struggled to try and sit up on her own, only to fall back into Ulrik's arms, too weak to rise. Stormy blue eyes briefly met his before she swooned. Ulrik smoothed the wet hair from the girl's face. She had small delicate features, almost fairy-like, her wet hair was long, her body small and gently curved. Even if this was a water spirit, she was the most beautiful thing Ulrik had ever seen.

#

She awoke and stared at the ceiling which was lost in heavy shadows. *"Strange,"* she thought, *"it must still be nighttime."* Her brow furrowed questioningly as she wondered why the formerly eggshell-colored ceiling, was now deep gray and made of what appeared to be heavy logs. Puzzled, she looked around the room and thought, *"They must have moved me during the night for some reason."* Casting her eyes down to where she lay, she found herself in a large bed, buried in miss-matched blankets and quilts, some of which smelled dusty and old, something else smelled like, *pine and wood smoke?*

She tried to raise herself onto her elbow and felt the familiar weakness of her frail body. Her hair, she realized, was damp and heavy, and her surroundings were completely strange. She tried to struggle into a sitting position pushing and unwrapping herself from the numerous blankets heaped upon her, but she ended up laying back, too weak to rise. The room was dark, but for a real fire that burned brightly in an unfamiliar fireplace across the room. A lone fish sizzled on a stick over the fire. She shook her head at the complete strangeness of it all. Her vision was slightly blurred, in and out of clarity, and she squinted at her surroundings.

As she tried to shake the cobwebs from her memory, she recalled a dream of a summer day, of drowning in a lake and being pulled out by a tall blonde man.

"More like a boy," she thought.

She recalled his deep, ice-blue eyes and the look of astonishment and concern as he carried her by the lakeside. Smiling she tucked the dream away in her memory and thought what a good story it would make to tell her old friend Gladys at the breakfast table in the morning. It had seemed so real.

A noise caused her to look over as the roughhewn door of the room opened and the same tall blonde boy, from the lake, walked in. His massive arms were laden with logs, obviously intended for the fire. Being as quiet as he could he squatted down and neatly stacked the wood by the fireside. Then he looked toward her, and his eyes lit up. She was awake and watching him. A slow smile spread across his devastatingly handsome face.

He rose slowly and walked toward her. She pushed back into the pillow, tipping her head to one side, and thinking how odd it was that he was dressed in suede boots and what appeared to be rough homespun britches. He had broad shoulders, a bare muscular chest, and powerful thighs. Two large, intricately carved, silver armbands on each bulging biceps glittered in the faint firelight. She simply stared at him as he slowly came toward her and stopped by the bedside. Then incredulity, exhaustion, and shock took hold of her again and she could no longer keep her eyes open. Her last fleeting thought was to chastise herself for being a dirty old lady dreaming about such a young and attractive boy.

Ulrik frowned, disappointed that the woman had swooned again. He pulled the blankets up to her chin and tucked them tightly around her tiny body. He had no idea what else to do for her. He stood staring at her sleeping face for a long moment then turned and went to check his dinner cooking on the fire. After he ate, he fell asleep in a chair while watching the sleeping woman from across the room.

Chapter Two – Second Chance

The sound of singing birds woke her. She blinked and stared at the gray wood ceiling and recalled her dream from the night before. Judging by the light coming through the window across the room, it was morning. She tried to stretch, but the blankets were tucked so tightly around her again that she could barely move. She took a deep satisfying breath and was surprised not to have to suck hard and cough to fill her lungs.

"*Hmmm, no rattle,*" she marveled inwardly as she exhaled.

She filled her lungs again with cool, fresh air that smelled of real pine and wood smoke, with no antiseptic and mothball scent. Rolling a little to the side she pulled her arms free and stretched. No pain. No aches. Again, she wondered at how good she felt. She could breathe freely, there were no stabbing pains in her chest, no catching of joints, and no arthritic aches through her hands and back. She took a mental tally of her body and realized she felt better than she had in many, many years. She felt *young again* and she smiled in astonishment.

As she struggled to sit up, she chided herself for being an old fool. Eighty-five, she remembered. Yesterday had been her eighty-fifth birthday. She untangled a little more from the blankets and swung her legs over the side of the large bed and stared at her new surroundings.

"*Where am I?*" she was completely baffled.

She found herself in what appeared to be some sort of cabin, but it was unlike any place she had ever seen before. It was shadowy inside there, but she could still see the walls were old, mismatched as if each of them had been removed from several different houses and stuck together in a rough hexagon shape. There was a small table, two chairs, a sink with an old-fashioned pump handle, and an old cast iron stove like she had seen in the movies. The fireplace that she had noticed from the night before smoldered with a few dying coals. The wall behind her was covered with yellowing wallpaper decorated with tiny purple Forget Me Nots. Nothing in the cabin seemed to fit together, neither the aged look of the walls nor the décor which appeared to be an eclectic blend of many different styles. At the end of the bed was an ancient cherry wood screen that, as far as she could tell from this angle, had oriental dragons carved in the wooden sides and painted on the screens. What was behind that, she could not guess. She could see the top of an old trunk just at the foot of the bed. She looked around for her pink robe but could not find it. Looking down she realized her nightgown was damp, wrinkled, and dirty.

Feeling a moment of panic, she quickly deduced that the assisted living home had moved her to an old, dilapidated hovel where they intended to let her die alone. She briefly thought about her nephew and wondered if he knew they had moved her and to where. Holding back panic and fear, she closed her eyes and shook those thoughts away. There was nothing she could do about it now but accept that she had been thrown away.

Standing a little wobbly, she was surprised to find her body felt different, without the familiar pinpricks in her feet and running up her legs. Shocked, she stood straight and did not hunch the least bit. She realized she felt too good to be eighty-five years old. Then the truth hit her, and she spoke out loud to the empty room.

"Oh, dear Lord! I'm dead! No pain! Feeling so good I could dance. I must be *dead*." She whispered out loud.

Swallowing hard she plopped back down on the bed shocked, and let the realization sink in for a few long minutes. Through the gloom of the cabin, she stared down at her young smooth hands and lifted her nightgown to look at youthful feet. At least they had not buried her or worse, put her in that yellow sweater.

Just then, the tall blonde boy came in the door.

"You're awake then," he said in a deep, gentle placating voice with a heavy accent.

She looked at him with wide eyes and an open mouth. He had to be well over six feet in height. She suddenly recalled the tan muscular arms that carried her and now noticed his long, shoulder-length, golden blonde hair. He was bare-chested, wearing the same suede boots she noticed earlier, and she now saw they were laced up with leather straps. Long, muscular legs were outlined by the same homespun britches she had also noticed the night before. He carried a spear and strapped around his narrow waist was a sword. Her eyes continued upward to his bare, sun-browned chest where a silver amulet hung on a thick chain. He also had two silver armbands on each of his biceps and *tattoos* she had not noticed before. The light from the open door highlighted a few days' growth on his chin, a sparse white-blonde mustache over full lips, and a strong, handsome face from which two piercingly ice-blue eyes stared back at her.

"Young man, can you tell me where I am? Am I dead? Is this Heaven?" She was startled at the sound of her voice, which was not the raspy croak it was yesterday but was almost sweet and musical today. Her eyes teared up realizing the truth, she must be dead.

He stared at her with a look that said he was afraid she was not right in the head.

"Young man, it's quite rude to stare and not to speak when spoken to. It's a simple question. Where am I?"

The man took a step forward and grabbed a chair, pulling it a few steps closer, he turned the chair backward toward her and straddled it, casually resting his arms across the back.

"Why do you call me, '*young man?*' I have more than twenty winters behind me, and I am willing to wager my sword, I am older than you."

She gave a little frightened laugh and said, "Well, you'd lose your sword then, I'm much, much, older than you, dear boy. Now can you please tell me where I am? Am I still at the home or have I been moved or am...am...I dead?"

The girl's face turned pale, and she looked at him as if she feared his answer. Ulrik was overjoyed at the sound of another human's voice but was not sure of everything she said.

"No, you are not dead! That is for sure, my Lady! And we will argue over who is older later. Are you hungry? Would you like to break your fast?"

"Break my what?" She gave him a puzzled look and hesitated because he had not answered her question. "Never mind. I think I understand what you mean. Yes, I am hungry. As a matter of fact, I'm quite famished."

Odd she was amazed, *"I have not felt truly hungry in what seems like years."*

"Could you please call room service and request one egg cooked over medium and some toast with butter, please? Oh, and some coffee would be lovely, with one sugar and two creams."

The young man gave his blonde head a slow shake and stared at her.

"I know not of what you speak, but if you will dress, I will get us some food."

"I, I don't seem to have any clothes." She clutched the lacy collar of her nightgown closed, suddenly aware that she was talking to a stranger while dressed so skimpily. The length of the gown hid her body and her legs, and the long sleeves covered her arms, but she still felt too revealed to his bright icy blue gaze. Fear clenched at her throat again and she could not speak anymore.

He rose to his feet, towering above her, and gestured toward the end of the bed.

"In that chest, you will find clothes. I think you can find something in there to wear. I will wait outside while you dress."

Swallowing, he stared at her for a moment, then turned and went out the front door, quietly closing it behind him, to give her some privacy.

After many minutes spent staring bewildered at the door, she gathered her nerves, stood, and walked to the chest he pointed out. Bending over she grasped the lid. Her surprise at not having any back pain was surpassed by how she easily could lift the heavy wooden lid of the chest. Inside were numerous lady's things. It looked as if this was a collection of costumes from a theater because all the items in the trunk were of ancient styles. She dug around until she found something simple and suitable, a white underdress of soft, thin cotton fabric. She had read enough romance novels to recognize it as a long chemise. She bypassed the stiff corsets and found a simple green bodice she would need to cover the thin material of the chemise and chose a deep blue skirt next. She could not find any panties or a bra but found thick stockings and soft dark brown boots at the bottom. The boots should fit well enough with the thick socks. Marveling for a full minute at the novelty of wearing such a costume, she smiled a little amused at the strangeness of what she was doing. Closing the lid, she placed the items on top and then turned to pull the oriental screen closed to conceal her from the door. Behind the screen, she found an ancient, full-length mirror that hung on a hinged stand. It was thick with dust but was reflective enough. She unbuttoned the top of her nightgown and pulled it over her head, folded it neatly, and placed it behind her on the end of the bed. Then she turned back, looked at her reflection in the mirror, and screamed.

Chapter Three – Tessa's Story

Ulrik impatiently waited outside while the woman dressed. A hard, sour feeling roiled in his belly as he feared that the only person he had seen in over two years, was not right in the head. Perhaps it had to do something with the lake and nearly drowning? She spoke very strangely. Maybe she cracked her head? He had not seen any bruises or bumps. She kept calling him *'young man'* and that made him feel very uneasy. His frown deepened as he looked down at the ground, he was not used to being nervous or unsure.

He paced, frowned more, and waited, not knowing if she would come out, or should he go in? He could knock and see if she was done dressing. How long could it take to throw some clothes on? He could look in the window and sneak a peek while she dressed, but no, no, no that would not be honorable he knew, although his loins stirred at the thought. He continued to pace outside, reminding himself he was an honorable man, and not knowing what to do with his hands. Then he heard her scream.

Protective instincts flaring, Ulrik ran and burst through the door. He did not see her at first but heard her breathing hard behind the dragon painted screen. He roughly pulled it aside and stared wide-eyed at the vision in front of him.

The girl stood completely naked. Her hands covered her mouth, eyes wide, while she breathed rapidly and stared at her reflection.

"By Odin! What is the matter?" His heart was pounding, and he flushed red.

"Look at me!" She whispered shakily while her eyes remained transfixed on the mirror in front of her.

Taking her hands from her mouth, she held her arms wide and then ran her hands down her smooth, flat stomach and then down across her hips. She felt the smooth, firm skin of her thighs and then they flew to her perky, firm breasts. In a daze, she could not believe what she was seeing. Just yesterday her breasts had sagged, two deflated sacks of flesh, and her entire body was mottled with age spots and hanging, dry, wrinkled skin. Now she looked at her face which was smooth and unwrinkled, alabaster white, clear of blotches, firm, free from the ravished signs of age. Her bright eyes twinkled with fascination as she gazed upon her young, shapely form.

Ulrik stared too. He could not look away from the beautiful young girl that stood completely naked in front of him. The *first woman* he had seen in over two long years. He took in the curve of her hips, smooth shapely backside, and then his gaze traveled to her reflection in the mirror landing on her firm breasts. His hands itched to reach out and touch, and he had to stop himself from stepping forward and taking her in his arms. His shaft immediately hardened painfully while he stared mesmerized by the seductive beauty of her.

Suddenly, she realized he was standing there staring. She squeaked loudly as she spun and grabbed up her nightgown off the end of the bed, covering herself. Her face burned red with embarrassment.

"Oh my! Get out!" She yelled. Ulrik reluctantly backed away, eyes wide, and then he bolted back out the door, breathing hard.

She dressed quickly while emotions whirled through her. While she could not believe she was young again, she could not deny how good she looked and felt. Shock filled her mind realizing, she could not feel this good and be dead, and then she realized she could not feel this good and be alive either. She pinched herself and felt the small prick of pain, she breathed in and out and felt the air in her lungs. She moved her arms and legs and jumped up and down watching her breasts bounce. Giggling a little, she decidedly was still amongst the living and appeared to be as healthy as she had been when she was about twenty years old. She was herself she realized, looking back at a young face that she had not seen in over sixty-five years. She looked exactly like she did at age twenty, slim, bright blue eyes, with long thick, blonde hair cascading to her waist. Only now she was *better*. Her face was smooth, and her lips were full, soft, and pink. She giggled into her hands and did another little dance. She decided, she liked Heaven very much, for that is where she *undoubtedly* had to be.

#

Ulrik paced outside the cabin once again reminding himself, over and over, that he was an honorable man. The sight of the naked girl was burned on his mind. Her beautiful face, smooth skin, and silky golden hair called to him. Those full red lips begged to be kissed and those curves beckoned to his hands for caressing. Ulrik shook his head vigorously and contemplated going to the lake and diving in, to cool the hot lust that burned through his body. It had been far too many years since he had lain with a woman. He was heavy and aching grumbling at the unfairness of it all. Finally, the gods had given him a woman, but he could not touch her, or he would scare her.

Just as he took a step in the direction of the lake to go and do so, the door of the cabin slowly creaked open behind him. The girl shyly stepped out into the sunshine and blinked as her eyes adjusted to the brightness of the day. She closed her eyes and held her face to the sun feeling the warmth on her cheeks. Then she opened her eyes and looked around with wonder and happy astonishment.

The outside of the cabin was more ordinary than the inside. It had shutters framing thick glass windows, and the door was battered, and weather-worn. Red roses climbed the walls in thick profusion. Deep purple lilac bushes bloomed next to thick clumps of irises that waved their delicate blooms in the gentle breeze. She marveled at all the different colors and types of flowers proliferating everywhere. Then her gaze fell on Ulrik who stood staring, mouth agape.

To him, she was a vision of beauty in a green bodice laced up the front and a blue flowing skirt. The white blouse peeked out from under her bodice with its puffy sleeves covering her arms to the elbows. Long blonde hair flowed freely around her shoulders and fell to her waist in a riot of golden waves. Blushing, she self-consciously pulled the locks forward over one shoulder and took a step further out of the door. She shook slightly as if she were afraid.

"Um, forgive me, I didn't mean to yell at you in there, I was just so shocked at…at…what I saw. I'm afraid, well, I don't know what I'm doing right now or where I am. I'm quite out of sorts." She smiled cautiously, "you mentioned you have food? I am starving!"

Food, yes, food was good and would offer Ulrik a needed distraction. Giving one tight nod of his head, Ulrik dodged around her and ducked into the house and a few moments later came out with a basket and a blanket. He walked over to a giant tree, placed the basket down, spread the blanket out in the shade under the tree, and beckoned to the girl.

She sat down reluctantly, arranged her skirt, and gave the basket a covert and hungry inspection. Ulrik reached in and brought out some apples and dried meat, two hard brown eggs, strawberries, and a skin of water to drink.

They ate in silence, not knowing what to say to each other. Every time she reached out to take something to eat, she would stop and stare in wonder at her hands. No age spots, no bent, gnarled, arthritic fingers, no broken, yellowed nails marred her slim fingers.

Ulrik did not notice the food but sat looking at the girl. He did not want to stare rudely but it was hard not to. She seemed to be trying to avoid looking at him but darted occasional looks from the corner of her eyes while eating hungrily. He kept thinking she was addlebrained and fumed at the unfairness of it all. She kept mumbling softly about being in 'Heaven' trying to convince herself of something he could not understand.

"What is your name?" Ulrik suddenly blurted out startling the girl.

It had been two long years since he had spoken to anyone and he cursed himself for acting like a smitten fool that he was having trouble even speaking to this girl. Ulrik never had any trouble with females before, not that there was a lot to *talk* about with females. He continuously reminded himself that it had been a long time since he had even seen another human being. Perhaps he had lost the ability to converse politely he inwardly mused.

"My name? Oh yes, my name. I am, was, am, excuse me, I am Tessa Danielle Vandallen and you are?"

Ulrik stretched his long legs out, crossed them at the ankles, and leaned down on one elbow, feigning a nonchalance he did not feel.

"I am Ulrik. My father was Ivar Wolfgarsson. I am a Norseman." He took a large bite of an apple and chewed, looking intently at her waiting for her reaction to his grand introduction.

"Ulrik, that's a very nice name. It is a pleasure to meet you."

Tessa looked down and folded her hands in her lap wondering if it was rude not to shake hands, but she was afraid to touch him. Well, not afraid but maybe intensely shy. Then, turning her hands this way and that, she admired her young hands and arms again. Inwardly she squirmed, she had never been very good at talking to men in her younger days, and long, drawn-out silences made her anxious. She squelched the urge to babble which was only made slightly easier by the strange predicament she now found herself in.

"Ulrik," she repeated and smiled brightly at him. Her blue eyes sparkled as she held his gaze.

Senses tingling from the sound of her sweet voice, Ulrik decided he liked the way she said his name. When she smiled it was like the sun peeking out from behind the clouds. It had been a long time since anyone had spoken his name.

"Tessa Dani..." he faltered and then said, "You have a very long name, what does it mean? I have never heard such a name. Where did you come from?"

"Please, just call me Tessa." She smiled another brilliant smile at him, but still felt awkward. "I am originally from a place called Oregon, but maybe you have never heard of it before? Where are you from?"

Pausing, he shrugged. "I am a Norseman," he said again as the extent of the response he was willing to give. He continued to stare, frowned, and then said in a deep husky voice. "From the north, Tessa of Oreeeegon."

Tessa giggled and shook her head.

"So, you're a Viking I gather by your clothing and the sword and your accent," she hesitated then her eyes widened. The smile fell from her face. "Oh no! Do you, um, rape, pillage, and plunder?"

Suddenly, realizing what she just said, she scrambled backward away from him.

"Oh, my Lord! You're not going to sell me into slavery or rape me, are you?"

She looked around trying to decide where she could escape to. Also, she suddenly wondered where the other people were.

Ulrik scowled and narrowed his eyes at her. He thumped his chest with his fist and said loudly, "I am a man of honor! I would never take a woman against her will. Well, *almost* never. Not anymore!" He puffed out his chest, "I do not have to take women by force! They come to me, begging for my caresses. By Odin!"

Ulrik did his best to look offended when in reality he was trying to hold back a grin at the thought of taking her. He considered once again that it had been so very long since he had lain with a woman, pushing his advances on her was not such a bad idea. He quickly shook these thoughts from his mind as unworthy and dishonorable. Inwardly, Ulrik knew he had to move slowly with this girl, the first he had seen in such a long, long time and she was so beautiful, he could have wept.

Tessa shook her head and closed her eyes in confusion. Here was a Norseman from Lord only knew what century, she was a twenty-first-century woman, and they were here, together somehow. Mentally, she gathered herself and taking a deep breath, calmed her nerves, and the trembling that had seized her. Tessa smoothed her skirts nervously and tried to make sense of it all.

"I'm sorry. If you were going to hurt me, I imagine you'd have done so by now. Forget I said anything. Can we start over?" She smiled trying to catch his eye. "Now, can you tell me where I am? Are there other people here? Is this Heaven?"

"No, I cannot tell you because I do not know where we are."

"You don't know?" She said incredulously. "Do you know how I got here?"

"You came from the Sacred Lake. I came here the same way, but that is a story for another time."

He spoke quietly and looked into her eyes for a long moment.

"I have been cursed by the Gods and they have banished me here alone. Until you came."

"Oh," Tessa spoke quietly but did not know what else to say. He looked so forlorn she felt sorry for him.

They finished the rest of their meal in silence each pondering their circumstances. Tessa waited for the old familiar stomach pains and twisting of her bowels that usually followed shortly after eating and was pleasantly surprised when the pains did not come. She felt agreeably satisfied.

"What is the last thing you remember before waking in the Sacred Lake?" Ulrik cleared his throat and spoke after a few silent moments.

"Oh that," she waved a hand dismissively and hesitated a while before saying, "well, it was my eighty-fifth birthday." She thought hard, her brow knitting in concentration, "I prepared for bed like I usually do. I laid down and said my prayers." She stopped, trying to recall. "I remember having a dream about my whole life. It flashed by in my mind like a bad dream and the last thing I remember was thinking, *"I wish I had a second chance."* There was a terrible tearing pain in my chest, and I couldn't breathe and then, I woke up gasping for air and drowning in the middle of a lake." Looking at him meaningfully she shrugged and stared with a faraway look in her blue eyes and then continued, "and then there was *you*."

After another long silence between them where Ulrik watched her intently, he finally spoke.

"You do not look eighty-five." His eyes flowed slowly from her head to her toes. "Forgive me for staring." Then he said more quietly, "I have been alone for a *very* long time."

Tessa blushed a flattering shade of pink.

"Oh, well, I supposed we'll both have to get used to my being here." She dropped her eyes and stared at the ground, contemplating. "You say you live alone? Where are the other people? Please tell me, how did you get here?"

Ulrik hesitated again, an annoyed look passing over his handsome features. "That is a story for another time." He was obviously bothered and held back some secret because he would not meet her eyes. After a few more minutes he asked calmly, "Was there a husband in your previous life? Children?"

Tessa pulled her knees to her chest and linked her arms around them. Waiting a while before quietly responding, "No, no husband. No children. I was alone except for a nephew. He brought me some cake and a yellow sweater for my birthday."

She nodded distractedly with a slight scowl but then brightened a little.

"But it was nice of him to remember me."

Ulrik stared at her. He only understood half of what she said. "You never had a husband in your eighty-five years?"

"No, I was a, oh, what would you call it? An old maid, a spinster, unmarried. Not that I didn't have a chance but..." she hesitated, seemingly lost in memories.

"But?" Ulrik coaxed her on.

"Well, I was engaged to be married once, but it didn't work out." She finally answered him after another long pause.

"What happened?"

"Oh, that is a story for another time. Maybe when I know you better." She repeated sadly, unable to meet his eyes.

"I am not going anywhere, and I have nowhere else to be. There is no one here to interrupt us. Tell me your story. It has been so long since I have had anyone to talk to. I like the sound of your voice."

Tessa looked at his cheerless handsome face. She felt a great welling of sympathy and understood his loneliness, but she barely knew him and did not want to reveal what she felt was her biggest shame.

"Oh, it is a sad, very private tale and we've only just met."

Ulrik pleaded with his large blue eyes and reasoned with her for what seemed like an hour. How better to get to know each other than by telling stories of their lives? Eventually, after much persuasion, Tessa acquiesced.

"Oh, I suppose I can tell you, even though I don't know you, but you will have to tell me *your* story, agreed?" She was starting to feel comfortable with Ulrik.

He just grunted and gestured for her to continue.

Tessa recognized a stubborn streak in this Norseman, and she gave in and began her story.

"I was engaged to be married once, but he broke it off. The end."

"That is not a story! Tell the whole of it!" Ulrik demanded gently, that stubborn streak showing.

"If you must know, the man I was supposed to marry, was a very jealous, possessive, and mistrustful man," she paled as she remembered.

Ulrik waited patiently for her to go on. Eventually, he waved his hand for her to continue.

Tessa went on slowly, "I thought he believed in me and trusted me. One night, a few weeks before our wedding, well, one thing led to another and I *gave* myself to him. After all, he was to be my husband and so I thought, why wait? I loved him and we were to be married." Tessa stopped talking and hugged her knees to her chest, "Well, as the days passed...I wasn't under his control at all times...I had to go to work. I had family, friends, and a wedding to plan. He accused me of lying and cheating on him. I explained that he was the first and only man I had ever been with. I had been a virgin, but his paranoia was too great, and he refused to believe that I was faithful to him."

She halted while memories assailed her, saddening her eyes.

"Go on," Ulrik prompted gently.

"He claimed to believe me but insisted that I quit my job and stay at home after we were married. As the wedding day drew closer, he accused me of cheating again and kept demanding to know the name of the man I was spending time with. Trying to continuously explain I was only doing my job and was with my family was pointless. Then a week before the wedding, he beat me in a jealous rage because I wouldn't give him the name of the man who I had been with. He called me a liar and said he could not bring himself to marry a whore. He canceled the wedding and he left me. End of story."

"That man had no honor!" Ulrik spat angrily watching her sad face.

Ulrik's indignation began to build. Being alone for so long had calmed his Viking spirit, but the thought of what the man had done to this beautiful girl, enraged him. He suddenly felt very protective of her. He laid a large warm hand over hers and lifting an eyebrow, prompted her to smile, his ice-blue eyes gently pleading.

Tessa felt ridiculous sharing such intimate details of her life with a stranger, but his gentle prodding had put her at ease, and it had spilled out. Now as she looked around the clearing, at the small cabin and the beautiful sunny day, she realized many years had passed and she should try not to allow it to ruin her lovely day here in Heaven. She tried to make her voice sound lighter and dismissive.

"There you have it, beaten by the man whom I thought I loved and was supposed to start a life with because he thought I was a liar and not trustworthy. Despite how cheated I felt by the whole situation, I never trusted another man again and that is the whole sad tale."

Finished with her story, she turned her face away and rested her cheek on her knees, looking away from Ulrik. A single tear escaped her eye and fell slowly down her cheek. The pain of such an old hurt still hid deep inside her.

Ulrik sat unmoving, giving her time, and did not say anything. He tried to understand everything Tessa said. He felt rage at the man who took her and then would not marry her. Shaking the story and unworthy thoughts it brought to his imagination, Ulrik jumped to his feet.

"Come!" he held his hand out to her.

Tessa did not move, so he gently reached forward, took her hand, and pulled her to her feet. As she stood, a little unsteady, she brushed up close to him. He was very tall, and her head barely came up to his shoulder. She slowly looked up into his intense blue eyes as they stood hand in hand. He wanted to pull her closer but did not want to frighten her. Slowly, he leaned down and gently kissed the cheek where the tear had come to rest. Then, as he turned and pulled her away, he licked his lips, tasting the salty tear, and silently vowed to himself, that she would cry no more.

Chapter Four – New Beginnings

Ulrik led Tessa up a gently sloping hill and took her for a walk in the splendid mountains. She shook off the melancholy of her past, marveled at the beauty of the forest surrounding them, and spent the entire time smiling and laughing. Trees with bright emerald leaves towered above her. Tall, white-barked aspen groves dotted the hillside. Shadows danced with beams of sunlight. Ulrik's hand was warm and strong in hers and the forest he knew so well seemed new to him, looking through her brightly sparkling eyes. Tessa was acutely aware of how strong and young her body felt and how good she felt whenever Ulrik touched her. She laughed feeling free and very happy, still half-convinced she had died and gone to Heaven. Whenever her thoughts drifted to her old life or to questions about how she got to this new world, she would shudder and concentrate on the here and now. She would think about the reality of her situation much later. For now, she was content to pretend she was living in a dream.

The muscles in Tessa's legs pumped easily as they ran through the forest and she breathed deeply, taking in the fresh air. A slight breeze wafted through the trees and she could hear the rustling of small animals and the singing of the birds. It had been so long since she could hear so clearly and see so far. Colors were brighter and more brilliant, and she felt astonished, again mentally recounting things she missed in her old uneventful life each time she saw something new here.

Ulrik showed Tessa the wonders of the forest. He pointed out a mother fox's den and told her how soon she would have pups to feed. He lifted her to sit on his shoulder to see a robin's nest protecting brilliant blue eggs high in a tree. They ran through a field and she braided a crown of wildflowers for her hair. They laughed and played throughout the afternoon as if they were old friends. His being an ancient Norseman and her a twenty-first-century modern woman, never seemed to be an issue they wanted to confront.

Finally, they reached the top of the mountain and Ulrik sat her down close to the cliff edge. He hesitated for a moment then pulled her close to his chest, arms going around her, keeping her warm. The position felt easy and natural. Together they watched the setting sun paint the sky with shades of pink, purple, blue, and orange among towering white clouds.

Behind them, a full moon rose in the distant sky and when it was almost fully dark, Ulrik said they should head back. He safely the led way down the hill back to the cabin, the luminescent moon brightly lighting their way.

When they arrived back at the cabin, Ulrik lit the fire and then they ate some dried meat and berries they had gathered that day. They sat companionably watching the fire and talking until Tessa fell asleep in the chair.

Ulrik rose and gently lifting her, carried her to the bed. He laid her down, removed her boots, and tucked the covers tightly around her. He returned to the fire, carefully placed on another log, and lay down before its warmth. His thoughts were chaotic and strange, the gods had heard his prayer for a woman as there she was, but why? He realized he could not understand any of the things that happened to him and stopped trying to make sense of it.

Ulrik watched the sleeping form in the bed and listened to her deep breathing, eventually, he fell asleep.

#

The next few days were busy with long hikes into the surrounding mountains. As soon as they both rose, Ulrik hurried them out of the cabin and into the forest. Ulrik was a hard worker and had many daily chores to do, but he took Tessa hunting with him and they did everything together. They snared rabbits and he shot a wild turkey with his bow. They spent the days lost in each other's company and fanning the flames of a deep affection that grew between them.

Despite the differences of their pasts, they found it easy to communicate and began to understand each other with a little effort. Secretly, Ulrik burned for Tessa and took every opportunity to touch her. Tessa spent long minutes covertly watching the play of Ulrik's muscular body as he moved and worked.

Tessa began to get used to being young again and took great pleasure at the feeling of having a strong, healthy body. It was as if God, or Heaven or time, had mysteriously thrown her back to her younger self so that she could start over again. Tessa tried numerous times to question Ulrik about how he got there, and all he would say was that he was cursed by the Gods and banished there as punishment. He did not say punishment for what, only that he came from the lake as she did. His face would cloud over with sadness mixed with anger, so Tessa did not push him. She knew that, in time, he would tell her his story.

Tessa woke early one morning. She realized Ulrik must have put her in the bed again the night before and tucked her in tightly. She rose quietly and decided she would make breakfast. She went to the kitchen area that looked as if it was torn straight from the 1900s. The pump over the sink looked like it might be coaxed to work, and she busied herself looking through the cupboards. To her astonishment, she found canisters with modern seals containing flour, oatmeal, and honey. On some shelves were jars of herbs labeled in faded, black lettering. She decided she would look those over some other time. Nothing in the cabin made any sense and it was like living in a place furnished with antiques. Everything from the depression-era plates and cups, to the cooking implements, even the dust-covered dishcloths were remnants from other time periods Tessa knew were very old. Though everything looked newly purchased as if from a mail-order catalog. Why Ulrik had apparently not used any of it was another mystery.

Tessa put some of the unburned wood by the fire into the cast iron stove and lit it with a match she found. Finding a bucket of water, she mixed up some biscuits with flour, oatmeal, and berries, and put them in the oven to bake.

Ulrik lay still on his fur by the fire. Through half-slit eyes, he watched at ease, as Tessa worked in the kitchen. Usually, he whisked her out of the cabin before she had a chance to look around, but today he decided to be content just watching her. As she put something into the big iron box, he never understood the use of it, she turned and found his eyes upon her.

"You're awake! Good Morning!" She smiled and the room lit up for him.

He rose on one elbow, crossed his muscular legs at the ankles, and smiled back at her.

"I don't suppose you have any eggs, do you?"

Ulrik rose in one smooth panther-like movement and strode barefoot to the front door, hopefully before Tessa could notice his morning erection. But she had noticed, and her eyes went wide, she quickly looked away, suddenly very shy.

Ulrik quickly went through the door and out into the crisp morning air. The coolness of the new day helped cool his skin and other parts of his body, and he went out back behind the cabin. It took some time, but he found where one of the wild hens laid three eggs and he took them into Tessa.

Tessa had found an old cast iron skillet and a pot. She also had some success with the pump and after quite a bit of pumping and spitting muddy water, succeeded in getting some clear water into a pot which she then boiled. She also found some herbs that smelled like she might be able to make tea with them. Overlooking the fact that they were probably old and stale, she used some of the hot water and made tea. Taking the eggs Ulrik brought her, she scrambled them, took the biscuits out of the oven, set out the honey, and poured some tea into two milky green cups she had found. Ulrik produced some dried meat and they had a feast.

Ulrik had not eaten like this for more than two years. He devoured the meal and grinned broadly at Tessa as she quietly sipped her tea and watched him. She was very pleased that he was satisfied.

"Ulrik, what is this place? You never speak of it. None of it *fits* together. It looks like all the parts of the cabin are from different time periods and places. Yet, it is all very well preserved. How long have you lived here? Where did the food come from? It is old but still eatable. Did you find all this and build it? Please tell me."

"I found this cabin, about two winters back. I was about frozen through when I stumbled on it after being spit out by the Sacred Lake. When I first got here, I searched through the place. It looked like no one had lived here for a very long time. There are many things I do not understand the use for, and I gave up trying. I only use what I need, mostly the fireplace, and that chair. I sleep there on my fur by the fire and the rest of the time I spend hunting and trying to survive." Ulrik paused and ran a hand through his long, tangled white-blonde hair. He did not want to admit that many of the things in the cabin made him nervous and brought strong superstitious dread to his mind.

"There is a small room in the back and it has a large bowl of mud in it. I have never been back in there since first coming upon it. I do not know what it is for. Watching you work over here now I understand that some of these things are meant for cooking. That thing that makes the water come out is a miracle."

"A small room, with a large bowl, with mud in it?" She repeated quizzically. "I wonder what that could be. Can you show me, please?" In her short time with Ulrik, she realized she had no opportunities for exploring more of the cabin either.

Ulrik stood, mentally shook away his superstitions, and led the way around the bed to the back wall with a short hallway and a closet. He came to a small door and slowly pushed it open. The door creaked on un-oiled hinges and silvery cobwebs parted, and lightly blew back. One hand on the hilt of his sword, he looked in first, and then held the door open wider for Tessa to see in. She looked and gave a small gasp of surprise clasping her hands together. Ulrik started slightly.

Smiling she said, "It's a bathroom!"

"A what?" Ulrik gave her a disturbing look.

"It's where you, um, well you go to the bathroom. Um, make water? Relieve yourself. Do you understand?"

Ulrik looked doubtfully at her then shook his head. "I know of what you describe, but I do not understand how this works."

Realizing a Viking from ancient times would not know about indoor plumbing any more than he knew about the cast iron stove or a water pump, Tessa went in. The small room looked to be from the early days when working toilets were first invented. A hole in the roof let in blowing dirt. There was a small wooden crate, layers of dust, many dried leaves, and an old toilet that used to work by pulling a chain. Doubting that there would be working plumbing, she pulled the chain as if to test it. Nothing happened. The bowl was indeed full of dried mud. After looking the thing over she determined that it would take a lot of tinkering and cleaning to get it working, and inwardly resolved to accomplish the task at a later date. She lifted the lid of the wooden crate and to her delight discovered a couple dozen bars of soap.

"Oh, this is wonderful!" She exclaimed holding one of the bars up to show Ulrik.

Ulrik bent his head forward and sniffed, "Yes, I found that, but it tastes terrible. It is useless."

"You don't eat it!" She laughed, "You bathe with it!"

He looked at her blankly for a long moment then a clever considering look crept across his handsome features. He tried to hold back a grin.

"Woman, I do not understand what you say," he grumbled with false severity.

Tessa bent her head toward Ulrik and took a tentative sniff.

"Yes, obviously, but I will show you!"

Taking a bar of the rough soap in one hand and Ulrik's hand in her other, they left the small room. Ulrik decided he did not care what the "soap" was for, as long as she continued to hold his hand. Tessa looked around and not finding what she was looking for, grabbed one smaller blanket, and one of the large ones off the big bed.

"Take me to the lake!" She declared with a triumphant smile.

Ulrik led the way to the lake where he had first found her. Upon arriving, she looked around shuddering at strange memories. It was a beautiful place with a cascading waterfall on one side. Moss covered the rocks on part of the shore and a wall of rock towered up the other side, making a nice hidden grotto. Reeds, long grasses, bushes, trees, and flowers made up the rest of the surrounding landscape and at the end, a rushing stream spilled downhill. Finding a fairly level spot in the grass beside the lake she spread the large blanket out. Going to the water's edge, she knelt and lathered her hands with the soap. It smelled faintly like lavender. It would do the job she determined.

"Now, you see, you rub it like this and get a good lather and rub it all over your body. Then it gets the dirt and sweat off you and then you are clean. Soap is for taking a bath! I can't believe you didn't have anything like it where you came from?" She looked at him with disbelief written all over her face. "I used to take a bath every day!"

"I do not see the need for the soap or the bath." Ulrik crossed his arms over his chest and tried hard to look severe.

"Well, you smell like you need a bath. It's wonderful! I promise, once you get used to having your body clean, you'll want to stay that way all the time. It's much more pleasant to be around a person who smells good. It is healthier for you and more appealing in every way. Now, I will return to the cabin and you get in the water, lather your whole body, your head, and your clothes, and dry them in the sun. Then when you are clean, we'll finish looking through the cabin for more treasures."

Ulrik grasped her by the arm as Tessa turned to go. "No! I am not letting you out of my sight. These woods are safe enough, but you're not leaving my sight and that is all there is to it!"

Ulrik did not want to admit that part of him feared she would disappear as easily as she had appeared and the other part of him just wanted to be with her.

"Well, I can't stay here and watch you bathe. It wouldn't be proper. I'll hide down the path behind a tree and you'll know right where I am."

"Not out of my sight! You may sit here in the sun on the blanket and I will bathe, but you must stay where I can see you at all times." The illogical superstitious part of him still thought she was a water spirit and might slip away from him now that they were back at the water. In reality, he used this as an excuse to keep her nearby.

Tessa handed Ulrik the soap, spread the blanket out, and sat down arranging her skirts. She tried not to blush at the prospect of seeing Ulrik bathe. Ulrik had no compunction against it though. He unbuckled his sword belt and placed it on the blanket beside Tessa, and then he unlaced his boots and tossed them aside. Next, off went the britches and a fur vest he sometimes wore. He dropped them to the ground and Tessa peered up, almost level with and, staring right at, Ulrik's large manhood. The only thing left "clothing" him were his two silver armbands and the Thor's hammer amulet he always wore. He took those off, tossed them onto the blanket and Tessa tried to look more closely at the intricate Nordic design tattoos encircling his biceps. She blushed at Ulrik's nakedness and quickly looked in the other direction, battling the fears that rose inside her breast.

His beautiful, tanned body rippled with muscles and the blonde hairs on his thighs and the darker hair between his legs curled invitingly. Blushing a scalding shade of red, Tessa turned her head away, raised her hand with the soap, and waited for him to take it and immerse himself in the lake.

Tessa realized, as her heart pounded fast and hard in her chest, that she was in unfamiliar territory. Stepping back into her young body, while it felt like putting on an old comfortable set of clothes, also brought a whole new set of sensations. Especially, upon seeing Ulrik naked, she strongly determined not to look anymore and help douse the fire that had begun to kindle within her body. Old fears from her previous life rose inside her heart and she felt a little sad and very afraid of her feelings, wants, and desires.

Ulrik took the soap, walked to the edge of the lake, strutted in a few feet, and then dove in, completely submerging his beautiful warrior's body in the lake.

Tessa could not help it, she peeked from the corner of her eye, as he swam with long easy strokes. He reached a large flat boulder that stuck out from the shore about ten feet away, and he lifted himself onto the rock. He clumsily lathered his hands and looked quizzically at Tessa. Tessa motioned washing along and under her arms and he mimicked her, grinning widely. She watched as he rubbed the soap across his broad chest and down his muscular arms and then, leaning back, over his lean, washboard stomach. Gratefully, he lifted the leg closest to her to block her from seeing him washing his more private parts. He looked at Tessa again with a wicked and provocative smile slowly spreading across his inviting mouth. She tried to ignore those full curling lips and motioned again washing her head. Ulrik frowned and again copied her motions. Leaving the soap on the rock he dove into the water only to come up again shaking and flinging his shoulder-length hair from side-to-side spraying water droplets in the sun. Then he dove again.

Tessa waited for him to come up again. After what seemed to be too long, Ulrik surfaced further away down the lake and stood up naked under the great waterfall. The water beat down on his long, tanned, limbs and chest and over his head, as he ran his hands over his head smoothing back his hair that turned dark gold in the water. He was like a water god she mused as she watched him.

Tessa's mind whirled and her heart skipped as she watched Ulrik, enthralled. Try as she might to give him some privacy, she could not stop looking at his beautifully sculpted body. Determined to look away she reached for his clothes and walking along the shore reached the boulder he had sat on that jutted out into the lake. Carefully, stepping on the river stones she made her way to where he had left the soap. She leaned over and began to wash his clothing. After she had satisfied herself that she had done as much as she could to clean them, they still smelled like wet dog she thought, she wrung them out and hung them on a nearby branch.

Ulrik swam up to where Tessa had been washing his clothes on the boulder.

"Did you not say *you* bathe every day?" He asked giving her a knowing and mischievous smile, raising one eyebrow.

"Yes, I did say that, but…" she said haltingly.

"You have not taken a bath today nor since you got here. Perhaps you should take one now. The day is hot and the water is cool."

"Um, well, I…" she faltered.

"You said you bathe every day. Now is the time for you to bathe."

"I usually prefer a hot bath."

Ulrik tilted his head and just stared at her. He beckoned impatiently with one hand.

"Oh, alright, I guess I would like to be clean." Tessa walked back to the blanket and began to undress. "You must not look though. Turn around please."

She circled one finger in the air and took off the green bodice and blue skirt. Standing in only her chemise, she turned and walked slowly into the lake.

Ulrik frowned seeing she had not fully undressed, but lazily swam back a few feet giving her room to enter. Tessa could not remember the last time she had bathed in a lake, if ever. The water was cool and felt welcome on the warm spring day. She stepped out a little way, frustrated that the cloth of the chemise either tangled her legs or threatened to float up and reveal her naked body underneath. She told herself she would just have to deal with it because being naked in front of Ulrik was not a good idea. Although, he had already seen her naked in front of the mirror that first day, she remembered, blushing. She quickly shook that memory away as it was causing her to grow warm and intimate thoughts began to invade her imagination. In her past life, she had never been this amorous.

Ulrik came up beside her and quietly warned her, "It gets deep here very quickly."

Of course, just as he said that Tessa stepped right off the underwater shelf she had been standing on and went straight under.

Ulrik caught her up in his strong warm arms and he pulled her to a shallower part where she could stand. Time seemed to stop as he stood with his arms around her. He caressed her face and gently pushed the wet hair out of her eyes. The sun shone down upon the two and Tessa realized her arms had instinctively reached around his neck.

"Tell the truth, you *knew* what a bath was and you know what soap is." She smiled knowingly.

Ulrik grinned wolfishly. "I bathe every few days, it is true. The soap as you call it is not like I have known before."

Then he turned serious his eyes darkening. They stood staring into each other's eyes, ice-blue meeting storm blue, and then slowly he bent his head to kiss her.

It was a soft tentative kiss at first. He was not sure how she would react, and he did not want to scare her, but the longer his lips remained on hers the more his control slipped. It had been *so long* since he had felt the curves of a woman. Ulrik pulled her closer feeling her small body pressed against his. Feelings raged inside him and burned through his chest like wildfire. He deepened the kiss, and she did not pull away although she trembled in his arms. As his tongue tentatively met hers, his hands seem to take on a life of their own as they smoothed down over her curves, trying to feel every inch of her at once and pulling her tightly against him.

Tessa gasped and clung to Ulrik as his head dipped and his lips ran along the edge of her jaw and down her neck. She realized that the only thing between their bodies was the thin chemise and his hard, erect shaft pressed into her belly. Her heart pounded and flipped in her chest. Her mind raced with the implications of what could happen between them. She was completely unsure of herself because her first experience with a man had gone so completely wrong, but she forced herself to forget that distant memory and relaxed into Ulrik's kisses. That was then and this was *new*.

Ulrik grew frustrated and he reached under the water and, in one swift motion tugged the chemise off Tessa, flinging it onto the rock. Then he pulled her close again relishing the feeling of her firm breasts against his chest, her soft skin under his questing hands.

"By Odin! You are soft!" He whispered in a deep husky voice, trembling and yearning for her. Fierce emotions battled within him and he longed to join with her.

Tessa smiled and put her hands on his chest, running them along his taut muscles. This was inevitable she knew and let go of all hesitation and doubt as they stared into each other's eyes. They became one mind in their passionate embrace. Ulrik lifted her off her feet and strode out of the lake, over to the blanket. He gently lay her down and looked into her glittering blue eyes.

"Tell me now if you want to stop this because, in a few moments, I will not be able to stop."

Tessa smiled shyly at him, but said breathlessly, "Don't stop."

Ulrik did not need to be told twice. His control shattered as he plundered her mouth and eased down beside her. One hand moved slowly under her wet head, the other slid along her side and caressed her smooth hip. When his hand went to her thigh, she shivered with delight, her skin grew warm as his large hand ran over the goosebumps on her skin. She tingled where he touched her, and her breathing quickened as her heart beat fiercely. Her hands slid over his chest, down his stomach, and over his lean hips. She copied his movements, and as his hand went to rest between her legs, so did her hand reach to grasp him. He groaned in ecstasy and she gasped with pleasure. As he caressed her intimate folds. She gasped his name, "Ulrik!"

The sound of his name coming from her passion-filled gasp drove away the last of Ulrik's loneliness and he could delay no longer. Heart leaping with joy, he moved to cover her, gently parting her legs with his knees while he kissed her lips. Her hands went to his hips and she pulled him to her. Ulrik guided his shaft into her tight opening and plunged.

Tessa arched back and gasped in shock and pain as something inside her tore. Ulrik stopped moving and looked into her eyes, his brow furrowed slightly, but the moment of pain cleared from her face and she smiled a little uncertain, then he could no longer keep from moving within her. She did not want him to stop. He undulated in and out of her, claiming her body with his. She let out another gasp of delight as the rhythm took hold of them and he surged against her.

Ulrik's heart slammed wildly in his chest. He could not hold back. Years of being denied the haven of a woman's body rushed through his mind and his blood rushed hot and urgent. He pushed deep inside her again and again, and they rode the waves of ecstasy that shook them both.

Suddenly, she cried out in a very different way and the soft, warm flesh of her inner sheath clenched hard around him, over and over again. The feeling and sounds of her pleasure undid Ulrik and he let out a growl of pleasure as his shaft pulsed and his seed shot inside her. They breathed heavily with their mutual satisfaction as he continued to plunge a few more times, prolonging their mutual release, until he shuddered and stilled above her, panting.

Tessa smiled at him and pulled his face to hers. She kissed him sweetly and Ulrik shuddered again. Slowly, he moved off of her and then pulled her into his arms exclaiming, "By Odin! That was good!"

They lay in silence warmed by the sun. Their breathing settled and their hearts slowed. Ulrik gently stroked her bare shoulder and Tessa, head resting on his chest, closed her eyes content for the first time in the many, many years of her existence.

#

The question hung between them. There had been that moment of searing pain when Ulrik had first joined with her. It was as if a barrier was there as if she had been a physical virgin, but they both knew she could not have been. He would not have been so forceful with her had he suspected it was her first time. Neither of them wanted to be the first to broach the subject, nor look down to see if there was any virgin blood.

Finally, Tessa slowly sat up and looked down. A small bit of blood-stained the blankets and smeared the inside of her legs. She gave a short laugh and shook her head disbelieving.

Ulrik rose on one elbow and glanced at the spot. "How is it that you were not a virgin, but now you are or were again? Perhaps you were mistaken about what happened?"

"I don't know." She whispered. "It shouldn't have been there after I was with…"

"The lake is sacred." Ulrik interrupted softly. Placing a hand on her shoulder as if to ease her distress, he said gravely, "it has strange powers."

They lay in silence for a long time. Till she finally spoke, "In my old body I was not a virgin as I told you." She could not look him in the eye for some reason. "I always felt so cheated! I had lain with my husband-to-be. Maybe this is not the same body as in my other life. Perhaps, I truly have been made new and given a second chance." She looked at him fearfully.

"Maybe I'm not really me." She looked baffled and gave a short uncomfortable laugh. Then she had a terrible thought. Fear streaked through her and she withdrew from him slightly.

"Are you angry? I didn't lie!" Ulrik shook his head, pulled her back down to lay across his chest, and smiled brightly at her. He hugged her closer to him alleviating her fear. After a few moments, she spoke again. "Although, I have to say being with him was nothing like this. This was so much better!"

Ulrik flushed with pride and pulled her over top of him.

"Just wait, the second time will be even better!" Ulrik kissed her slowly and they began again.

After the second time, they got back in the lake and swam and played the afternoon away. Eventually, Tessa got out and announced, "I'm starving!"

Ulrik's stomach grumbled in agreement.

They went back to the cabin, prepared dinner, and sat outside eating under a huge oak tree as evening began to fall.

"Ulrik, I know you don't want to talk about it, but won't you please tell me how you got here?" She pleaded gently. "It might help me figure out why I'm here and maybe *how* I came to be here."

Ulrik looked grim as he paused, thinking long and hard, and then he came to a decision.

Chapter Five – Ulrik's Story

"I am a Norseman as I told you. I was a Jarl, a war chief, on a voyage to follow a man named Leif Ericson to new lands he had been boasting about. There was a terrible storm. The worst we had ever sailed through. The waves were as large as mountains and we fought for hours to remain afloat. Eventually, the ship floundered, and a great wave flipped the ship over. Everyone on board was swept into the sea. I struggled to swim to the surface, but I was pulled down by my heavy clothes and the sword on my hip. I went down and down into the depths of the ocean drowning. The next thing I knew, I was pushed up through clearer water in this lake and I could breathe. The sun was shining, the water was calm and fresh, not salty like the ocean. I was able to swim to the shore. I was there and now, I am here. I thought the gods were playing a funny joke on me. After a long time alone, I wasn't laughing anymore."

He drew a deep breath before continuing his tale.

"That was about two winters ago. I wandered around the mountains and I lived in the forest for a long time. No matter how far I wandered I came back to this Sacred Lake. When I went up the mountain, I found the cabin. It was almost winter. I did not wait to see if anyone lived there, because the snow forced me inside for shelter. I have been here ever since, alone."

The last word hung in the silence that followed. Eventually, Ulrik began to speak again.

"The cabin was stranger than anything I have ever seen. I am ashamed to say I was afraid of many of the things inside. I felt like I should not disturb anything, in case the owner ever came home, but no one has come. Until you," Ulrik hesitated, looking meaningfully into Tessa's eyes.

"You must have been so lonely!" She whispered her hand rising to cover her mouth. Her blue eyes sparkled with unshed tears for him.

Ulrik did not answer, he just looked away as if to admit it would make him less of a man.

"Ulrik, how old *were* you…when you…at the time of the storm before you got here?"

He hesitated for a long moment, "I had seen more than sixty winters. I was still strong and a great warrior. I had the strength to swing a war axe and could best any man with the sword. I had most of my teeth, except on one side, because I lost those in a fight years earlier. When I got here, I had all my teeth and none of the battle scars from my old life. Now I am as I once was, as a young man of only twenty winters." He took a deep breath, shrugged, and then went on.

"My men respected me and I them." He hesitated before saying slowly. "They were my brothers. We had been on many raids and had been through many battles together. I owned a great ship, treasure, lands, and many sheep."

"Why didn't you want to tell me any of this?"

"It is my greatest shame to lose my ship and all of my men and only I live. If I had done things differently, commanded better, or given different orders? I have been through it over and over in my mind many times, what I should have done to save us all. Now, I am cursed by the gods because I failed my men and they all died because of me. They did not die in battle and are denied Valhalla because of my failure as their Jarl." He ran a hand through his hair and shook his head, looking outward as if seeing the past.

"I too should have died in battle with a sword in my hand so that I could sit at Odin's table in Valhalla and feast with my brother-warriors for eternity. But I did not, and now I am here, banished, shamed, and denied a place with my forefathers in Odin's Hall."

Tessa placed a hand on Ulrik's shoulder, and he closed his eyes as if in defeat.

"I'm so sorry." She whispered, feeling bad for making him talk about something he felt so ashamed about. She carefully slid forward and placed a kiss on his bare shoulder.

"I don't think you are to blame. You couldn't command the storm or know that the waves would sink your ship. It wasn't your fault. I know you did everything you could to save your men." She consoled him.

Ulrik held still staring into the distance deeply in thought.

"Did you leave a wife and children behind?" Realizing after she asked the question that she may be adding salt to his exposed emotional wounds.

Ulrik gave a wry smile. "Oh, I left a wife, if she could be called a wife," then he said more quietly, "No children."

"I'm so sorry." She said again, feeling helpless to ease his pain. She felt slightly embarrassed that she had slept with another woman's husband, but she banished the thought as this was plainly a new life for them both, and the other wife was long gone.

"My *wife* was Ingrid, a witch if ever one walked the Earth! She was a girl from my village, whom I had known since I was a boy. For years she never noticed me until the first time I came back from a very successful raid with a large share of the treasure and I had won my ship. I learned too late that when she found out how much gold I had returned with, she began to pursue me. She began serving me at the feast table, pouring my mead, brushing her breasts against me. Walking through the village, she would suddenly appear and pull me behind a lodge, kiss me, and then run off laughing. Once when no one was looking, she even put her hand down my breeches and caressed me until I spilled my seed in the dirt. She promised me her body in words and deeds. I was young. I was a man and I thought her very comely at the time.

I did not protest much. I thought she wanted me. I needed a wife and sons. So, I asked her to be my wife."

Ulrik stopped that faraway look never left his eyes. He blinked, shook his head, and then took a deep breath and continued.

"We were married, but on our wedding night, a man named Snorri Sigurdsson came to our bedchamber. He had been her secret lover. They planned to murder me in our wedding bed, take all of my gold and silver, and claim thieves had done the deed. They would take everything for themselves and no one would know the truth. She could claim my treasure, my ship, and my lands by right of marriage and make up a story about my dying protecting her. They had not counted on my being the better warrior. I slew the bastard! The witch, I forced to bed, as was my right as her husband. She tried to slip a knife between my ribs."

Ulrik pointed to his side where a scar used to be but was now only smooth, tanned, skin.

"After that, my life was a living nightmare. She was a hateful demanding shrew, refused my bed, and would not give me sons. She constantly threw Snorri's death in my face and told me how she hated me. I lived in misery with no hope of ever having an heir. The only way I could get her to bed was to force her. Very quickly, I lost all desire for her."

Ulrik took another deep breath and turned to take Tessa's hand. Now that the story had begun to flow, he could not stop telling it.

"After many winters of suffering with the witch, I set her aside claiming she was barren because we had no children. The Lawmakers took my side and Ingrid seemed to hate me even more for setting her aside than she did for killing Snorri. I was glad to be rid of her. After her, I had no more desire to marry again. I spent most of my time on the open sea and had very little time for women. So, I grew old alone. I had the fastest ship on the seas and great wealth, but no sons of my own."

Tessa stared at their hands entwined between them. His hands were tan, large, and calloused by hard work. Her hands were soft, small, and white not yet tanned by the sun. The trees around them rustled in a gentle breeze and evening began to quietly descend. All she could think to do was kneel in front of him, lean forward, take his face in her hands and kiss him tenderly. Ulrik kissed her back. Taking her in his arms they held each other in silence while the past blew away with the breeze.

That night Ulrik slept with Tessa in the bed, but before sleep took them, he moved over her, slowly and gently parted her knees with his, and entered her. Looking into her eyes he pushed deeper into her and together they moved in a slow rhythm until their passion demanded they plunge and plunder each other's ecstasy. Afterward, while Ulrik's hardness grew soft inside her, he kissed her gently and ran his finger lovingly over her lips. Then he gently withdrew and moved to her side, pulling her close against his body.

Tessa nuzzled Ulrik's neck and took a deep breath. She inhaled the exotic scent of his sweat and their lovemaking. She felt his warmth and knew in her heart that he was why she was there. They fell asleep, arms and legs entwined, and let peaceful dreams take them.

Chapter Six – Discoveries

In the days that followed, Tessa and Ulrik explored more of the cabin. This was something they had not done earlier out of a false sense of respect for the previous owners. They found more clothes that looked like a collection of period costumes and some that were plain and more serviceable. Most were men's and Ulrik soon sported a new pair of what Tessa knew as, black, leather biker pants, that hugged his hips very nicely. Tessa found a sundress that looked as if it were from the 14th century and she put it aside for future use. She also found a pair of men's denim pants too small for Ulrik, those she wore instead of the skirts she had been wearing. Ulrik protested saying he liked her in the skirts so he could catch glimpses of her bare legs but conceded when he saw how the pants hugged her small behind. Laughing, they moved onto another crate, shoved further into the shadows, back against the wall. Tessa squealed with delight as she opened it and then pulled out book after book.

She read some of the titles exclaiming with joy, "I *am* in Heaven!"

These were novels; King Arthur and the Nights of the Round Table, Sir Ivanhoe, Peter Pan, a book on herbs and plants, one on animal husbandry, and a small, black, leather-bound Bible.

"These will help long winter nights pass much more pleasantly." She exclaimed.

Ulrik put his arms around her, kissing her neck, and said, "I know how to pass long winter nights very pleasantly and it has nothing to do with these things you call *books*."

"I don't suppose you know how to read do you?" Tessa looked at Ulrik doubtfully.

"I can read maps and the stars. I can read runes."

"Well, maybe someday I can teach you to read these books."

"I do not know what you are talking about. Maybe later you can explain it to me. For now, I need to hunt, or we will have nothing to eat today."

"Oh, alright."

She smiled fondly and set the books aside for later letting her fingers longingly brush the covers one last time.

Ulrik took Tessa outside and down the hill a very short distance to a place where a garden grew wildly in all directions. It was overgrown with weeds, but after a little pulling, they discovered ripening carrots, green beans, some cabbage, huge summer squash, pumpkin, and watermelon. She took a mental inventory of what was there and even picked a few vegetables for dinner later.

Tessa squealed in delight as she found herbs growing profusely in and among the weeds. As they moved closer to the forest edge, they came upon a wooden door buried in the dirt and hidden by thick vines. Strangely, during Ulrik's time at the cabin, he had not stumbled across this before. It was hidden well, and he had to cut and dig and eventually was able to pull open the door. They descended into the dark. The smell of dust, mud, and decay assailed their senses. They came to a dirt floor barely illuminated by the sun spilling in from above and there they found the previous owner of the cabin.

A desiccated skeleton in molding rags lay at the bottom of the dirt and stone stairs. Strangely, it looked as if the tall body had been covered with a blanket. Ulrik nudged the bones with a toe and then bent to look closer lifting the blanket partially off.

"Looks like he fell and broke his neck. I will get a spade and we can bury the bones down the mountain."

Tessa gasped, "the poor man!"

Ulrik replaced the blanket over the bones so that Tessa wasn't troubled by the sight.

"Sounds like a good idea. Let's see what else is down here before we go." Tessa whispered as a shiver ran down her spine and she looked into the darkness ahead.

With a last sympathetic glance at the bones, they walked further into the dark cellar, but could not see anything in the blackness and decided to return to the cabin and retrieve a lamp.

Later, they returned to get the bones. They folded the skeleton into the blanket before taking the lamp and exploring further.

The lamplight flickered faintly on many dark bottles of various colors, sizes, and shapes. Taking one from the wooden shelves and dusting off the grime they discovered it was a storeroom for wine, pickles, and some smaller jars of jam. Beeswax seals still held tight and Tessa decided later she would take a couple of the jars back up to the cabin to see if the food inside was still good.

The cellar was huge. It went deep into the mountain and revealed a variety of hidden rooms containing stacks of items. There were a few miscellaneous furniture pieces and decorations galore, rugs, paintings, a vast number of knick-knacks, and clothing. In the deepest part of the cellar, where it was coolest, there were more food stores too, jars and canned goods, boxes of tea, and coffee that were kept fresh by the coolness underground. There was row after row of wine bottles, casks of beer, and even some whiskey. Tessa and Ulrik had no idea how long these supplies had been there. It appeared to Tessa that the previous owner had been a collector of antiquities and had hoarded his treasures here.

The room that grabbed Ulrik's attention was decorated with weapons from all different centuries. It looked to be a collection of knives, swords of all kinds, several crossbows, and piles on top of piles of arrows and rusting useless pistols. Another room held tools, saws, hammers, axes, and boxes of nails. Many of the weapons were decorative, but a few were functional. Tessa had to explain the usage of many of the tools and Ulrik's eyes gleamed as he understood the value of the treasure they had found in this room.

Tessa's eyes gleamed for different reasons. One room held a vast library with a tremendous variety of books. They were neatly stacked on shelves, piled on the floor in mounds, and covered every chair and table in the room. Tessa lit another lamp she found on a small table and wandered around the shelves, reading the titles. Approaching a large desk, she found it piled high with books and papers. Centered on the desk was a black leather-bound journal. She reached for the journal, blew off the dust that lay thickly upon it, and read the title in gold letters: "Dr. Jeremiah David Tennbaum, Journal X."

"This must have belonged to the man who used to live here. I bet that's him we found at the bottom of the stairs. Poor man!" Tessa's voice was full of sympathy. "It looks like there are more of them because this one is labeled number ten." She opened the journal carefully, cringing as the pages crackled, but withstood her perusal. She read a short way and then carefully flipped through the pages. Determining that it would require much better light and concentrated study, she decided to take the journal with them when they left. Her scrutiny returned to the titles of the books and she discovered volumes with subjects such as Science, Mathematics, numerous Medical books, and books on horticulture and animal husbandry. Tessa looked for journals one through nine and upon discovering them, grabbed them to take along. Ulrik grew impatient with the books as he saw no real use for them. Seeing his impatience, Tessa quickly grabbed the dusty journals, blew out the lamp, and they left the room. The exploration of the rest of the cellar took them well into the afternoon. Finally, they decided that it was time to go.

Ulrik stopped in the weapons room and chose a long dagger, a shovel, and an axe, and took them with him.

As decided earlier, Ulrik took the bones wrapped in the blanket, down the mountain. They dug a grave and carefully placed the bones in the hole. Then they covered them back up with dirt and made a cairn of rocks. Tessa instructed Ulrik on the design of a cross and they made a plan to construct one and return and place it later.

Ulrik buried the bones and turned to go but Tessa stopped him, "Wait shouldn't we say a prayer or something."

"What needs to be said? He is long past caring about words said over his bones. He died from a broken neck with no sword in his hand, so he did not go to Valhalla. What is left to be said?"

"Well, a prayer, like, oh, I don't know, ashes to ashes, dust to dust, we commend this poor soul, we think he was Dr. Jeremiah David Tennbaum, back to the Earth. We hope he is in Heaven and we thank him for leaving his wonderful cabin to us so that we may live. Amen!" Tessa smiled, very pleased with the short ceremony, and bent to place some wildflowers she had picked, onto the grave.

On the way back, they checked Ulrik's snares and found a rabbit in one. They returned to the cabin and with some of the vegetables and herbs Tessa picked, she made rabbit stew.

#

The summer was warm and gentle. Ulrik and Tessa fell into a routine and began a peaceful, but busy life together. Their days were spent with Ulrik hunting, preparing his kills in the small smokehouse next to the cabin, and taking care of the furs, and a few animals they managed to domesticate. Ulrik was also a good carpenter and he fixed holes and leaks in the roof and more firmly shored up the front door. He also built a coop and caught some of the chickens that scampered wild along the mountainside. He imagined the foxes in the area were not too happy with that, but Tessa was glad not to have to hunt for hidden nests to find eggs for their breakfast.

Ulrik also captured two temperamental wild goats and kept them in a pen with a plan to build more of an enclosure before winter as Tessa refused to let them stay in the house. He showed Tessa how to milk the goats and they soon had fresh goat's milk and she learned to make cheese.

Even though Tessa was a modern twenty-first-century woman, she took to mountain living as if she were born to it. She completely forgot the 85-year-old woman who had gone to bed alone and heartbroken and woke up with a second chance at life in a strange land. She kept the cabin clean, washed and mended the clothes, and did the cooking. She learned how to make goat cheese, dry herbs for various uses, and tea, and also read in the book on herbs about some of their medicinal applications although neither she nor Ulrik ever got sick.

At night after they finished their dinner they would sit by the fire and talk until it was time to go to bed. They would make passionate love and lay close together, falling asleep in each other's arms.

Chapter Seven – Dr. Jeremiah Tennbaum's Story

Tessa undertook studying Dr. Jeremiah David Tennbaum's journals and discovered the truth of why and how they got there. With passionate awe, she told Ulrik an unbelievable story once she had it fully pieced together from the ten journals.

"It seems Dr. Tennbaum was a scientist from thousands of years in our future, sometime after the year 3,000. He invented a machine that would transport him to a different time and dimension of Earth. He discovered that this particular dimension transported him back to a younger age, and he writes about how much longer his life was extended. Apparently, he lived here for hundreds of years going back and forth from this dimension to the Earth you and I knew." Tessa laughed, "He called it *"youthening"* instead of aging." She laughed, "Dr. Tennbaum was a real character I judge from the style of his writing."

Tessa shook her head smiling and continued her story. "Anyway, anything that he brought back, like food, clothing, books, furniture, and so on, was affected the same way. They age very, very slowly, that is why the food stores in the cellar are still good to this day. Lucky for us."

"This machine also appears to be able to go back into another age of Earth which makes sense that this is the Earth we both knew because the moon in the sky is the same one we both recognize from our previous lives. It seems Dr. Tennbaum traveled back through time and, as an antique lover, collected the things we found in the cabin and cellar. This cabin and its strange configuration of walls and items from different periods throughout time were sort of an experiment. He fashioned it together during the early trials of his machine. It was eclectic and interesting, so he decided to keep it as it is, all mismatched."

Ulrik frowned, "Do the journals say how we came to be here?"

"Yes, it is very interesting! It seems he used his machine to experiment with searching through time. He was looking for his DNA, his ancestors. In fact, he was quite obsessed with them. He went back and forth from there to this other Earth casting back in time to meet his ancestors. One journal has pages and pages of the Tennbaum family tree. It says here…" Tessa paused and grabbed another one of the journals, opening it.

"What is dee-en-ey?" Ulrik interrupted, intrigued by the story.

Tessa smiled and paused over the page she was looking for, "D-N-A, it stands for Deoxyribonucleic acid. It is the genetic map that constitutes who and what you are. It self-replicates as people reproduce and makes up the fundamental and distinctive characteristics of who you are, what you will look like, blonde hair, blue eyes, and so on. Those characteristics are passed down to your children and your children's children."

"So, how did we come to be here?" Ulrik leafed through the pages looking at pictures of the machine that brought them there.

"Well, that is another fascinating part of Dr. Tennbaum's invention. He discovered this dimension of our Earth's past and decided to live here traveling back and forth through the dimensions, forward and back in time. After many years of building this place, he decided he was lonely. So, he programmed the machine to look for the perfect mate for him through Earth's time and dimensions. The journals say it found her and one day, here she was! The machine brought her. The journals go on to say they lived here together for many, many years. It does not say what happened to her." Tessa shook her head sadly, "We know what happened to him. He fell down the stairs and died from a broken neck. We have no way of knowing what happened to the woman after that and he never discussed her in any of the other journals or mentions any other people living in this dimension. All indications are that this dimension is of a very, very young Earth at a time before people inhabited it. A simple way of explaining traveling through time is like going back to yesterday and reliving it or doing things differently."

Tessa pulled out one of the journals, removed a folded paper, and spread it out in a very long line. It was similar to a map but reflected a timeline instead. It listed dates throughout Earth's history by hundred-year marks and had lines and arrows drawn from one point in the year 3,000.

"This looks like a record of Dr. Tennbaum's time travels. The arrows point backward in time. Somehow, he had the technology to go back and forth, come here and build the underground storage and this cabin and bring back all the things he collected along the way."

"That still doesn't explain how we got here? Where is this machine that travels through time? I still do not understand." Ulrik said bewildered.

"I don't know either. Perhaps the machine was left running in the future and kept looking for Dr. Tennbaum. In a way, you are him or at least a very, very distant ancestor. You at least probably have some of his DNA. Maybe the machine transported you here and because it provided Dr. Tennbaum with a suitable wife, it eventually brought me here. I don't know. I might be related to his wife somehow, whoever she was."

"Do you think it will bring more people here? Why did it drop us in the middle of a lake? We could have drowned." Ulrik shook his head, indignation and, then concern crossing his face. "Could it send us back? I do not want to go back."

"I don't either. I just don't know Ulrik. The journals don't reveal where or more accurately *when* the machine is located, somewhere thousands of years in the future I guess. I suppose it is possible it might still deposit another one of our ancestors here, but somehow, I doubt it. I'm only guessing, but we are two, just as with Dr. Tennbaum and his wife. Since there are two of us, maybe that fits the machine's programming or completes what it was told to do. I wouldn't go back to my old life! Not for anything, but as we don't know where the machine is or how to shut it off, I guess we'll just have to see."

Ulrik stared into the fire and quietly contemplated all of what he had learned while Tessa continued to read through the journals. She resumed the conversation after a while.

"These explain a lot about this place, why this dimension is so much like the Earth we both knew, but not even a little bit more about why you and I are here."

Ulrik's brow furrowed in thought and finally, he let out a frustrated sigh.

"Yes, you and I are here, and we are happy, and I have no wish to return to my old life." Ulrik rose and pulled Tessa into his arms. "You are mine and I will never let anything happen to you." He kissed her gently on the lips and then pulled her toward the bed, blowing out the lamp as he laid her down. "Let us not worry about what was or what might be, but just live."

This was the first time Ulrik had spoken to Tessa with such emotion and any indication of how he felt about her. He said, *"you are mine."*

Tessa was overjoyed as she rested her face on the warm skin of his chest and whispered, "I agree, my Love."

Ulrik made love to Tessa thoroughly and desperately, pouring all his passion into every kiss and every touch, every thrust.

Early the next day as they ate their morning meal, Tessa asked Ulrik if he had ever seen any other people.

"My first summer here I traveled for three days in each direction away from the cabin. Then I returned here. I went north over the top of the mountains and only saw more mountains stretching as far as my eyes could see. I traveled south down the mountains and came to fields stretching out to the horizon. The same was true for the east and west. I never saw any sign of villages or people. There is nothing out there at least within three days' journey. Each time I came back thinking someday I might travel further, but there is no need." He shrugged his shoulders as if his word was law.

"That is strange. I can't for the life of me think that we are the only ones on this entire planet. Maybe Dr. Tennbaum found a completely ancient Earth before people populated it. He offers no explanations in his journals."

Ulrik rose, moved over to her, and pulled her close.

"I am just glad you are here. I was beginning to despair of seeing another soul ever again. I was just asking the gods for a woman when I looked out over the Sacred Lake and there *you* were."

Tessa pressed close and wrapped her arms around Ulrik's waist.

"I've been thinking. Maybe we are like Adam and Eve, the first people put on this planet and this is the Garden of Eden."

"Who are Adam and Eve?" Ulrik spoke into her hair and he nuzzled her neck, distractingly kissing her smooth skin.

"Who are…I guess you might not have heard that story. I will read it to you tonight."

That night Tessa took out the black leather-bound Bible they had found weeks earlier and she read the story of Adam and Eve to Ulrik. For a long time afterward, he said nothing but remained lost in his thoughts.

Much of what Dr. Tennbaum's journals revealed did not make sense to Ulrik. The Bible's explanation of how the world was created, about God the creator, and the first man and woman on Earth, he could accept. Though the story was different from the way his Norse religion taught, something felt truthful and reverent about it.

The journals did not reveal how Ulrik and Tessa had come to this place, anything about the Sacred Lake, why there were no other people, or what purpose they might serve. Ulrik kept everything he learned tucked away in his mind. The truth was Ulrik was happy now Tessa was with him despite the fact she was from a more modern time. There were no rules to follow, no enemies to threaten them or take what they had. He had no need for gold or treasure and no wish to change anything about his current life. He did not need to strive or struggle and no longer wanted to look back at the past or lament over his failures. Ulrik tallied his needs and responsibilities simply; food, water, shelter, wood for the fire, and Tessa were all that he needed.

#

The next day, Tessa and Ulrik went back to the lake. They undressed and swam across splashing and playing under the hot sun and vast blue sky. They washed each other with soap brought from the cabin and rinsed off under the waterfall. Swimming back to shore, Ulrik pulled Tessa close, wrapping her legs around him, he entered her in the cool of the lake, and they rocked together, kissing passionately. Ulrik carried her out of the water and still linked inside her, gently lowered her to the blanket. One hand on each side of Tessa, he held himself over her and gently, slowly made love to her savoring the feel of her, until their mutual satisfaction was found. Then they lay down beside each other as the early afternoon sun coursed its way across the sky. A slight breeze wafted around them making the trees sway calmly.

"By all the gods, I can never get enough of you! I also never get any work done with you around that is for certain." Ulrik said in a mock chiding tone.

"Yes, and my poor body can't get a moment's rest from you either." Tessa teased him back.

Then she straddled him and kissed him passionately until he was hard again. After they made love once more, he stated it was time to pick berries and check the traps. They dressed and strolled hand in hand down the mountain.

Ulrik went to check his traps while Tessa moved among some raspberry bushes filling a basket she had brought for that purpose. She spied some wild blueberries in a field close by and went to pick some of those too. As she knelt among the blueberries, she heard a great crashing noise coming from the nearby brush. Looking up, she saw lumbering toward her, a huge black bear. Tessa screamed, dropped her basket, and ran yelling for Ulrik. The bear bellowed as he reared up on his hind legs and then lunged after her. Tessa kept running. Ulrik came bolting out from the trees drawing his sword. He ran straight toward the bear swinging the sword over his head with two hands. Yelling, he struck the bear in the neck with a mighty downward stroke. Blood spurted and sprayed over Ulrik. His momentum carried him just past the bear that bellowed in pain and turned quickly. The bear's massive, long-clawed paw managed to catch Ulrik with a tearing swipe. In a snarling, rolling mass of blood, teeth, and fur, they collided and fell backward tearing at each other. Tessa watched hardly breathing, terrified Ulrik would be hurt or killed. The bear roared. Ulrik grasped him by the throat with both hands and, muscles bunching and sweat pouring down his face and mixing with blood, he pushed the bear's head back. In a blur of motion, he plunged his long dagger into the bear's eye and its brain. The bear stilled and Ulrik rolled off of it gasping in huge gulps of air. Tessa sprinted to his side and ran her shaking hands over him gently, trying to see how badly he was injured.

"We will be having bear meat for supper." Ulrik gasped and grinned.

"Ulrik, you're hurt!" Ulrik had numerous scratches and a bite on his upper arm. She helped him sit up and gasped in horror. The skin on his back at the shoulder was torn open with three long gashes. Blood streamed down his back.

"It was a good fight!" Ulrik proclaimed rising. He grasped the bear by the black hairy arm and turned it over, thinking to butcher it right on the spot.

"Ulrik I've got to get you back to the cabin and clean those wounds. You are going to need stitches. You are losing a lot of blood."

"The meat is too good to leave for the scavengers and we can use the fur. I am not hurt that bad." He continued to work.

Tessa gazed at him open-mouthed, but seeing that it was useless to argue, his stubborn streak was showing again, tried to help him. The entire time she begged him to leave the bear and let her tend to his wounds first. He would not listen, saying the meat was vital to survival and he was stalwart when it came to providing for them.

When they finally arrived back at the cabin with a huge side of bear meat, Ulrik fell heavily into a chair. Tessa ran to get a cloth to make bandages and put water on to heat. She boiled everything she could to make it as sterile as quickly as possible. Ulrik slouched in the chair exhausted, sweat running down his pale face.

Tessa cleaned the bite wound first then moved to the claw marks on his back. She gasped as she examined the tears in his flesh. The wounds were swollen and oozed blood. Tessa washed the gashes, pouring hot water over them. Ulrik hissed in pain as she worked. Putting a hot cloth over the wounds she went to get the bottle of wine they brought up from the wine cellar. She gave it to Ulrik and had him drink half the bottle down.

"I wish we had some of the whiskey from the cellar." As she began to sew up the claw marks on his back, Ulrik did not flinch once he only took long gulps of the wine. When she was done stitching the three long gashes, she cleaned away the rest of the blood and wrapped bandages around his shoulder and arm.

Ulrik stood shakily to his feet. "I will go and finish butchering the bear."

"You'll do no such thing! You are going straight to bed! You're too badly wounded!"

Ulrik staggered a bit, partially drunk and exhausted. She stripped him and helped him to bed. He lay down on his good side, closed his eyes, and fell asleep immediately. Tessa moved a chair next to the bed and watched Ulrik through the night. He moaned a little and woke for water once. Tessa fell asleep in the chair, exhausted herself.

The next morning Tessa awoke in the bed and Ulrik was gone. She sat up straight when she realized he was not there as she looked around the cabin. It was early morning. The birds were just starting to sing outside, but Ulrik was nowhere to be seen. She got up quickly and went to look for him. She found him in the smoking shed where he was busily cutting up the bear meat. He had dragged the rest of it up to the cabin on a hastily erected lean-to, finished preparing the meat, and the large black fur lay to one side. He worked quickly and deftly with his sharp dagger as if he had not just had the flesh of his shoulder nearly stripped away by the bear's claws.

Tessa went up to him, stood on her tiptoes, and placed her hand on his forehead. "You're burning up! Ulrik, get back to bed this instant before the fever gets any worse!"

Ulrik smiled a crooked smile at her, grabbed her with one arm, and gave her a lusty kiss. "I am almost finished here. Go back inside and make us something to break our fast, and I will be in when I am finished."

"No! I said get back to bed now! You have a fever!"

Ulrik just looked at her, grinned, "Only if you come with me," and continued to cut and hang the meat.

Tessa moved to stand in front of him, placed her hands on his chest, and stared at him.

"Ulrik, I couldn't stand it if you got sick and died. I couldn't live without you. You need to rest and get better for me. Please, get back in bed."

Ulrik let out a huge sigh and then hung the rest of the carcass up, checked the smoking fire, and then went to a pail of water, washed the bear blood off of his hands and arms, and only then followed Tessa back to the cabin. Tessa's brow creased with worry. She contemplated getting one of the medical books she had seen in the cellar library and decided later she would go down there to see if one of the volumes would help her treat his wounds.

Back in the cabin, she undressed Ulrik and he lay propped up on the bed. Tessa got some cool water for him and he drank thirstily. She unwrapped the bandages and looked at the angry gashes she had sewn up in his shoulder the night before.

"You're going to have three lovely scars. I need to clean this up a bit, you've torn the stitches in a couple of places, but I don't think I should re-stitch them. I'll also need to take a look at that bite again."

Ulrik just grunted and watched her face as she dabbed at the fresh blood and re-wrapped his shoulder. She looked at the bite wound which was bruised, swollen, and beginning to ooze a yellowish puss. She cleaned it with hot water, scrubbed it vigorously, and then re-wrapped it too. Fluffing the pillows behind Ulrik, she gently pushed him back to rest in the bed. Tessa returned to the kitchen and began to make tea and throw some breakfast together. When she turned back, Ulrik was fast asleep.

It took Ulrik a week to get back on his feet again. Tessa insisted he stay in bed for the duration. He wanted to be up and working the next day, but as his fever got worse, Tessa won the argument. Ulrik stated he would not mind staying in bed if she would join him, but that just earned him a disapproving look. Tessa busied herself around the house and read to Ulrik when he was awake and restless. Eventually, they went down to the lake and bathed being careful not to get his wounds wet, but the cool water seemed to chase away the last of his fever and Ulrik was soon his hearty self once more. They made love under the tree in their favorite spot and napped in the sunlight.

They fell back into their routine with the constant reminder that life was fragile and could be dangerous. Ulrik and Tessa spent their days working and playing. Tessa went hunting with Ulrik and soon became an excellent shot with a bow and arrow. Ulrik tended to the meat and hides he hunted, while Tessa gardened, cooked, and sewed. At night Tessa read to Ulrik from one of the books that they had found in the cabin or from the underground library. They did not discuss Dr. Jeremiah David Tennbaum or his machine again because the subject bothered Ulrik greatly. Tessa continued to wonder where the machine was but decided it was left turned on somewhere in the future. Why it deposited them in the lake also remained a mystery. They both accepted that they were there and left it at that.

Tessa completely forgot the 85-year-old, twenty-first-century woman whom she used to be. She left behind all her old psychological hang-ups and stopped speaking so formally to Ulrik. Ulrik wanted nothing, but to please Tessa and provide for her. Together they made a home.

Once a month when Tessa had her monthly menstruation, she wondered why she had not conceived. As much as they made love, she had expected to be pregnant by now. Although the idea elated and frightened her at the same time, she could not hide the disappointment from her face during her monthly period. Ulrik would gently take her in his arms kiss the top of her head and hold her while she silently cried.

"Do not worry. It could be my fault. I never fathered a child in my life before."

"I want to give you a son, Ulrik. I want it more than anything."

Ulrik would hold her close, pressing his face into her hair or rubbing his cheek against hers. He would take a deep breath and then kiss away her sadness. Tessa began to despair of ever conceiving.

Chapter Eight - Summer Harvest

The summer season was long, but fall would eventually threaten to appear. Ulrik began to talk about taking a trip.

"When I traveled three days to the south just out of the mountains, I saw fields of wild grain. We should go there and harvest some before winter sets in. I can show you how it is done and then we will have enough grain to get us through the winter months."

"That would be wonderful! We can camp under the stars and have a vacation!"

"What is a vacation?"

"Well, it is where you go away from home and visit a place you've never been to before. It is like taking a break from work so that you can rest and relax."

"It will be hard work to gather grain for the winter. If you want to call it a vacation, then I will not argue with you."

Tessa and Ulrik prepared to go. She sewed bags for the grain and rolled up some bedding to sleep on and packed enough food for a long trip that might take a couple weeks or more. Tessa dressed in pants, a warm overshirt, and a soft undershirt. She wore her sturdiest boots, braided her long hair, and carried her pack, a bow, and quiver of arrows. Ulrik carried the rest. They closed the door to their little cabin one morning and headed down the mountain. Tessa turned to take a last look before they entered the trees and tried to squelch the unbidden feeling that she might never come back.

The forest was a magical riot of color and the late summer day was warm. Rich brown barked trees dressed in emerald green leaves surrounded them. White aspens stood regally in vast groves. Colorful wildflowers bloomed everywhere and mushrooms of all shapes sizes and colors pushed up from the deep black soil.

Ulrik and Tessa traveled quickly following a game trail to make the going easier. Ulrik was an excellent woodsman and seemed to know exactly where he was going. He was always on the watch for bears, mountain lions, or wolves, and kept his sword strapped to his hip, his long dagger sheathed tightly to his thigh.

Sometimes as they walked Ulrik would tell Tessa stories of the adventures he had in his other life as a Norseman. Upon hearing them, Tessa marveled that he had made it to sixty years old. Tessa never shared stories about her previous life but told him what she knew of the Viking culture, and of Leif Ericson. Ulrik would grow a little quiet and moody after they talked of his previous life, but nothing seemed to keep him down for long. He did not seem surprised to find out that Vikings were thought by many to have discovered the North American continent. Ulrik seemed to have unending strength and vast knowledge of how to survive in the mountainous wilderness.

They had a good night's sleep under the stars in the deep forest. Then the next day they came to a cleft in the mountain where a natural hot spring bubbled up from the ground. It conjoined with a cold brook that eventually formed a pool nestled in the tall pines and aspen trees that thickly covered the mountainside. They bathed in the pool's hot waters and eased their tired muscles and sore feet.

The next day, much refreshed, they resumed their descent down the mountainside. Eventually, they reached a place where the Aspen trees thinned out considerably, and soon, they saw a vast stretching plain of swaying grasses. They traveled another hour bordering the thinning rows of trees and then came to a vast wild wheat field extending as far as their eyes could see. The golden stalks swayed gently in the breeze making a soft swishing sound. Ulrik tested a stalk twirling the seeds between his fingertips and pronounced the grain good enough for harvesting. They cleared a flat area on the ground, laid out a blanket, cut a row of stalks, and began to beat the wheat on the blanket. Soon, they had a pile of golden grains.

They picked out pieces of stalk and other inedible pieces and scooped the grains into bags. It was hard and slow labor, but they worked steadily at it together and soon had a respectable amount of grain to show for their efforts. Carrying it all back up the mountainside to the cabin would slow them down, but it would be worth the hard work.

That night they slept under a vast sky of twinkling stars but rose early to resume their work.

Ulrik stopped to wipe the sweat off his brow and glanced toward the eastern horizon. The hair on the back of his neck prickled. He gave a sudden curse and bolted toward Tessa.

"Ulrik! What is it?" She asked shocked and scared at the way Ulrik grabbed her hand and ran.

"Riders!" He yelled pulling her toward the trees.

"WHAT!" Tessa exclaimed looking back as she ran, astonished at seeing other *people* coming toward them and scared at the same time. She could see in the distance at least ten horsemen riding straight toward them at a furious pace. They were waving weapons in the air and shouting. There was no chance that they had not seen Ulrik and Tessa out in the open field. All they could do now was hope to outrun them and lose them in the trees of the forest.

As they approached the line of trees where their camp was, Ulrik turned, drew his sword, and pushed Tessa behind him.

"Run!" He shouted at her.

"What are you doing? You can't fight that many!"

"You have never seen me fight before! Now RUN! I can hold them off while you escape. Go back to the cabin and I will come as soon as I deal with them." Ulrik's chest heaved as he caught his breath and planted his feet in a fighting stance. Half turning his head, but not taking his eyes from the riders, he yelled at her again, "Run! *Now!*"

"I'm not leaving you!" Tessa bent and grabbed her bow and arrows. She doubted she could hit a man moving on horseback but vowed she would give it a good try.

"Tessa run! I will not let them take you. I can give you time to get away, but I cannot fight all of them with one eye on you. Now go!"

The distance closed quickly as the riders moved toward them at a threatening pace.

"Maybe they are friendly? We don't know. I can't just leave you. Let's try and talk to them."

"Tessa, I will deal with them whatever they intend and join you as soon as I can. Please go!" Ulrik's voice rose loud and filled with anger.

Tessa finally turned to go then turned back demanding, "You come as soon as you can! Promise!"

"I promise, *now run!*" The thunder of hooves grew closer to them.

Tessa reluctantly turned and ran. By now the horsemen were upon them and Ulrik turned to stand and fight.

As the riders approached, Ulrik swore and spit, "Picts!"

The men rode in strange saddles or bareback on tall, sleek horses, they were painted with blue designs and they yelled in a language Ulrik did not understand. The man at the head of the pack gestured to his right and then left, and the other riders spread out surrounding Ulrik.

Ulrik took their measure quickly. They had drawn wicked-looking knives made of black shiny stone and some had black stone axes. Ulrik knew his huge Viking steel sword could quickly cut through their inferior weapons. He smiled grimly and waited for them to come at him knowing instinctually that they were not friendly. The leader gestured toward the forest where Tessa had disappeared into the trees. Ulrik shouted and ran at two blue-painted men who took off after Tessa, but they surrounded him quickly. Swinging his sword, he chopped down splintering the stone axe of the first man to get too close. Then he took off the man's head on the backswing, blood arched up, as he turned toward his next attacker.

The blue-painted men yelled and darted in and out at Ulrik, slashing and swinging their stone weapons. They never got in close enough for Ulrik to land another killing blow. Ulrik fought smoothly, each stroke battering the men back. It proved to be a lesson in frustration though because as soon as they got in close enough for Ulrik to strike, they would leap back out of the way and never engaged him in real combat. Ulrik cursed them as cowards and taunted them, beckoning them to come into striking range. The blue-painted men shouted at him in their strange language and he barely dodged a thrown spear.

Sweat ran down Ulrik's face, but he regulated his breathing and began to make fewer strikes with his sword conserving his energy. His blue eyes stormed with anger. He quickly realized that they were baiting him and trying to wear him out. Ulrik settled in for a long fight knowing he *had* to outlast them all and hoping to present a big enough challenge that they would forget Tessa. Silently, he prayed to Odin that she had gotten away.

The leader of the blue men seemed to realize that Ulrik was not going to go down easily. He wheeled his horse around behind the other men on foot, pulled out a long thin tube from his belt, put it to his mouth, pointed it toward Ulrik, and blew. A blue-painted dart streaked out from the end of the tube, so fast, that Ulrik did not see it coming toward him. It took him in the neck. Ulrik grabbed it as it pierced his skin and wrenched it free, but enough of the poison in the dart reached his blood and had done its work quickly. After a few moments, Ulrik fell to his knees as his eyesight went blurry. He pitched forward and darkness took him.

Chapter Nine – Taken

Ulrik woke to find himself slung over the back of a horse. The animal's jostling gait caused Ulrik's head to bounce up and down and he cursed aloud as the motion made him feel nauseous. A rider approached and then another poison dart struck deep just above his hip and he fell into oblivion once again.

The next time Ulrik awoke he was in a tent. He was laying on his back, arms out, legs spread, bound firmly to stakes into the ground. The dark interior of his prison indicated it was nighttime. Ulrik did his best not to moan in pain, as he slightly moved his head to attempt to see his surroundings. He was not sure if he was alone or not. He sensed stirrings and someone moved toward him from out of the shadows. There was a scuffling sound and then Ulrik could just barely make out the form of an old woman. She came close, bent toward him with a cup, and poured some liquid into his parched mouth. Cool water filled Ulrik's mouth and he could not help but drink greedily. She filled the cup again and gave him more before moving away. Ulrik could hear flint striking and soon a small fire dimly lit the interior of the tent.

The woman was very old. Ulrik could make out dark blue robes covering her thin body. Her gray hair hung in many braids and was decorated with beads and painted with blue streaks. She smiled and nodded her head at Ulrik mumbling in a strange language. Patting her chest, she said, "Mohem, Mohem."

Ulrik guessed that was the old woman's name and nodded his head once that he understood. Then Mohem gestured toward her mouth, making an eating motion, and brought some food to Ulrik's mouth. She stuffed a piece of some kind of heavily herbed meat into his mouth and cupped his chin making him chew. Ulrik choked down the meat and some more water. After a few more mouthfuls, the old woman named Mohem rose and left the tent.

Ulrik quickly tested the leather straps around his wrists and ankles, but they were tied very securely. He tugged at the stakes with all his strength thinking he could pull them free, but they were long and thick, and deeply embedded into the ground. Still, he fought at his bindings until his wrists and ankles were rubbed raw and starting to bleed. He felt dizzy and sick from the aftereffects of the blue darts and quickly realized he was making absolutely no progress getting free. He lay back and stilled, wondering if Tessa had made good her escape, praying to Odin and all the Norse Gods that she had made it safely away. He was filled with a restless fear for her and not knowing what happened to her made him want to roar with anger. Eventually, he had to calm himself and a dreamless sleep finally took him.

The next morning the old woman woke Ulrik as she bustled around the tent. She had some kind of milk, cheese, and bread, and fed Ulrik again as she had the night before. She made tisking sounds as she discovered his bloody wrists and, picking up a rock, she gave the stakes a couple of weak whacks seemingly trying to demonstrate how firmly he was held and unmistakably indicating that there was no escape, with sharp words he did not understand. Then, she pulled aside the flap of the tent and pointed to two guards directly posted outside the tent, speaking calmly in her strange language to Ulrik as if to show escape was not possible. He was well guarded.

Now that it was daylight, Ulrik assessed the rest of his surroundings. The tent was made of shades of blue canvas-like material. There was a small brazier where a fire crackled and many pottery jars of all sizes, a few bowls of food, sacks made of leather, and a worn drum. Everything was painted with blue symbols. When the sun shone on the tent from the outside, the inside of the tent was cast in a blue gloom.

As time passed, Ulrik began to grow even angrier and worried about Tessa. Then he began to get restless wishing they would just come and begin whatever they had planned for him.

He waited for what seemed like hours hearing the sounds of people and animals outside the tent. Near midday, the flaps parted and three old men, and the old woman named Mohem, entered the tent. The men were old, small, and stooped, dressed in blue robes. They had multiple strands of beads and bones hanging from their withered necks. Their thin hair was braided and painted in blue streaks just like the old woman's.

For a long time, they sat around the fire and argued, gesturing, and pointing at Ulrik. Eventually, they seemed to come to a decision. One of them said something to Mohem and she moved toward Ulrik. She bent over him and pulled one of his eyelids open revealing his bright blue eye then pulled his lip up showing his strong white teeth. She smoothed his long white-blonde hair admiringly and pinched his biceps muscle, all the while keeping up a string of conversation. Then, she moved down and unlaced his britches. Ulrik started cursing her and tossed his body as far as his bonds would let him and he, ineffectually, tried to move away from her. She reached into his pants and pulled his large penis out. Ulrik cursed her so loud that she had to reach over and stuff his mouth with a piece of cloth.

The old men bent forward and made begrudging sounds of appreciation. Ulrik continued to yell, promising retribution through his gag, not caring that they could not understand a word he said. The old woman gave his penis a soft pat and stuffed it gently back into his pants, pulling the laces tight. They stood listening while Mohem animatedly rambled on in their strange language, obviously trying to convince them of something. Ulrik knew nothing of what was going on. Finally, the old men mumbled together for many long minutes then turned and left without a backward glance.

Mohem smiled showing surprisingly nice, white teeth, and resumed a string of conversation with Ulrik that he could not understand. Every once in a while, she would cover her mouth and giggle into her hand in a youthful gesture that made her look half her age. She worked purposefully around the tent, dipping into the jars and sacks, and was mixing something in a large bowl. She pulled out a handful of deep blue flowers from an ornately painted pouch. Giving them a long appreciative sniff, she put them in the bowl and began to crush them with a blue-stained stone.

That night just outside the tent Ulrik was held in, he heard what sounded like a gathering of the entire tribe of blue people. The glow from a large bonfire flickered and danced and lit up the interior of his prison. There was some sort of meeting going on and he could hear shouting and men's angry voices talking over each other. Mohem's voice frequently rose loud and clear giving long speeches. The discussion seemed to go on for hours. Ulrik gave up paying any sort of attention to it because he could not understand what was being decided.

The following morning the old woman fed Ulrik and held a gourd for him to relieve himself in. Ulrik cursed her often and continued to pull at his bonds. She reprimanded, shaking a finger at him then smiled and continued with her mixing, mumbling, and gesturing over the mixture. To him, it looked almost like she was casting a spell and the hair on the back of Ulrik's neck stood on end. He was vastly superstitious about witches and he shuddered to think about what she was going to do to him.

As the hours passed, Ulrik stared at the roof of the tent and waited to see what they had in store for him. Night fell and he slept. His dreams were of Tessa and their mountain home.

The next day Ulrik did not have long to wait to find out what the blue people had in store for him. Mohem undressed and washed him and combed out his long hair. Carefully cutting away the seams of his clothing with a black stone dagger, leaving him completely bare. He was lying on many thick furs, so he was not uncomfortable, but being naked made him feel vulnerable and that was not a feeling he was familiar with nor one that he liked. His mind raced with what this could mean, and he wondered what tortures they had in mind for him. He could endure almost anything as long as he knew that Tessa was safe, but there was no way to know.

Mohem held a cup to his lips saying, "Meadwhey."

Ulrik filled his mouth with the liquid and then spit it in her face just to be difficult. The old woman calmly wiped her face off then firmly plugged his nose with her thumb and forefinger and forced him to swallow another draught. The liquid was tinged slightly blue, tasted sweet, and had a spice to it that Ulrik could not recall ever tasting. His belly was otherwise empty, and he felt fine after drinking it and began to think it was nothing to be suspicious of. Maybe she had not poisoned him as he first thought. He began to feel slightly drunk after she made him drink more and more of the stuff. Then his vision began to go hazy and his head spun. The silence of the tent roared in his ears and he felt very strange and *very* drunk.

Soon the tent flaps parted and Ulrik's eyes went wide upon seeing five young girls enter the tent. They were all dressed in short blue tunics split at the sides to reveal tan, shapely legs, their long dark hair was fashioned in many twists and braids and was streaked with blue. Their faces were painted delicately in the same blue, with swirls and strange symbols. Some of the girls openly stared at him, smiling widely, while others looked shyly from under blue-painted eyelids and dark lashes. They all stared wide-eyed at his nakedness.

Ulrik suddenly began to feel the drink the old woman had given him, which made him grow rock hard as he had an erection that became heavy and horribly painful. His blood burned fiery in his veins and his head swam as the Meadwhey worked. His eyesight grew blurry and everything looked strange in the blue gloom of the tent. Incredibly dizzy and feeling very drunk, he fought at his bonds clumsily and he shouted at the women with slurred speech. Mohem crouched down beside him. She talked gently to him like one would talk to a child. She filled his mouth with more of the Meadwhey forcing him to swallow or else choke, then offered a draught to each of the girls who drank eagerly. Finally, she gave a long string of instructions to them, gesturing, almost lewdly.

Ulrik had never in either of his lives been this drunk and as the Meadwhey surged through his veins, he passed out. The sound of drumming invaded his befuddled dreams.

#

The following morning Ulrik woke up with this head splitting as if he had been hit with an axe. He lay gasping as the effects of the Meadwhey slowly left his system. Strangely, he felt raw, used, and exhausted. He tried to remember what happened the night before after he had been forced to drink so much of the Meadwhey that he lost consciousness. His mind was blank except for flashes of tanned limbs and firm breasts that seeped into his memory. The overwhelming feeling that something very wrong happened with the five girls who entered the tent that night, turned Ulrik's blood cold. He struggled to recall exactly what had happened, what he had done, but his memory was a hazy blue fog. Reality hit him like an axe blow, Mohem's witchcraft had ensnared him leaving him incapable of recalling fully what he had done.

Rage and embarrassment filled him. All his thoughts were of Tessa. Had he betrayed her with the blue-painted girls? Ulrik shuddered with fury, indignation, and shame.

Mohem came into the tent and cleaned him, head to toe. Her surprisingly strong hands massaged his muscles. Then she put salve on his wrists and ankles that were raw from pulling and then fed him. She took care of his every need except the need for freedom. He tried talking to her several times and asked about Tessa, but their language barrier only allowed the most basic understanding. Ulrik rested the next day. The effects of the Meadwhey she had given him completely wore off and he was grateful for that, but his shame over what might have happened had not worn off. He continued to struggle to remember.

The following day, it all began again. The old woman forced Ulrik to drink the Meadwhey, but this time he sputtered and choked, spilling much of it down his chin and neck. Patiently, Mohem gave it to him again, holding his head and pinching his nose so that he was forced to swallow it down. He coughed and fought, but the liquid continued to flow down his throat. Then five more young girls came into the tent. The strange ceremony began again. Ulrik was in a drunken delirium and felt as if he were floating outside of his body. His mind shut down, but his body participated when the drum's erotic beat took over.

#

In the days that followed, Ulrik became almost frantic wondering how long his captivity could go on and what was happening to Tessa. He struggled to remember what happened each time he was forced to drink the Meadwhey to the point of passing out. He thought it was even in the food Mohem fed him as the same spicey flavor permeated everything. If his suspicions were correct, they were using him in some sort of ceremony, to what purpose, he could not guess. His memories contained flashes of naked, blue-painted female bodies.

He also thought long and hard about the, *ten* girls it would be now, who could potentially have gotten pregnant during the ceremony. In nine months, could he have ten sons? Or would it be ten daughters? Most likely it would be a mixture of both. However, he had not gotten Tessa pregnant in the many months he had been with her so it was entirely possible he could not father children. He also wondered what the blue people would do with him after they were finished with him. Why was this barbaric tribe forcing him to do this?

The next day Ulrik was allowed to rest. In addition to a break from the ceremony, some men came in and unbound him from the stakes. He instantly tried to escape, but despite his superior size and strength, his legs had been unused for many days and were very weak. They easily stopped him. They tied his arms tightly to his body and tied his ankles together just wide enough for him to walk then put a rope around his neck to pull him out of the tent.

Bright sunlight momentarily blinded him. The guards each had a spear with a long wicked looking stone blade on it. They led him to a river where Ulrik, still bound, was washed, and taken care of by young girls, some of whom Ulrik thought he recognized. They laughed and splashed Ulrik, washing his hair, and fawning over him as if it were a game. Ulrik looked at them angrily and refused to give them any satisfaction by looking as if he was enjoying their antics. He also looked around under lowered eyelids, watching, and calculating. He made numerous attempts to escape, but all failed because of his bindings. His guards were diligent and frequently jabbed at him with their spears, stopping just short of cutting him.

The camp was fairly large consisting of dozens of blue tents of many different hues. Men and women were working, making weapons, eating, and just lounging around. There was a pen of horses that appeared to be well guarded and further down the river some women washed blue clothing. All of the people wore blue clothes and were painted with blue decorations. Most went about their daily lives as if Ulrik was not there. However, Ulrik noticed many of the men cast him vicious looks full of hatred. Them, he intentionally cursed and taunted. He also noticed no little children were running around which seemed to suggest a lot.

Ulrik's eyes searched the camp for Tessa. His emotions were conflicted because seeing her would be a balm to his heart, but he truly did not wish her to be a captive as he was. Not seeing her, meant she had gotten free and he ultimately hoped she was safe back at the cabin. His promise to return to her weighed heavily on his heart. Ulrik decided to make a break for it at his first chance, but he feared the blue darts which noticeably hung at every warrior's hip. He had no choice, but to wait and watch for his opportunity.

The guards eventually walked him back through the camp to the tent where they held him captive. He sat down and tried to convince them to leave him tied sitting up and not staked to the ground as before. Mohem would have none of that and they bound him to the stakes lying on his back again.

Just as they finished tying him up, the flaps of the tent flew open and a man and woman stalked in. They appeared to be in the middle of a heated argument. Ulrik recognized the man as the leader of the riders that had taken him prisoner.

The woman was very beautiful. She had long chestnut braids richly decorated with beads and small bones. Her blue-painted arms and ankles were adorned with bracelets and her short tunic accented a slender figure and large firm breasts. Her attitude suggested she knew how beautiful she was, and she was using all her wiles on the man, Ulrik guessed was her husband. She kept gesturing toward Ulrik making a string of demands that got louder and more desperate. The man stood stubbornly with his arms crossed over his chest. He remained unaffected through her tirade and only shook his head "no" in the end.

Finally, the woman realized she was getting nowhere. She stamped her foot and pleaded one last time with her husband, who did not budge. Finally, she left the tent in a huff. The man turned toward Ulrik. Wrath painted his strong features, hatred burned in his eyes, and he looked as if he would like to throttle Ulrik. Then Mohem entered the tent. She placed a consoling hand on the man's arm and spoke gently to him. Ulrik guessed he was some sort of Chieftain. The man gave a short curt demand to the old woman who nodded her head agreeing. After casting a malevolent look at Ulrik, he too left.

Ulrik could guess what that conversation had been about him, and he was glad that the Chief said, *"No!"*

Chapter Ten – Chieftain's Wife

Night fell. Mohem fed Ulrik and forced him to drink the Meadwhey by pinching his nose and forcing his mouth open. The drink seemed more potent than before and he quickly became drunk. Part of his mind knew he was not hallucinating when three blue-painted girls came into the tent. He thought he recognized them from the very first ceremony but could not be sure as everything had turned into a blur. The oblivion that came with the potion was welcome and all Ulrik knew was the erotic beating of the drum as darkness covered his mind.

Hours later Ulrik lay drunk and exhausted. His head still swam from the Meadwhey and he was sick at heart struggling to remember what he had just done under its influence. Something was different this time and he forced himself to clear away the fog that was his memory. As before visions of tanned limbs, flowing dark hair and firm breasts were all he could see. Trying harder to recall, it suddenly struck him. After the drums stopped and he was finally left alone, a beautiful face swam before his mind's sight. It was the chieftain's wife!

He tried to think clearly and pull his splintered memory into a coherent order and uncover what happened. Ulrik had fallen under the Meadwhey's power and he lost time and consciousness again. The drums had stopped after the initial ceremony, but he felt as if he was still dreaming when the tent flaps had parted, and the beautiful Chieftain's wife silently glided into the tent.

The firelight showed the determined look on her face. She moved slowly toward him. He remembered she released a tie at her shoulder and the garment she wore fell to pool at her feet. She stood completely naked before him. Her beautiful body was painted with blue designs up her arms and down her outer hips and thighs that were illuminated by the firelight.

She searched through the old woman's things until she found the bag with the Meadwhey in it. She moved to where Ulrik lay and then straddled him. She held his mouth closed and plugged his nose so that he would have to swallow. Ulrik, too out of awareness to fight her, fell into oblivion again and knew no more.

Now as he lay there forcing himself to face the memory, he could guess what happened. His last vision was of watching her as she dressed, smiling, very pleased with herself, and she left without a backward glance.

Ulrik shook his head trying to sober, staring into the gloom of the tent contemplating everything that happened to him after the drum silenced and the Chieftain's wife came to him. Gritting his teeth, hating every minute of his captivity he prayed he was indeed hallucinating that the Chieftain's wife had not actually been there. He pulled at his bonds with all his strength and could not break the tough leather straps that bound his wrists and ankles.

The Chief's wife was not a maiden and it was obvious she desperately wanted a child and Ulrik was evidently chosen to give her one. He could find no pity in his heart for her. Inside his head, fury added fuel to his determination to escape. *Somehow*, he had to get free, but until he knew if Tessa was also a prisoner, he could not leave. He lay lightheaded and shaky with the effects of the Meadwhey and sick at heart from what had happened.

Later that morning Mohem returned to check on him. She took one look at Ulrik who lay awake. His eyes were red-rimmed, angry, and miserable. She mumbled something to herself, picked up a bowl of water, and cleaned his bloody wrists. She gently patted his cheek and spoke calmly to him as if he were a child. Ulrik turned his head away and refused to acknowledge her. He understood that what happened with the Chieftain's wife was not part of Mohem's ceremony or a Meadwhey-induced hallucination. It had been real and for once he was glad no more details rose to the surface of his mind. He shut the memory out and continued to plan an escape.

Another day passed and five guards came to take him outside. They led him stumbling through the camp again and took him to the river. It was a gentle, early fall day and the sun shone brightly on the thickly wooded area where the camp spread widely. Ulrik looked at the leaves on the trees and saw that they were just beginning to turn red and gold in anticipation of falling. The prospect of spending the winter with these people did nothing to improve his mood as he looked for other signs of the seasons changing. He frowned at all the women he passed even growling at them when they tried to wash him. He stepped out as far as the rope on his neck would allow and dunked his head in the clear cool water.

The effects of the Meadwhey Mohem gave him were starting to linger and his mind felt fuzzy all the time and his vision was slightly blurry. His memory was confusing and Ulrik was not sure of anything. The cold water helped to dissipate the effects and he drank deep and shook water droplets from his eyes. That is when he saw her.

Tessa was downstream with the other women. They had dressed her in one of the short blue tunics and had twisted and painted her golden hair with streaks of blue. She had spotted him as well and stood transfixed watching him stand in the river. A look of delighted relief crossed her face and she acted as if she wanted to run to him. It was then Ulrik noticed that Tessa was kept under guard as well and had a long rope tied around her neck. Although, her hands and feet were free so that she could help with the clothes washing. She also had a large purple bruise under the eye that was on the side of her face turned away from him. Ulrik was enraged to see she had been hurt. Tessa gave him a smile, filling it with all the love in her heart, and held his eyes for a long moment. Then one of the blue women gave her rope a vicious yank and Tessa fell to her knees in the river.

Ulrik roared and lurched toward Tessa, but the guards and the rope around his neck would not allow him to get any nearer to her. He was yanked back no matter how hard he strained. They dragged and prodded him out of the river with spears and he was taken back toward the tent. He fought hard, but it was useless. Ulrik craned his neck as long as he could just to keep sight of Tessa. His guards led him back toward the old woman's tent, his prison. At least, he had one question answered, Tessa too was a prisoner.

As they walked through the camp there was a loud clamor and soon about twenty riders galloped into the camp. Ulrik and his guards stopped to watch the newcomers as they rode toward them on tall sleek horses. They were more of the blue men. About ten male riders surrounded a wagon that had about seven girls in it and about ten more riders following behind that wagon and a second wagon, piled high with what looked like supplies or trade goods.

These men were dressed similarly to the others and had the same blue paint on their hair and bodies, but the designs were different. One of the riders walked his horse forward. Without dismounting, he leaned forward and spoke to the Chief whom Ulrik had met twice now. They greeted each other with cold civility, although they shared similar features and appeared to be brothers. They spoke for a few minutes and the Chief gestured toward Ulrik. The other leader got off his horse and walked to where Ulrik stood. It seemed that word of Ulrik had spread.

The guards tightened their hold on Ulrik's ropes and pulled him forward for inspection. As with the three old men weeks before, the newcomer checked his eyes, his hair, and teeth, pinched his muscles, and made many gestures admiring his height. Ulrik wrenched away and tried not to stand still as if he were a horse being inspected for stud. These people had evidently never seen a blonde, blue-eyed Norseman before. The leader of the new group of men gestured and the second wagon was wheeled forward. The hides that were covering the second wagon were yanked away to reveal blue cloth, pottery jars, bags of grain, and various trade goods. The new leader gestured toward the first wagon of girls and then at Ulrik. A bargain was struck, arms clasped to seal the deal, and the two chieftains walked away satisfied with themselves. The wagon of girls was also taken away and the girls giggled behind their hands, smiling, and watching Ulrik with great interest.

Ulrik quickly surmised what was going to happen. He was to play stallion to this new brood of women in the Meadwhey ceremony, but he would have none of it. He wrenched and strained at his bonds and tried to run away. He yelled at the two chiefs.

"If you think I am laying with your women think again! I am a man, not a breeding stallion! Cursed Picts!"

Ulrik started swearing at them and kept yelling as the men walked away. One of the guards jammed a spear into his stomach and one hit him across the back, another hit him in the back of his knees. Ulrik fell forward and landed hard. As he did, he saw the two chiefs a couple of tents away giving Tessa the same evaluation. Ulrik had had enough!

"NO!" he roared and surged to his feet straining at his bonds, pulling his guards forward.

"Not her! Tessa!"

Ulrik rammed one of his guards in the gut with his head, but with his ankles bound he could not get but a couple of steps away. He fought and they continued to beat him with the ends of their spears until the old woman came and loudly chastised them. They dragged him, still struggling, and yelling for Tessa, back into his prison tent.

Tessa fought her guards too and shouted for Ulrik, but she was more easily pulled away.

Inside the tent, Ulrik lay bound to the stakes again with even more ropes and straps. His chest heaved with his exertions, he was bruised and battered, dirty and bloody, but not badly injured. He cursed his captors loudly, shouting in his native Norse language. He jerked and pulled at the stakes and raved until he fell back exhausted. Mohem threatened him with a blue dart and he quieted a little. She tisked and mumbled and cleaned his cuts and bruises. She tried to feed him, but he refused, and she gave him water to drink.

During the night, Ulrik decided to take a different approach and try communicating with Mohem. He asked for Tessa saying her name over and over. He tossed his head in the direction of the tent he saw her go into and even begged anything to get her to listen. She nodded her head up and down as if she understood and mumbled a long string of words in her strange language. She patted his shoulder as if to assure him and gave him a sad smile. She could have been telling him anything he realized. He gave up, praying to Odin, Tessa's Jesus, and any other god he could think of, that Tessa was safe and was not being put through the same torture as he was.

#

For five days Ulrik was allowed to rest before he was forced into the ceremony again. Four of the new maidens were brought in and like before, he was forced to drink the Meadwhey and became so drunk that he passed out. The drum started beating and the ceremony went on. He was delirious and blacked out.

Ulrik's shaft was raw from all the friction of the many different women. He was covered in sweat, maiden blood, and stickiness from his seed. He was revolted at what they were making him do and felt, turning his head to the side, heaved the sparse contents of his stomach out. Mohem would clean him up and change the furs beneath him. With a worried look on her face, she seemed to pronounce him in need of rest, and the next day when more women came, she turned them away. Ulrik seemed to have earned a reprieve because he was not used in the ceremony again for almost two weeks.

At night, he heard drums and singing as the two tribes celebrated and carried on late into the night. He slept and mentally planned.

The old woman let him sit up, cleaned him all over, and gently rubbed his raw penis with a soothing salve. She fed him and took care of him. Ulrik physically healed but remained sick at heart over this forced betrayal of Tessa. Though thankfully his memory was foggy of the specific details of the ceremony his body knew what he had been up to.

He did not know how much more of this he could withstand. He was frantic with worry for Tessa. According to his limited view of the camp, he guessed he had been with every woman in the camp except the last three of the newcomers. There was no telling how many more tribes of the blue men would come bringing their daughters for him to impregnate *if* that were truly what the ceremony was meant to accomplish. It was the only logical explanation he could come up with. To have to continue to do this much longer was inconceivable. The whys of the need for his seed disturbed him and he did not think he could stand it. His thoughts were only on Tessa and his imaginings over what was happening to her were inconceivable and maddening.

One thing was for certain, she could only get pregnant one time whereas he could impregnate many women, but she could be used repeatedly. When he saw her, she looked well cared for and not abused, except for the bruised eye.

Ulrik was desperate to make this torment stop. The superstitious dread of Mohem tore at his mind and the fragments of his memory tortured his heart.

Although his head was fuzzy, his body felt anxious with the need for movement. He continually forced his mind to try and fully unravel what happened each time he passed out drunk and the drum began. He thought he was untied during the ceremony. That meant he participated freely, but his heart could not accept that possibility. Regardless, if he had the use of his hands, he could get free. He thought long and hard about how to stay awake and or pretend to pass out. If they really did untie him, perhaps he would have enough strength or a frenzy of rage to free himself. It was a plan made out of desperation.

Ulrik was not given the opportunity though. After an extended rest of about another week, the last three girls from the other tribe were brought in. Mohem gave him even more of the Meadwhey. Ulrik fought but was forced to drink it down and passed out cold despite his attempts to remain awake. The drums beat and the spell took Ulrik where he would not want to go if he had full control.

Resting for another two or even three weeks Ulrik tried to guess by counting the nights, but his head was muddled from the effects of the Meadwhey in the beginning and he had lost count. He was allowed to sit up, stay dressed, and was taken to wash every few days but, to his great relief, he was not forced to participate in the ceremony again. Ulrik grew desperate and decided the next time they let him out of the tent he would fight his way free or die trying. The next opportunity would be the chance he would take. Somehow, he would find Tessa and they would escape this place for good. He would slaughter anyone in his path to be free. So, Ulrik ate everything the old woman gave him, remained calm, tried to gain his strength back, and waited for his chance.

Ulrik had completely lost track of how much time had passed since the first ceremony with the first five girls. He was sure his food was tainted with the Meadwhey and they easily forced him to complete the ceremony two more times with some of the girls he had been with before and with six new ones. More time passed between ceremonies until eventually, it all stopped. All totaled he estimated he had been with at least twenty-five girls, some of them more than once, and the thought horrified him.

One day many girls were ushered into the old woman's tent. There was a great crowd of girls and more waiting outside. Ulrik grew fearful that he would be forced to be with them again, but he was still sitting up and clothed, so he just watched. Each girl came forward and Mohem would ask her questions, weigh her breasts, and place her hands on the girl's stomach. The old woman would close her eyes and turn her head as if listening. She made a great show of her examinations then she would nod sagely, and the girl would cry out and clap her hands with joy. It seemed Ulrik was to be a father many, many times over. He could not feel any happiness or pride at this news but was grateful that he did not have to suffer the ceremony with them again. In fact, it was all strangely curious that they all conceived so quickly when Tessa had not. Ulrik could only blame it on Mohem's witchcraft and the Meadwhey.

After all the girls had left bubbling with happiness, their hands pressed protectively to their abdomens, the tent flaps opened again. In stalked the Chief's wife who did not spare a glance for Ulrik. Mohem repeated the questions, weighed her breasts, listened to her womb, and then said something to the Chief's wife. She held her chin up and barked something at the old woman. Mohem nodded sadly. The Chief's wife smiled a wicked smile and triumph filled her eyes. She turned and headed toward the door, but she stopped at the tent flap. She turned back and looked at Ulrik. He guessed the old woman had given her happy news. She looked at him for a long time, almost like she was committing his face to memory as her eyes danced over his face and his body. Ulrik called her a whore in Old Norse again and cursed her loudly. She left, not understanding nor caring about what he said. She had received what she wanted from him.

Ulrik rested, waited, and watched. Gratefully, no more girls were brought to him to perform the ceremony and the drum was finally silenced. Ulrik was allowed to stay sitting up but was still bound tightly to the stakes and his ankles were tightly bound together. Guards stood outside his tent and escape seemed more and more impossible.

Chapter Eleven – Mohem's Story

A week after the first girls had received the news that they were pregnant, Mohem shuffled up to Ulrik and he turned to glare at her. In every way, she was responsible for all that he had suffered. His anger had not subsided and his worry for Tessa was painful.

Ulrik's five guards came and helped him to his feet. Only tying his hands behind his back, they led him from the tent at spear point, and this time took him in a different direction away from the river. They approached a large gathering of men who stared at him with hatred and parted as he approached to let him by. The men stood around a large fire, at least fifty sharp spears pointed at him. They watched as Ulrik was brought into the center of the gathering. At the other side of the circle, the men parted, and Tessa was led out. She was dressed in the clothing of the blue people and her long hair was intricately twisted and braided, the white-gold length had been streaked with blue dye and the top intricately weaved into a skull cap. She had three long strands of blue stone beads and crystals around her neck. She shined like a beautiful gem among dull plain rocks. Some of the other women came forward and stood beside her. Her hands and feet were not bound and when she saw Ulrik she ran to him, throwing her arms around his neck. Ulrik felt his bonds cut from his wrists. He clasped Tessa's body tightly to him and he just held her, burying his face in her hair, and covering her face with kisses. Likewise, Tessa clung to Ulrik and kissed him back not caring that the company of blue people watched their affectionate reunion. Their joy at seeing each other again was overwhelming.

Ulrik quickly looked Tessa over examining her for any injury. They had painted each arm from shoulder to elbow with blue dye in intricate designs. The swirling vine pattern had small moons and flowers intertwining with a copy of what looked like Ulrik's Viking sword in the center. The short side split tunic she wore revealed they had also painted her from outer hip and thigh to her knee, in matching designs.

Ulrik growled but quickly came to the realization this was his chance to escape with her. Keeping her in the shelter of his arms, he looked around. They were thickly surrounded by men with spears, but free of bonds. This was a start. Despite his weakness from his long captivity, he was tense and ready to fight. He would show them that this Norseman could not be easily held any longer.

The people parted again and Mohem came forward. All of the people bowed paying great reverence to her and mumbling her name. She approached closer and in a strong clear voice that belied her age, she spoke.

"You have to understand Ulrik we *needed* your seed."

Mohem's accent was strange, but there was heavy inflection on the word *"needed"* as if she could explain everything in that one sentence with that one word.

Ulrik stared at her, eyes blazing, his mouth fell open in shock and he yelled.

"All this time you could speak my language! *You old witch!*"

He took a menacing step toward her bringing his hands up as if he would like to strangle her. Tessa stiffened at Ulrik's side and stared up at him, head tilted and eyes wide with shock. The blue men circling them also stepped forward spears raised to protect Mohem.

Mohem just smiled and nodded her head up and down. She shrugged one shoulder as if to say none of that mattered.

"We are the Alahemwhey," gesturing around her she went on. "That roughly means, 'The Beautiful People of the Blue Flowers' in your tongue. The Alahemwhey call me Mohem which means many things like leader, healer, and wise woman." She paused gesturing around her.

"The Alahemwhey race is ancient and is swiftly dying out. We have bred within our tribe for so many centuries that our women rarely conceive and the few children we do have among us are girls, any males are weak, deformed, or die young from sickness. You have brought new life into our tribe and to our brother's tribe. We truly meant no harm, but we had to have new seed to plant in our women so that our race will grow and survive. When the Chieftain found you in the grain fields and you killed one of his warriors, he wanted to put you to death. I convinced him and the Elders of the tribe that you could be put to better use and replace the life you took. In many ways, I saved your life."

"What did you do to Tessa?" Ulrik could barely control his anger as he spoke to the old woman through gritted teeth. "You could have asked me! Instead, you worked your witchcraft on me!"

"Would you have cooperated had we asked? No! You are a man of honor and loyal to one woman and I can see that you two are bound beyond this life. You would not have agreed. I pretended to make great *magic* for the Alahemwhey because it is what they believe in and understand. There was no true witchcraft, as you call it, and your soul was never in danger.

As for Tessa, I slept in the same tent with her every night so that no harm would come to her. I kept her safe and unmolested in every way I could until you were done helping us. Now, you are to be freed but I felt I owed you some explanation."

It was true. Ulrik would not have chosen to betray Tessa with other women even if it meant the extinction of this race. Even though he was not completely willing, it was still not right, not honorable, not his choice. Despite the fact that Mohem saved his life, his chest tightened with frustration and confusion. Ulrik looked at Tessa and she shook her head in silent agreement verifying Mohem's words that she had protected Tessa. He pointed toward the Chief's wife.

"That whore, she did not come with the others."

The woman lifted her chin as Ulrik pointed at her, realizing he was talking about her. She gave a self-satisfied smile.

"That is the Chief's wife. He forbade her to lay with you. She was childless and so took matters into her own hands. She wanted to bear a chief's son, but it was too soon. I warned her, but she would not wait. Now, she will give birth to a daughter."

Ulrik spat at the Chief's wife's feet and called her a "whore."

"We are leaving, and *I want my sword!*"

Ulrik looked back at the old woman. He gritted his teeth in anger and spoke through his bared teeth.

"My sword!"

He would be damned if he would leave good Viking steel with warriors who only had stone knives.

Mohem turned toward the Chief, spoke to him in Alahemwhey, and demanded in their strange tongue that the sword be brought and returned to Ulrik. The Chief argued fiercely but eventually, begrudgingly, complied sending a warrior to fetch it.

"Please sit and let me explain some things." The old woman seated herself on a nearby log, gestured to another log, and pleaded, "*Please*, while we wait for your sword to be brought."

Reluctantly, Ulrik sat stiffly and pulled Tessa protectively against him. The old woman began her tale.

"My name was Dr. Eleanor Ann Tennbaum. I am, oh, over two hundred and sixty years old. I stopped keeping count." She chuckled and shook her head. "I came to this planet as you did, brought here through the time and dimension travel machine in the mountains when I was in my late sixties. When I arrived, I woke up young again, in my early twenties. I lived for many years with the man who became my husband in the cabin built with artifacts stolen from time." She stopped, took a deep breath lost in memories, and seemed to steal herself to go on with the tale.

"My husband, Dr. Jeremiah David Tennbaum, was a brilliant scientist and a physicist who had discovered how to travel to this dimension, another *alternate* Earth if you will. I know you two came into this world the same way."

Ulrik did not offer confirmation or reveal any details from his past. He just remained stiff, ready, acutely aware of the men surrounding them with their spears, and tried to listen to the old woman. Tessa shook her head slightly and smiled at the old woman. Ulrik decided Tessa appeared to have been treated well enough but would not relax.

"Tessa has told me a little of her old life on Earth. I also understand you found Jeremiah's journals, so you know a little of what I am talking about." Mohem smiled fondly at Tessa.

Mohem paused looking back and forth between the two, then continued.

"I lived for over forty years in that cabin with my husband and seemed to age only a year. One day he disappeared, and I waited for a long time for him to return. I thought he had gone back through to the other dimension, back to Earth. Sometimes he did that for supplies and things we wanted or needed, but he never returned. Tessa told me you found him in the underground cellar with his neck broken. I confess, I eventually found him down there too, but he was already dead. I couldn't move his body by myself and decomposition had already set in, so I covered him with a blanket and left our home."

The old woman paused and took a shuddering breath. Her eyes glistened with tears and her voice shook a little.

"Thank you for giving him a proper burial. Tessa told me you took him down the mountain to a nice glen. He would have liked that."

Shaking her head after a moment as if to chase away sad memories she returned to her story.

"Eventually, I found the Alahemwhey. They took me in as their Mohem, and I have lived with them for over two hundred years. You see, we age very, very slowly in this world. You two will live long, happy lives together as well. There is no going back."

Ulrik sat, stunned, staring at the old woman and what she was telling him. Tessa hugged him close to her and he felt he was on the verge of finally being freed, in more ways than just from this place. He shook his head not willing to be mollified by the woman's story. He fixed his angry stare on her and let her speak. Mohem continued with her story.

"In my previous life, I was a Geneticist and a Scientist."

Ulrik shook his head slightly, not understanding the words but guessed it was some kind of healer or priestess.

"I brought my medical expertise to these people and they have given me a good life. The two Chiefs are my sons. I have come to deeply love these people, but I feel the end of my time approaches. As I have said, the tribe has grown weak, interbred too much, and too many killed in battles with neighboring tribes. All that I have done has been to assure their survival. I've tried for years to get them to breed with other friendlier tribes, but they stubbornly refused, though they are not above stealing children from other tribes. I do not agree with that practice. Perhaps in time, they will give in. When they captured you both in the fields, you were so strange looking they brought you to me. As I have already revealed, the Chief wanted to put Ulrik to death because of the warrior he killed, but I convinced them to spare you. It was your blonde hair, blue eyes, and powerful body that helped me convince the men of the tribe to allow this. The blue flowers that grow so abundantly here, have many medicinal properties like none I've ever seen before. However, they don't work on the Alahemwhey men because they've grown immune to it over hundreds of years. It worked wonders on you Ulrik and your seed will produce strong sons and daughters, and the Alahemwhey will survive and thrive. You see blue is considered great magic and a strong attribute, your obvious height, and strength will imbue this tribe with new life. The Alahemwhey have never seen such a hair color and your children will be revered with their blue eyes and blonde hair. Hopefully, they will be able to have children with the Alahemwhey women and the tribe will grow and survive. It may take many, many years, but I have no doubts it will work."

Tessa had remained quiet all this time. She finally sat up taller and looked around at all the women in the circle surrounding them, the realization that Ulrik had *been* with them all was not lost on her. She shrunk away from Ulrik imperceptibly. Ulrik too, knew that she now understood but he did not know how to tell her of the strength of the Meadwhey and that he had never once been willing. He wanted to hang his head in shame.

"Tessa, Ulrik had no choice in the matter of helping us. It was *I* that forced him to drink the Meadwhey until he lost consciousness and then I let nature take its course. The girls got what we needed from him in order to save the Alahemwhey from extinction."

After a few silent moments where the realization of what Mohem was telling her sunk in, Tessa spoke up.

"You are or were a Geneticist?" That was all she asked in a tight voice.

"You understand this word?" Ulrik asked her, happy to distract her from the other subject.

"Yes, I can explain later." She turned back to the old woman, "How do you know these women will bear sons? How do you know they will all have blue eyes? There could be a recessive gene in his ancestry, and they could be born with a different hair or eye color or end up with coloring like the Alahemwhey. Many Norsemen had black or red hair. What will these people think of a child born with their brown eyes or red hair? It is false to think you can predict with one hundred percent assurance that all the children will be born male, with blonde hair and blue eyes. Why is that so important? How do you know that the children will be accepted within the tribe being sired by a stranger?"

Mohem clapped her hands together, "Ah! So many questions! I see you understand some very basic genetics. It is true, nothing is guaranteed. Looks are not important, what *is* important is that new blood will be born into the tribe and they will mate with the other Alahemwhey and have strong children assuring the future prosperity of the tribe. I only used Ulrik's coloring and strong physical stature to convince the Elders to go along with my plan. It is what they understand. What is important, is that the Alahemwhey will live and thrive after I'm gone. We revere all life and children are sacred. So, I can assure you they will be well-loved and taken care of."

By now the warrior had returned with Ulrik's sword which he handed to the old woman with a slight bow. She turned and presented it to Ulrik. Before relinquishing it to him she said, "You have two choices Ulrik. You and Tessa can stay here and live among the Alahemwhey, or you can return to your life at the cabin. We will not stop you, nor will we follow. You have done us a great service and we will always be deeply in your debt."

He rose, took the sword wordlessly, and strapped it to his hip. He momentarily pictured himself cutting all of them down in a berserk rage, but instead, he turned and spoke to Tessa.

"Let us leave this place." Tessa nodded and took his hand.

Mohem rose slowly to her feet and gestured. The crowd parted and three horses were led forward.

"These are for you. The best animals we have. We can never repay you for what you have done for us but hopefully, you will at least consider it a small token of our gratitude."

A huge black stallion pawed at the ground. He had an ornate saddle in the style of the Alahemwhey and his long mane and tail had been twisted and dyed with blue streaks. The other horse was a black and white spotted horse whose long white mane and tail glistened in the sunshine. She too had her mane twisted into ropes and dyed in blue streaks. Following the other two was a red roan packhorse piled high with gifts and supplies.

Ulrik led Tessa by the hand and lifted her onto the black and white horse. Then he leaped onto the black stallion. Mohem approached him and reached within her robes pulling out a small clay vial. Holding it up, she offered Ulrik the vial.

"Take this. It has many medicinal purposes, and you may need it someday." Mohem's eye sparkled as she closed Ulrik's hand around the vial.

At first, Ulrik was going to refuse it, but he looked at Tessa whose expression was unreadable and then decided he would take it. He knew it contained the Meadwhey that had been the bane of his existence these past months of captivity. He turned his horse's head to leave. Mohem walked over to Tessa and gave her a huge smile.

"Thank you, my child," she spoke quietly, "Someday, I will be there when you need me."

Tessa gave her a curious look wondering what she was trying to impart. Mohem raised her hand in farewell. The Alahemwhey parted to let them pass. Tessa gave a small smile to Mohem then turned her horse to leave beside Ulrik.

Suddenly, hot rage grew in Ulrik's chest as thoughts flooded his mind over what had been done to him. He was relieved Tessa had not suffered as he had and that they were now on their way home, but he turned his horse back and walked it over to the old woman. "What these women carry in their bellies, *my children*," He stopped almost speechless with rage.

"Mayhap I will return someday and take what is mine." His hand grasped the air in front of her and his fist clenched white as he shook it at her.

Mohem shook her head smiling.

"Vikings! You think everything belongs to you and that you can solve everything with violence. We are a nomadic people and will be long gone. You will never see the Alahemwhey again. I am truly sorry for the treatment you've had to endure." Her eyes sparkled and she smiled mischievously, "Most men would have loved to comply, but it was all for the greater good of the tribe. You *must* believe that Ulrik."

Ulrik held her eyes for a long moment, "There was no honor, no love in the conception of these children, and I hope your plans do not turn to evil on you. Remember they will be half Norseman!"

With Tessa finally beside him once again, he nudged his spirited horse in its sides and together they rode away at a fast gallop.

Chapter Twelve – Home

Ulrik and Tessa rode for a full day toward their mountain home. Ulrik constantly watched behind them to assure they were not being followed. They did not speak of what had transpired during their captivity, but Tessa smiled beautifully at him, every time he looked at her. Although she was silent and introspective, he tried to judge what was going through her mind and heart. Was there any blame or sense of betrayal in her eyes? Soon, they came to the place where they had been captured. They came across their camp and it was as they had left it although their things were scattered and covered with dirt and leaves. They quickly packed their belongings, dispersing them evenly on the packhorse and on Tessa's horse. Ulrik swung Tessa onto the black and then climbed up behind her. They let the horses slowly pick their way up the gently sloping mountainside while Ulrik held Tessa tightly in his arms and buried his face within the soft locks of her sweet-smelling hair.

As the day progressed, they remained silent, but Ulrik held her close to his chest, kissed her face, and hugged her tightly. Tessa breathed a sigh of contentment. Internally, Ulrik battled with all the things he needed, wanted, and was afraid to say to her. Eventually, their path led them to the river and a low waterfall.

Ulrik dismounted, lifting Tessa down. He let the horses move off to drink and crop at the fresh mountain grass growing beneath the trees.

They stood, bodies close, hands tightly clenched, looking into each other's eyes. Ulrik reached up and slid his hand to the back of Tessa's neck and lowered his mouth to hers. Without hesitation, she kissed him back and the kiss went from tentative, to passionate. Ulrik tasted her and swept his hands down her arms and across the small of her back. He pulled her closer into his embrace. Tessa's arms went around his neck and she leaned pressing her hips into him.

He broke the contact suddenly and with one swoop, lifted Tessa up into his arms. He carried her over to the water. After setting her down, she stood silently waiting to see what he was up to as with swift but gentle motions, holding her gaze, he untied the beaded belt from her waist and, raising his arms to her shoulders, he slid the blue Alahemwhey tunic down to her feet. She stepped away from the blue garment and stood breasts exposed to him. Then Ulrik lifted the strands of blue stone beads from her neck and over her head, dropping them next to the clothes. Tessa waited, completely revealed to his hungry eyes but for some small pants covering her feminine place. She slid those to the ground, stepped out of them, and was bare except for the blue-painted Alahemwhey designs on her arms, and down the outside of her thighs.

Ulrik unbelted and dropped his sword to the ground, stripping off his shirt and removing his boots, and trousers, he lifted Tessa under the legs and held her close to his chest. He carried her into the gently moving water. The heat of the sun had warmed them and Ulrik gently lowered Tessa so that she could stand in the water. They moved toward the waterfall and he guided her under. She gasped as the cold sheets of water cascaded over her head. Ulrik smoothed his hands over her hair holding the twisting braids in the water, watching the blue wash away. He rubbed at the designs on her arms and thighs, gently scrubbing, trying to get the blue dye off. The brilliant blue designs were not affected at all but seemed permanently tattooed on her.

"Maybe it will wear off in time." She spoke quietly for the first time since they stopped.

"I want it off now!" He said with some vehemence. Grasping her by the arms. "I want to forget that place and..." emotion caught in his throat and he suddenly hugged her to him holding her so tightly against him she gasped for breath.

Tessa wrapped her arms around his waist and held him until he roughly breathed out his emotions and frustration, she could feel his heart beating hard in his chest. "Tessa, Tessa," he repeated over and over whispering in her ear and rubbing his face against her neck and her cheeks, kissing her. Caressing every inch of her body with his hands, they stood in the water until they shivered with cold and had to move back toward the shore. Taking a blanket from the horse, they laid down to dry in the sun. Their nude bodies glistened with water droplets. The blue designs still stood starkly against the white skin of Tessa's arms and thighs, but faint blue streaks were all that remained in her hair. Ulrik made no move to make love to her he just held her close, the warmth of the sun drying them.

After a while together, Tessa rose and went to her horse's pack. She pulled out her old clothes that had been cleaned and packed for her. Quietly, she dressed and went to look for some food. Ulrik watched her every move. She found a bag with fruit and dried meat, a large wheel of cheese, and a skin of Alahemwhey wine. Taking it to Ulrik, he smelled the wine to make sure it was not Meadwhey. They sat and ate in the quiet afternoon. Ulrik could hardly look her in the eye, could not eat. He seemed to be waging an internal debate. As before when they first met, he seemed reluctant to tell her anything about what happened to him during the past months they had been with the Alahemwhey.

"Will you tell me what happened to you?" Tessa said quietly. "When I first saw you weeks ago, you were bound and didn't look very well. I tried to go to you. I asked and asked for you every day, but they would not let me see you." Her voice broke full of emotion and a tear fell slowly down her cheek. Her lower lip quivered and Ulrik ached upon seeing her cry.

Ulrik's hands shook a little as he set an apple aside that he had been rolling around in his hands and not eating. He started slowly and described what had happened to him. He told her everything because she deserved the whole truth. Ulrik told her of the darts that pricked him and left him unable to move, of the Meadwhey they forced him to drink, and the effect it had on him. He told her of the drumming and the ceremony, the blue swirls painted on the breasts of the girls and how they got him so drunk on the Meadwhey he passed out. Ulrik told her he could not fully remember what he had done but revealed what he suspected happened. Leaving nothing out, he described the rage and despair he felt at not knowing what had happened to her.

"I fought them as much as I could. I did not want to do it, but the Meadwhey the old woman made me drink, left me without a choice. It was like nothing I'd ever experienced before. I was given so much of the Meadwhey to drink and in my food, and it made me so drunk that everything went black. I woke the next morning fearing what I had done."

Ulrik dropped his head in his hands and shuddered with the memories. Tessa knelt before him and covered his hands with hers. She drew his head up until his eyes met hers. Leaning forward she planted a lingering kiss on his forehead.

"I don't fault you for what was done to you. I'm truly sorry you suffered and that I could not be there to help you. I tried reasoning with Eleanor. Every day, I begged and pleaded with her to let me go to you, but she kept me closely guarded and would not allow it. She spoke of the man you killed and how she was trying to convince the Chief to let you live. She also said she needed you and that you were safe and assured me we could leave soon. Any man that tried to come at me, she protected me. She told me of the Alahemwhey and their lives. We talked about my previous life and she told me of her years at the cabin." Tessa's voice caught and she blinked back tears. "She didn't tell me what was happening to you, just that we would be released soon and that you were safe."

She took a deep breath, "Ulrik, I love you and *nothing* will ever change that. Though I don't completely understand it all, I know you did not willingly lie with those girls. I'm just happy to have you back safe in *my* arms." He looked at her for a long time and his eyes were tormented by the memories of what had been done to him.

Tessa smiled her most beautiful and loving smile, "Let's go home."

Ulrik consented with a nod of his head and they packed up their few things and continued on foot leading the horses. They camped that night, they did not make love but held each other under the starlight sky, trading soft kisses.

At the end of the next afternoon, they reached the cabin. They originally had only planned on being gone for a few days, but still, everything was mostly as they had left it. The chickens were loose, and the goats had gotten out of their pen. It took an hour or so to gather them all back in and feed them, but eventually, everything was back in some semblance of order. Ulrik stabled the horses as best they would fit in the small barn and stored the feed the Alahemwhey had sent with them. He estimated they would have enough feed for the winter, but beyond that was not sure how he would go about feeding three horses. Leaving that problem for another day, he wandered about their mountain home looking for things that needed to be done. The smokehouse stood unharmed, but the meat inside was spoiled. He left the meat there to deal with later.

Going to the chopping block he began to chop wood. He swung his axe and split each piece with one blow. It felt good to strike, to work his muscles again. He felt alive for the first time since their capture. Soon, he glistened with sweat. He worked out some of his frustrations and anger on the chopping block and eventually had a large pile of wood which he stacked neatly against the house.

He looked around to see what else needed to be done. The sun was setting swiftly, and shadows harkened the end of the day. The weather was turning chill signaling winter was coming. Inside the cabin behind him, warm light spilled through the windows beckoning him inside. He could smell dinner cooking. Moving to the full rain barrel, Ulrik took his shirt off and dowsed himself with cold rainwater. He realized he was intentionally delaying going inside and confronting the night and being in bed with Tessa. Everything was different now that they were home. He thought that Tessa would expect things to return to normal. He wanted that too but was afraid he might not be able to forget what had happened, his betrayal, his shame. When he could put it off no longer, he grabbed his sweat-stained shirt, combed back his long, wet hair with his fingers, and went inside.

Tessa was waiting for him. She had combed out the twists from her hair and although it was still faintly streaked with blue, it hung freely and rippled golden in the firelight. She had put on one of her dresses. Mother of pearl buttons lined the front and the creamy white flowery material flowed almost to the floor. She wore a white shawl over her shoulders and Ulrik knew that she covered the blue designs on her arms and legs. Not for the first time, he worried that they might be permanent and somehow *his* Tessa was not the same anymore. He looked to his biceps where he had Nordic runes and designs tattooed in bands around his arms and he tried to console himself that they were at least similar where the Alahemwhey had tried to copy some of the designs.

Wordlessly, he closed the door behind him, and went to sit at the table and eat supper. Tessa tried to make conversation but Ulrik remained moody and quiet. He avoided her eyes. Truly, he did not mean to be rude, but he was pent up with too much emotion, fear, and anger to make small talk. It was hard to believe they were home and Tessa was safe and with him but how to pick up where they had left off? When she was not looking, he drank in the sight of her beautiful face and slim form.

Tessa cleaned up after dinner and Ulrik went to sit in his usual chair by the fireplace. The fire was built high for light and warmth, and a lamp was lit and left on the table. The cabin felt like home and Ulrik let out a long sigh of relief, allowing himself to find contentment that they were finally safe and together.

The night grew older and eventually, Tessa rose and went to get ready for bed. Ulrik watched her through lowered eyebrows and wondered what he should do next. Would he desire her after all the sex he had been forced into these last many, many weeks? Would she still want him after what he had done?

He watched as she undressed and washed in front of him as she always had. The warm golden light from the lamp table caressed the curves of her body. Ulrik looked away from the blue tattoos on her arms and legs and stared hard at her breasts and at the golden juncture between her legs. He was completely surprised to feel himself grow hard, his stomach taut, watching her, he warmed with desire for her. A feeling of great relief descended over him. He rose and went to her.

Tessa turned and stood waiting, watching Ulrik with her large blue eyes. His eyes flickered with yearning for her and in two strides he was crushing her against him. He flooded her mouth with kisses and pulled at her tongue, dancing in circles with her lips. Her hands fumbled at the laces of his britches and his hardness burst forth from confinement. She pulled his hand and stepping out of the clothes that pooled at her feet, he let her lead him to the bed.

She pulled the sheets back with a yank as she lowered herself down onto the soft mattress. Her hand had not released his and she tugged at him. Ulrik took a moment to stare at how magnificent she was, her pretty round breasts and smooth curves. Then he lowered himself to the bed looming over her. Taking his time, he kissed her lips more gently as he ran his hand down her arm, her side, and the swell of her hip. She gasped into his mouth and arched up as he cupped her velvety warmth. She began to slowly move with his soft caresses and each tiny intake of breath drove Ulrik mad with desire for her.

Ulrik realized how afraid of this moment he had been, of her reaction to him after all of the other women, but he gave up the fear and found relief in her arms.

Moving over her, she gently eased her legs apart welcoming him in. As he entered her, moving slowly at first, he committed himself more with every thrust. Lifting his chest, he looked down where they were joined, and watched as his shaft pulled out and plunged into her warmth. Tessa gasped as her climax rose. Her hands went up to caress his chest and he burned where she touched him. He plunged and pulsed, and spilled his seed inside her as she cried out in joy.

As Ulrik spent himself inside Tessa, he watched her eyes and felt surprise and relief at the love he still saw in the blue depths of her gaze.

"I love you," she whispered as he lowered himself down, still sheathed within her, and kissed her. He felt the length of her body beneath him, felt her legs wrapped around his hips, felt how she pulsed around his cock still joined with her.

"And I will love you forever, no matter what has been or what is to come," he replied quietly.

Tessa held him tighter. Their lips met in another long, sweet kiss and Ulrik sank to her side. Pulling her close, she fell into a peaceful, satiated, sleep. Ulrik held her and traced the blue stains that now seemed permanent on Tessa's arms and thighs. He conceded they really were beautiful and if Tessa was not bothered by them, he would not remind her of the ugliness of his captivity by hating the marks it left on her.

Chapter Thirteen – Winter

Ulrik and Tessa prepared for the long winter as the days grew shorter and the nights colder. They tried to forget what had happened with the Alahemwhey and pick up where their lives had left off. Fall went by swiftly as they worked to prepare their little mountain farm for harsh weather. Ulrik made the stable bigger and weatherproof to accommodate the three horses and they gathered as much feed as they could. A month after their return, the farm was more secure and ready for the hastening cold. Soon it began to lightly snow and then it began to snow very hard.

One blizzard-filled morning Ulrik came in from tending the animals and Tessa lay snuggled in the bed. He removed his snow-covered bear cloak and clothes and crawled into bed beside her, his cold skin warmed by her soft body. A fire crackled in the fireplace and they spent a lazy day making love while outside the wind blew, and foot upon foot of snow accumulated.

They played under the sheets and blankets and made love. Eventually, they talked of the winter. Ulrik had been through winters there before, but it was Tessa's first. He assured her they were well taken care of, but that at some point he would have to get out of bed to eat and tend to the animals and get more firewood.

Tessa drew Ulrik's hand to her lips and placed a kiss in the palm of his work-hardened hand. Then she placed it on her belly. "Ulrik, around early summer, I think we will have another mouth to feed."

Ulrik stilled and the smile fell from his face. His hand felt warm on her belly and he left it lying there as if he were trying to feel the life that he now knew grew within.

"When," He stammered, "when did you…"

Tessa said gently, "I think I conceived right after we returned home. I didn't say anything until I was absolutely positive. I waited to tell you but now that I am starting to show more, I think I am about two months along, maybe a little more or less."

Ulrik let out the breath he was holding, threw back his head, and whooped loudly, genuinely pleased. He clutched her against him, and they fell to kissing and caressing all over again.

The winter months passed without incident. It was frigid. The snow was heavy, and the days were long and dark. Tessa read to Ulrik and worked on teaching him to read. Ulrik did not see the point or when he ever would need to use reading or writing, but he settled into the task to please Tessa and to help the cold days pass. Tessa's stomach swiftly grew fuller and, during the nights, they talked about their child.

It was impossible to estimate what month in the year it was or if time ran the same here on this alternate Earth. She guessed they harvested the wheat around the beginning of July and were held captive with the Alahemwhey for about two and a half months possibly three. Which meant Tessa could have conceived sometime in October. This timing was all guesswork on Tessa's part and thus counting, thought in late June or early July they could expect the baby to make his or her entrance into the world. In time, Tessa was indeed huge with child.

One afternoon, Ulrik came in carrying firewood and stacked it by the fireplace. Tessa called him over, took his hand, and placed it on her large belly.

"Wait…feel that? There he is. He is playing kickball with my internal organs." She moved his hand over to feel a small round protrusion on the other side.

"Feel that?" She said placing her hand over his. "That is the other one's head. He is kicking his brother." Tessa glowed with happiness.

"The other one? What do you mean?" Ulrik's face revealed his shock. "There are *two* of them?"

"Yes, I think so. I am overly large, and I grow more uncomfortable each day." Tessa smiled at him, stretched, and then went on, her face turning serious. "There are definitely two babies. I can feel them when they wrestle and push on my sides." She paused, "I have never had a baby, let alone *two* babies at once. There are some things we will need to do to prepare. I've written down a list of things we need, and I looked through some of the medical books we brought up from the library to see if I can get some idea of what will happen. Of course, I've watched births before, but I've never been the one doing the birthing. You will need to do much of the footwork."

Ulrik grinned at her and said, "I have helped the goats give birth and once helped with a cow *and* a horse. We will work through it together, just tell me what you need me to do and I will do everything." His face clouded over with worry. "You are strong, but many women die in childbirth. I could not bear to lose you, Tessa." His hand smoothed her cheek and he leaned over to kiss her on the lips.

Tessa looked back at him. All the love in her heart was in that look. "Well, I choose to think positively about this matter. I think we will be fine."

Ulrik turned and said, "I have a surprise for you." He went outside and came back a few minutes later carrying a cradle he had built and carved with his own hands. The front sides were decorated with protective Nordic runes and pictures of animals ran along the slats at the sides, it stood on two curved bands of wood for rocking.

"You will have to make a blanket for it and I will have to get busy to make another one!"

"Go then because I think you will not have much time!" Tessa laughed.

Ulrik shook his head in wonder saying over and over, "Two sons, *two* sons!" as he walked out the door then he stopped in shock. "Or two daughters!"

Tessa rose from her chair and went to bed. She did not have any ideas about what she was doing and hid the fear that threatened to consume her. She lay down in the bed and slept, her mind whirling with everything that needed to be done.

As the day approached, Tessa took material from unusable clothing and blankets and prepared clothes and diapers for the expected babies. She even tried her hand at knitting some wool they had found amongst the cabin's treasures. She rested and waited for the impending births.

Winters lasted long this high up in the mountains and a final spring snowstorm hit and it snowed lightly outside the warm cabin. Tessa moved restlessly trying to get comfortable. Her swollen belly stretched, hardened and the labor pains started to come harder and harder. She labored slowly, willing herself to relax and breathe through the pains as she had read to do in the books. Ulrik bustled around the cabin, jumping from task to task. He boiled water for later and dabbed her forehead with cool water. As the night progressed, Tessa labored through.

Morning came and so did Mohem. Ulrik had spent a sleepless, worried night tending to Tessa as she writhed in pain. He thought his mind was playing tricks on him when he heard a knock. Wearily, he rose and opened the door and there she stood. Ulrik's mouth fell open in stunned amazement.

She pushed her way in uninvited, dropped a large bag on the floor, shook the snow off her shoulders, and went directly to Tessa's bedside as she removed her heavy blue cloak. Ulrik stood with his mouth gaping open staring at the old woman. He did not know whether to feel relieved or angry at seeing her again. He stepped outside to check if she was alone and all he saw was a small shaggy horse tied to a tree.

He closed the door and went over to her, "What are you doing here?" He spoke angrily, not letting any sign of the relief he felt spill into his words.

"You'll be happy to have my help, I think. It looks as if she has two in there." Mohem placed her hands over Tessa's swollen belly and felt around gently.

"How did you know?" Ulrik gapped unbelievingly.

Ignoring his question, she lifted one shoulder and shrugged, and then she turned to Ulrik. "Ulrik, be a dear and tend to my horse. It will be a while yet, I think."

Mohem turned back to Tessa and began asking her many questions. Ulrik did as he was asked, silently relieved that he had help with the upcoming births and furious to see the woman who had caused him so much grief. He closed the door after taking a last look at Tessa, feeling better that she too smiled and looked grateful to have the old woman there.

Tessa labored through the day and as the night came her water broke. Mohem busied herself preparing for the births. She gave Tessa a drink of something that brought her great relief and after that Tessa relaxed. Then the pushing began. Ulrik paced nervously and did what he could to help, bringing water and clean cloths.

Ulrik stood by Tessa's side holding her hand as Mohem deftly worked. "You're going to have a nasty tear." She said as she smoothed a strong-smelling salve on Tessa's straining opening.

Tessa gasped and cried out. "I think I have to push!" She gasped and strained up, crying out.

"Sit behind her and hold her legs up Ulrik that helps her push." Mohem demonstrated as she commanded. Ulrik wordlessly did as he was told and Tessa strained gritting her teeth and bearing down.

"There's the head! A little more, push now!" Tessa pushed and the baby boy slid easily into the world. Mohem grabbed a waiting cloth and wiped him down, she gently blew into his face and the baby gasped, taking his first breath and crying out in a strong high-pitched wail.

"Take your son, Ulrik the other baby is right behind."

Ulrik took the crying baby and stared into his pink, blood, and goo-covered face, then he placed him in the cradle and returned to Tessa not yet having the time to enjoy his first few moments of fatherhood.

Tessa strained and screamed again.

"PUSH!" cried Mohem. Tessa bore down and again heard Mohem proclaim, "Here comes the head! A few more pushes, you can do it! Tessa, push!"

Tessa took a huge breath in, held it, and pushed. The other baby slid into the world with a gush. Mohem turned toward Ulrik and held up the second baby who let out a wail. "You have another son! Congratulations my boy! Now take him and wrap them both snugly, not tight, just snug. I will tend to Tessa."

Ulrik awkwardly held his second son and cast a worried look at Tessa. He went to her and placed a kiss on her sweaty forehead. Then he moved over to the cradle with the other. He had not had enough time to finish the second cradle yet, but both boys would fit in the one for a while. He wrapped them as instructed, then with one large hand, he scooped up the other boy and took them to Tessa. He placed one boy in her arms and held the other so that she could see their tiny identical faces. Tears filled his eyes as he looked at his family. Both boys had his long thin nose. The twins were identical and were almost bald except for a slight dusting of white fuzz.

Tessa's sweat rolled down her face and she still breathed heavily from her exertions, but she smiled gloriously at her sons. "Two boys." She whispered hoarsely.

"Ulrik, are you pleased?" She cried tears of joy.

"I will be pleased when you are through this and I know you are safe." He beamed, "Two sons! No father could be prouder than I." The slightly larger one of the boys, the firstborn, began to wail. Tessa reached for him, pulled aside her nightgown, and brought him to her swollen breast.

"That is good! Breastfeeding will help shrink your swollen womb. I am going to have to do a little bit of sewing down here. Tessa, I will prick you with a blue dart so that you don't feel any pain. You will feel numb from the waist down, though."

Tessa nodded in complete trust, not taking her eyes from her feeding son. Mohem sterilized a needle and some fine blue thread and began her work. Tessa finished feeding one infant and then held the second son to her other breast and fed him. Ulrik took his first son and walked to his chair by the fire. He held the new baby boy and marveled at how beautiful he was. His little face held contentment as he smacked his lips twice and went to sleep. Ulrik ran his large hand over the tiny head and felt the soft white baby fuzz. In the background, the old woman kept up a stream of conversation, describing to Tessa everything that she was doing. She spoke of keeping the area clean and eventually removing the stitches. She warned against signs of infection and even advised as to how long Tessa and Ulrik should wait to have "relations" again. Ulrik fell asleep in the chair and did not even feel it later when the old woman carefully took the baby from his arms and put him gently in the cradle next to his tiny sleeping brother.

As Tessa, Ulrik, and their babies slept, Mohem stood, turning in slow circles she looked around her old home. She smiled with nostalgia and contentedly went to fall asleep by the fire herself.

In the days that followed the twin boys' births, Mohem was essential, helping take care of Tessa and the babies. Tessa had a slight fever after the births and the old woman fussed over her, giving her healing draughts to drink and wiping her forehead with cool wet cloths. She cleaned Tessa and took care of the babies. She seemed tireless and one would have never known she was over two hundred and sixty years old as she said.

Ulrik helped where he could, but eventually was shooed outside and told to stay out of the way. He busied himself around the mountain farm and hunted. Tessa improved and eventually she was on her feet again.

Mohem gave her advice on how to take care of the babies, how to keep enough milk flowing to feed them both, and how to take care of her nipples so that they did not get too painful. Tessa beamed with the joy of motherhood and was very grateful to have Mohem there.

After a month, Mohem announced it was time for her to leave. Both babies were healthy and thriving, and Tessa was healing nicely. After due time, she removed Tessa's stitches and pronounced her healthy enough to bear many more children.

On her last night there the three of them sat at the kitchen table eating their last supper together. She asked, "What will you name the boys?"

Ulrik went to the cradle and picked up the tightly swaddled twins. Holding them gently, but protectively in his large strong arms, he walked over to show the two boys to Mohem.

"This one," he said indicating the eldest and slightly larger boy, "Is to be called Hunter and his brother will be Archer." He beamed proudly at his boys.

Mohem clapped her hands with joy. "Perfect names and I know they will grow up to be great men and live up to those fine strong names!" Mohem went to her things and brought out a skin of Alahemwhey wine.

"I have something to celebrate with." Pouring three cups she raised her glass and said, "Let us toast to the good health and long lives of Hunter and Archer Ulriksson."

The crisp summer morning came, and the old woman packed her things. She gave Tessa written instructions on how to make medicines for coughs and fevers. She told her what herbs helped other common childhood sicknesses and showed her how to make the numbing darts. She told Tessa they would need to search out the blue flowers for it, but at least she left her with the knowledge that she could do it.

Then she slowly turned and took a long last look at her old home. "You've kept it well Ulrik and I thank you for letting me help with the birth of your sons. Now, I must go. I can't be away from the tribe any longer."

Tessa came out holding Archer in her arms. She wished to say goodbye, but the wise old woman knew that Tessa had many other things she wished to say. Tessa turned to Ulrik and handed him the baby.

"Take him inside will you please so that I can say goodbye?" Ulrik took the babe frowning, but only moved far enough away to stand watching from the door.

Tessa went toward Mohem. They walked a few paces away and she embraced her tightly. "I can't thank you enough for all you've done to help us. I don't know how I would have been able to get through this without you. Despite what happened in the past...I am very grateful." Tessa hesitated a moment and went resolutely on, dropping her voice, "Eleanor, I *have* to know. The other babies, Ulrik's other babies. How did things turn out?"

Mohem took Tessa's arm and pulled her a few more steps away, out of Ulrik's hearing.

"You and I come from a modern time and I think you understand what I tried to do for my people."

Tessa hesitated and then reluctantly nodded, "Yes."

"Well, I was right! The women of my tribe have given birth to twenty strong sons and five beautiful girls. Most of them have blonde hair and blue eyes. And, I was also wrong, there are about five of the children with darker golden hair and brown eyes, but they are clearly from Ulrik's seed. Tahala, the Chief's wife, you may recall, who went against my good advice and went to Ulrik too soon, bore a daughter, a daughter with fiery red hair and large blue eyes. As you suggested that day you left, there must have been a recessed gene. That one will be a spitfire like her mother. The Chief is not pleased, but the mother dotes on her. All of the children are healthy and strong, they are guarded fiercely by their mothers. The fathers have come to accept them as their adopted sons and daughters for the good of the tribe. They are well and good, part of the Alahemwhey. Now, I must go, I have a long road ahead of me and these old bones don't travel as well as they used to."

Mohem embraced Tessa one last time, took her horse's lead, and began the slow journey down the mountain with a last wave at Ulrik, who brooded darkly in the shadow of the door.

Tessa turned, went to her husband, and kissed him.

#

As Mohem picked her way slowly down the mountain, she felt a sense of peace that comes with the feeling of accomplishment. She had delivered her share of babies these past few months and being with Tessa and Ulrik and their two sons had been a welcome break. She stopped and seated herself on a large stone and waited. As she knew he would, Ulrik appeared quietly from out of the woods. He had his bow and arrows as if he was out for his daily hunt.

"I knew you'd come." She said, squinting up at Ulrik who stood with the sun to his back. He had a dark look on his face. "Go ahead. Ask me what you came to ask." She folded her hands in her lap and waited, resolute.

Ulrik let out a sigh of exasperation. "I am grateful for all you have done for us." He said halting and with obvious difficulty. "Tessa asked you, didn't she? About the *others*?"

"Yes, would you like me to tell you what I told her?" She smiled again.

"I would know." He growled, squatting down to her level so that he could look into her face and judge if she lied.

"The women of my tribe have given birth to twenty strong sons and five beautiful daughters. Tahala, the Chief's wife, I'm sure you will remember her, she was the one who went against my advice and her husband's wishes and went to you. I told her to wait another week for a son, but she wouldn't listen. Her husband the Chief, who is one of my sons, did not want her to go to you at all. But, Tahala had her own agenda. She bore a daughter, a daughter with fiery red hair and the most amazing blue eyes. Tell me did you have any relatives with red hair?" The old woman looked quizzically at Ulrik.

Ulrik thought a moment. "My grandfather had red hair and a red beard, as did a few of my cousins. It was said his mother was an Irish woman, stolen in a raid. She had fiery red hair."

"The Chief is not pleased with his redheaded daughter, but the mother loves her fiercely and I will protect her. All of the children are healthy and strong, and part of the tribe. What I didn't tell Tessa, but I will tell you because you deserve to know the full truth, the boys and girls with your white gold hair and blue eyes are held in *more* esteem than the rest. Already, they hold status above the others. I fear that, when I'm gone, I just don't know how that will affect the tribe. Oh, I think the children will be safe enough, but I fear, I have brought a significant change to the Alahemwhey culture that I had not predicted. Some changes have happened very quickly where I had planned they would take years, but I did what I could so that my people would not die out."

Mohem paused looking saddened and took a swallow from her drinking skin. Her face grew weary, but she rose slowly and moved toward Ulrik. She placed a hand on his arm.

"I am deeply sorry for any pain or harm I have caused you, but as I told you, I did what I thought I had to do. Now, return to your wife and sons and I will be on my way."

Ulrik had a strange sensation flow through him and he realized it was forgiveness for the tiny old woman and for what she had done to him. He towered above her, hefted his bow, and arranged his arrows more firmly on his back.

"Come, I will take you to your husband's grave."

"Ah!" Mohem said with a smile, nodding as if that is what she had waited for, and followed. He led her down the mountain to the place where they had buried Dr. Jeremiah Tennbaum's bones. Tessa had insisted on making a wooden cross to mark the spot. The old woman sat down heavily next to the grave. Without looking at Ulrik, she sighed and simply said, "Goodbye Ulrik, and thank you."

Ulrik took a long, last look at the old woman sitting by the grave, then turned and silently disappeared into the woods.

Chapter Fourteen – Adventure

Hunter and Archer grew into strong and healthy boys. One year after their birth, on a full moon night, a little sister arrived. They named her Emmer. The family thrived and the years passed quickly on the little mountain farm.

As the family grew, so did the little cabin. Ulrik, with the help of his growing sons, built a loft onto the top of the cabin and extended another two rooms off on the sides. The boys were mischievous and active, while Emmer was sweet and gentle, the very image of her mother.

Tessa and Ulrik, as Mohem had revealed, did not appear to age. Tessa still looked like a girl in her early twenties. Ulrik looked like the same young man who had pulled Tessa from the lake. The children grew at the normal pace at which children grow.

Hunter and Archer were rambunctious but worshiped their father. Ulrik taught them to fish and hunt and work on their mountain home. Hunter excelled at tracking and was a superior hunter. He also took a great interest in becoming a skilled healer. Any hurt bird or animal they came across, Hunter was the first to nurse them back to health and he took great pleasure in releasing them back into the wild.

Archer, as his name revealed, was very skilled with the bow and spent hours shooting and crafting arrows. Both boys learned to wield a sword under Ulrik's instruction and became proficient in using all weapons.

Emmer grew to be a sweet girl with pale hair the color of moonbeams and flashing blue eyes, like her mother. She was the apple of her father's eye. She learned to sew and cook with Tessa and though she was the youngest of their clan, was also taught hunting, fishing, and swordplay.

Although Ulrik managed to put the Alahemwhey and what happened during his captivity out of his thoughts, he was diligent in teaching his family to defend themselves and be wary of danger. It was frequently in the back of his mind to protect his wife, sons, and daughter from the harm men could bring to his family.

For the most part, Ulrik's family was happy and busy trying to survive in the mountains. Times were lean at different points during the years that passed and abundant at others, but Ulrik made sure they all prospered. If Ulrik and Tessa had ever felt lonely before the children came along, they had not noticed until their house filled with their noisy presence. It was enough for Ulrik to have sons, something he was denied in his previous life.

The boys, almost identical in appearance, grew to tower above their mother and sister. They had long white-blonde hair worn in the old Norse fashion as Ulrik did. Tessa often reflected that, if there were any girls around, they would be considered extremely fine-looking young men. They were loud and boisterous, quick to smile and slow to anger but were in constant competition with each other. Who could run faster, wrestle better, hunt more game, who was better with the staff or the wooden sword, and who was more accurate with the bow and slingshot, were constant topics of conversation.

Tessa taught them all to read and write and they took turns reading from the books that Tessa had discovered so many years ago in the cabin and from the cellar library. Although Archer, who just wanted to play and have fun, thought it was a complete waste of time, he did it to please his mother. Hunter showed the greatest interest in the medical books. Emmer was an avid reader and spent most of her free time pouring over King Arthur and the Nights of the Round Table, Romeo and Juliet, and the story of Tristan and Isolde.

One early spring day, as the family sat around the dinner table, Archer kicked Hunter under the table and widened his eyes at his twin, slightly nodding his head as if to impart some secret meaning. Hunter glared at him but cleared his throat as if he were about to ask a difficult question.

"Mother, *Archer* wants me to ask you, what those markings are on your arms and legs?"

Ulrik stopped lifting the food to his mouth in mid-air. Tessa looked at him with wide-eyed surprise as if to ask, *"what should I say?"*

Ulrik cleared his throat and asked gruffly, "Why do you ask?"

"Well, we were…" Hunter started.

"…just curious." Archer finished Hunter's sentence as he often did.

Emmer looked intently from Ulrik to Tessa and waited, interested in hearing about the markings too.

"They are called Ohhem," Tessa spoke quietly.

Both boys looked interested and Emmer leaned forward anxious for more explanation.

"Where did you get them? They are really beautiful." Archer asked, "Father has tattoos on his arms, but we've heard a hundred times how he earned those in his previous life, which by the way, I think I've earned a few tattoos myself!"

Hunter guffawed, "If you've earned a few, then I've earned at least a hundred!"

"A hundred! You brag like a braying horse!" Archer retaliated.

Hunter for once did not rise to the taunt but turned to his mother.

"Will you tell us about them?"

Tessa looked at Ulrik and waited. Ulrik rose from the table without looking at any of them. Steeling himself he said, "After dinner, *I* will tell you the tale."

Emmer and the boys hustled to clean their plates, gobbling down their food, and rushed to clean the table and the dishes. Tessa took her place in the chair across from Ulrik's and the boys jostled each other for a place next to the fire to listen to the story.

Ulrik stared into the flames, not quite knowing where to start. So, he began at the beginning. He told them of their capture and how he killed one of the blue men because he was going after Tessa but he was vague on specifics about the treatment he received at the hands of Mohem and the Alahemwhey maidens. He did reveal the meaning of what happened. The boys grew still, and anger flushed their cheeks thinking of their mother and father in danger, thinking of what Ulrik hinted he had endured. Emmer's eyes filled with tears and she moved closer to lean her head on her father's knee.

Tessa took up the story.

"The Mohem of the Alahemwhey was protecting me by tattooing me. In their culture, the designs mean that I am a married woman. It is not a painful process and they were meant to bring health and happiness in my marriage to Ulrik, and lots of children." She smiled beautifully at them. "To be marked so is their *highest* honor to a woman and was meant to save me *for* Ulrik so that no Alahemwhey man could claim me as his, as is done in their tribe with unmarked women. I am marked as belonging to your father. Within the designs are some Nordic runes similar to those on Ulrik's arms. Mohem, their wise woman, knew a great many things and instructed the designs. As his wife, I am blessed as a married woman, to him only as the Ohhem signifies, in the Alahemwhey culture at least."

Ulrik looked at her for a long time, his face unreadable. This was a new revelation to him and was the most she had ever spoken about the tattoos.

After Ulrik's story, Hunter, Archer, and Emmer remained silent, until Hunter could no longer hold his tongue. "You mean we have brothers…"

"And sisters somewhere out there?" Archer finished Hunter's sentence.

"No!" Ulrik spoke sharply. "They are not your brothers and sisters. They are just-*others*." Ulrik stopped, shaking his head as if at a loss for words.

Archer spoke up next, "But there are people out there. Should we go and find them?"

"Meet them and maybe we could just...*find* them?" Hunter finished.

Ulrik surged to his feet. "No! No one will be going to find the blue people! They are people without honor. They take what is not theirs to take."

"But you said what they forced you to do was to save their people from extinction. Maybe they were desperate and didn't know what else to do." Emmer spoke for the first time, her musical voice full of pity and understanding.

Ulrik was speechless and angry and stalked away from his family. Tessa rose to follow after him but hesitated. He stormed into their bedroom and slammed the door.

Tessa turned to her children, taking up the lamp. "Please go to bed now and let's not speak of this again until, well, I don't know. Good night." She looked at them a long moment, poured her mother's love into her smile, and then turned to go to her room.

Emmer rose dutifully and went to her bed and the boys climbed up to their loft. The usual preparation and before-bed antics were dispensed with and they swiftly grew calm, each lost in their individual thoughts.

Tessa entered the bedroom. Ulrik sat on the edge of their bed and stared at his hands. She placed the lamp carefully on the side table in the small room.

"You never told me the meaning of the tattoos." He said quietly.

"I didn't want to upset you by talking about it. They are not like tattoos I was familiar with in my life before. I honestly thought they would wear off with time. I am sorry. I should have told you, but I wanted to put the whole matter behind us.

Then we were home, and the boys came, and then Emmer and I just let the matter go."

Ulrik rose and pulled her close to him. Her head barely came up to his chin and he stood for a long moment with his arms around her, holding her tightly. Then he moved to the table and turned up the lamp brighter. He returned to her, untied her laces, and pulled the dress off her shoulders. He ran his hands down along her arms feeling the softness of her skin. He cupped her breasts amazed that she was still as beautiful as the day he had first met her. There was no indication that she had borne three children. Her belly was flat, and her muscles were still taut, her breasts still round and firm. Some magic of this world kept them both young. He bent his head and kissed her. She trembled in his arms and he shook with longing.

Tessa slowly began to lift the shirt from over Ulrik's head. She undid the laces of his trousers and slid her hands within the material to grasp his firm behind. He pushed her back toward the bed. Tessa moved and pulled him between her legs and clutched him to her. She spread her hands over his broad back, and he guided his erection into her. He thrust into her with a ferocity that claimed her again and again, with each stroke, each plunge to the hilt of his shaft, with each kiss. They loved until their passion was spent. As he pulsed inside her, she gently bit his shoulder stifling a moan as she climaxed. Afterward, she lay in the protection of his arms.

"Ulrik?" Tessa spoke later.

"Hmmm?"

"Our sons will need wives." Tessa ventured, "Eventually, Emmer will need a husband. We can't deny them the love and companionship that is vital to life when we know there are other people out there. What are we going to do?"

Ulrik let out a deep breath. "I do not know." His voice rumbled under Tessa's head and he stared at the ceiling where the lamplight danced among the wooden beams.

"As I told you when I found you, I walked for three days in all directions. That is not to say there are no other people further away, but the only people on this planet that we have met were the blue people. I would not have my sons, nor my daughter meet *them*. Who can tell what would happen? I would like to keep them from danger. Perhaps the Sacred Lake will provide them with mates as it did for me." He pulled her a little closer.

"I don't know. I just don't know what to do, but I'm afraid they will eventually go hunting for the Alahemwhey or other people on their own." Ulrik could hear the strain in Tessa's voice.

"The same fear lives inside me as well." Ulrik clutched Tessa to him and he kissed the top of her head. He ran his hands over her firm body again. "Hunter and Archer have seen nineteen winters and are past the age they should be marrying. Emmer eighteen winters, she seems too young, but women of my people were married at fifteen or younger and already had children by her age." He paused, pain and indecision crossing his handsome features. "I will think on it."

Tessa nodded and snuggled into Ulrik's arms and eventually went to sleep.

Ulrik did not sleep. He relived a memory when Hunter and Archer had gone out into the dangerous woods on their own. Ulrik had regaled them with a story from his youth about hunting alone in the wilderness and they must have taken it as a challenge because the next day they were gone. They had barely been twelve years old at the time, full of themselves and over-confident in their abilities to hunt and survive in the wild. Part of Ulrik's heart fumed and wondered why the stubborn boys felt they had to prove themselves to him. The other part of Ulrik's heart shriveled that day worrying about his boys in the mountain wilderness alone. Forgetting to take food, water, and clothing in case of harsh weather, they ventured out on their own trying to prove their abilities to their father. Tessa begged him to go look for the twins while she stayed home with little Emmer.

It had taken Ulrik half a day to track the boys as they ventured deeper into the mountains to the southwest. As it happened, he was not the only one tracking them. Large paw prints showed a mountain lion stealthily following the boys. Judging by the size of the tracks it would be large enough of an animal to take down a boy. Ulrik shuddered and quickened his steps.

The loud raspy roar of the mountain lion had Ulrik sprinting toward the sound and the sight that met his eyes froze his blood. His two sons stood with their backs to a large rock facing the hungry lion. The lion's tail thrashed from side to side. Its ears laid back, hair standing on edge, the lion was ready to leap. The boys stood together. Hunter's knife was out and pointed toward the lion and Archer struggled to notch an arrow in his bow. Ulrik came charging out of the trees with axe raised and he threw. The lion, hearing Ulrik shout a battle cry, turned right as the axe buried in its shoulder. Ulrik's momentum caused him to crash into the lion and they rolled together. Ulrik's large dagger plunged, once, twice, and then the lion lay twitching.

Breathing hard, bloody, and dirty, Ulrik pushed the lion's body from him and stood. The twins watched wide-eyed and terrified. Hunter and Archer dropped their weapons and flew to their father's side, crying out in relief at seeing him. Ulrik loomed over them both. He took them by the scruff of their necks and frowned down at them. He was overjoyed to find them and glad they were not harmed, only cold and hungry, but he knew he needed to teach them a lesson.

It was true that on their own, they traveled further than Ulrik had ever taken them and before the night began to fall, must have quickly tried to build a fire but failed. The appearance of the mountain lion had surprised them. Ulrik crashing out of the trees, shouting, and battling the animal had surprised them even more.

Ulrik tried not to shout at the already frightened boys.

"Why did you not light a fire? The lion would not have approached the flames."

"We tried, but the wood…" Hunter began.

"Wouldn't catch and…" Archer went on.

"Then the mountain lion tried to attack us." Hunter finished

Ulrik let them go and strode over to the pile of twigs they had attempted to light. He squatted down and looked at it then and turned to survey the place they chose to stop for the night. It was out of the wind and a good place to camp but for the mountain lion stalking them.

"I thought I taught you better than this? This wood is green and damp. You have no kindling. No wonder it wouldn't start."

"We were cold and in a hurry." Hunter defended them.

"And then the mountain lion came," Archer repeated.

Ulrik just glared at them. He turned away and gathered dry pine needles, pieces of bark and smaller dry sticks then started a fire for them. Hunter and Archer huddled together close to the fire's warmth looking miserable.

"This is my fault. I have treated you both like children and not men. When I was your age, I worked the fields, hunted to help feed my family, and went raiding with my father and brothers. I should have left you two out here to fend for yourselves, but your mother is not from my time and does not understand what it takes to turn a boy into a man. I have only followed you two because she begged me to."

Sitting close together, Hunter and Archer were intent on his every word but hung their heads in unison at the mention of worrying their mother. Ulrik fell silent but turned to stare at the dead mountain lion. He picked up Hunter's knife and Archer's bow and arrow and handed them to each boy.

Coming to a decision, he fetched the pack he dropped before the fight with the lion, dug inside, and then handed each boy some dried meat.

"In the morning you two will skin the mountain lion and bury the meat because is not fit to eat. You will not return home without the pelt. From this day forward you must be men and not impulsive boys. Learn from your mistakes! That means if you go out to hunt on your own you tell your mother and me when you are leaving, take proper provisions, and know for certain how to start a fire. Most important, always watch your backs and never drop your weapons even if you think you are safe."

The next morning the boys woke alone with the coals of the fire barely smoldering. Ulrik had left at some point during the night leaving them to find their way home. Though he told them to keep the sun to their right and made a clear path for them to find the way home, he felt he had to leave them so that the boys would learn a valuable lesson. If they were going to go out on their own, they had better be prepared to survive on their own and defend themselves.

When Ulrik returned home the next day and told Tessa that he found the boys and what happened, she was greatly relieved. Though, she became furious with him that after going to the trouble of finding them, he would just leave the boys to fend for themselves anyway by leaving them alone.

Ulrik swore under his breath and was loath to explain himself even to Tessa but insisted the boys needed to learn to become men. Tessa knew in her heart that twenty-first-century thinking could not prevail in this situation. Ulrik understood the necessity of preparing their sons to survive in the wilderness. Life could be precarious in the mountains as Tessa had learned when Ulrik was wounded by the bear and so she had to agree with Ulrik's methods many times and did not continue to argue for the sake of being right.

Later that day before supper, Hunter and Archer came stomping in the door. Bloody, dirty, tired, and hungry, they dropped the mountain lion pelt to the floor at their father's feet. That day the boys had become men.

\#

The memory released Ulrik as he stared into the darkness and listened to Tessa's even breathing. The fact that Hunter and Archer were now grown men past nineteen winters, was not lost on Ulrik. Tessa was right, they would need wives and Emmer would need a husband. Their family had been happy but solitary on the mountain top and he did not want that to change. In the end, he feared, nature would not be denied.

The following morning after Ulrik revealed the story of the Alahemwhey, the family gathered at the breakfast table as usual. The twins came in from doing their chores. Ulrik took a long hard look at them. A smattering of soft blonde hair was beginning to show on Hunter and Archer as their facial hair began to grow. They were tall, lean, and capable young men, not twelve-year-old boys trying to prove themselves.

There was an uncomfortable tension among the family and Tessa could hardly stand it, but she remained silent. Ulrik did not eat, just stared at the table in front of him trying to ignore facts.

"Father?" Hunter began, "Archer and I, we've been talking, and we want to go find the Alahemwhey. We've never seen other people. We are men now and we..."

"want what you and mother have, we want..." Archer finished his sentence,

Ulrik slammed his fist on the table clattering the dishes. A glass fell to the floor and shattered.

"No!" He shouted into the stunned faces of his family. "By Odin! No one will go."

He stood quickly and turned to leave but stopped at the door and looked back at each of them with a meaningful glare.

"No one!"

Hunter and Archer looked at each other and Emmer's eyes filled with concern for her father.

Tessa placed a motherly hand on each boy's shoulder, "Let him think about it. Be patient. I will talk to him when the time is right, and we will figure this out."

Hunter stood anger clear on his face. He grabbed his big hunting knife and stalked toward the door. Archer, grabbing his bow and arrows, followed his twin from the cabin. Tessa walked over to Emmer and placing her hand on her cheek said, "Don't worry Little One. All will be well, *somehow.*"

Tessa stared through the door where her men had stalked away in anger. She realized that without societal mandates and cultural norms, life on their mountain was determined by the basic needs to survive, food, water, and shelter. There was no competition for resources, no expectations or strife, or prestige. The elements and nature were their providers and many times, their biggest enemy. As a family, they worked together and played together but ultimately, Ulrik was the law.

In the days that followed, Hunter and Archer remained quiet, and strain coursed through the family. One morning Tessa woke and went to make the morning meal. She noticed right away that Archer's bow and arrows were gone, and Hunter's long knife and a double-bladed axe were missing. Although her logical mind argued that they had probably left to do chores or to hunt, her mother's heart knew they had gone. After the incident with the mountain lion when they were twelve, they never left without telling Ulrik where they were going. Tessa rushed to Emmer's room and looked for her. Emmer was calmly dressing. She sat on the end of her bed slowly tying her boots but refused to greet or look at her mother when she entered.

"Emmer! The boys? Have they gone hunting?"

Emmer remained silent still looking guiltily at her feet. Tessa fled back to her bedroom and threw open the door.

"Ulrik! The boys are *gone!*"

Cursing, Ulrik dressed quickly yanking on his shirt and grabbing his boots. He stomped past Tessa and left the cabin. Less than a half-hour later he came back. He sat at the table and Tessa handed him a hot cup of tea.

"Well?" she asked fearing the answer.

"They must have left sometime during the night. They are on foot headed south toward the edge of the mountains." He stopped his voice dropping low, "It is not hard to figure out they have gone to find the blue people against my wishes."

He hesitated and ran his hand through his long hair then confirmed, "they have taken swords as well as an axe, Hunter's long knife, and Archer's bow and arrows."

Tessa covered her mouth with her hand, "Oh, no!"

"I will go after them. I can catch up to them quickly if I hurry."

"We will go with you," Tessa replied immediately.

"No! I can make better time by myself."

"*No*, we *will* go with you. If they are intent on finding the Alahemwhey, then nothing will stop them. They are stubborn and determined like their father. Perhaps I can help convince them to come home."

"I will convince them alright!" Ulrik looked grim. "You stay here with Emmer. I will return in a day or so."

"No!" Tessa stood with her hands on her hips and gave him a fierce look. "We will go as a family, and then we will *all* go find the Alahemwhey. The boys will not stop until they find them anyway, even though it is next to impossible. The Alahemwhey are nomads, there is very little chance they will find them. Let's just go and show them it is futile to look and bring them home as soon as possible. Then their curiosity will be satisfied, and we can go on with our lives."

"What if they find the blue people and are captured and forced to...what if they do to Hunter and Archer what they did to me?" the look of horror on Ulrik's face was quickly replaced by fury.

"I will quickly pack some supplies and we will be off as soon as possible. If we go on horseback, we can catch up to them in no time." Without answering Ulrik's question or waiting for a further response, Tessa turned and yelled for Emmer. Emmer walked out of her room smiling sheepishly, holding a pack already prepared to go on a trip. In less than a half-hour, they were ready to go.

Ulrik was furious because his hand had been forced. He reluctantly saddled three horses and mounted. They headed down the mountainside. Hunter and Archer had at least six hours of lead time they guessed, but Ulrik was determined to catch them.

Chapter Fifteen – Hunter and Archer's Story

Hunter and Archer knew that as soon as their absence was discovered, their father would be after them. Being skilled woodsmen, taught by Ulrik himself, they traveled quickly down the mountainside leaving no sign of their passing. Side-by-side, keeping up a steady trotting pace they quickly covered the miles. They had left the horses at home, thinking it would be harder to track them if they were on foot.

They were determined to find the Alahemwhey although they had little information with which to start their search, they headed south to where they understood the fields of grain were. Their buckskin clothing offered a little camouflage, and their soft boots left few prints in the dirt. They kept up the pace and put a great distance between them and their mountain home, bringing their destination closer.

Eventually, darkness fell but the twins traveled through the night knowing their father would be pursuing them. By morning, they gained the fields described by their mother and father, in the story of the Alahemwhey. They looked at each other, grinned, and headed straight ahead, hoping that luck would take them where they desired to go. They traveled another day without stopping to rest. They stopped briefly at a stream to drink and snatch a quick bite and an hour's rest. Re-energized they loped on and continued for most of that day and the next.

Hunter and Archer jogged along at a steady pace that they could easily keep up for hours on this flat land. They were alert for signs of any riders or people. From the story their parents told them about the Alahemwhey, they did not expect to meet up with anyone for at least a day or more, possibly weeks would pass before they found them. The two of them had discussed their plan to find the Alahemwhey in detail. There were many unknowns about the blue people.

They planned to stay hidden if they found them and just watch and decide what to do. Confident in their abilities in hunting and tracking, they were sure they would see signs of the Alahemwhey before they would come across them. Their father had taught them the skill with the sword and although they had never fought with anyone but each other and him, they were the sons of Ulrik the Norseman and were confident they could hold their own. They itched to test their sword skills against real foes. This was the adventure they had always hoped for and was similar to the Viking adventures their father had told them stories about.

They knew the Alahemwhey were a nomadic tribe and expected to spot their tents from a great distance. After leaving the mountains and traveling almost three days, they came to a stream and rested briefly. They did not expect to be followed by their parents for at least a day or two more because Emmer was supposed to tell them the boys had gone hunting and give them time to get a good distance away. Regardless, they hurried on. Emmer had never told a lie before and they were not sure she could pull it off.

Hunter crouched down and drank from a stream they stopped at. Archer dug through their pack to find some food. They had rested and eaten very little before they felt the ground begin to rumble. They had been spotted. As one, they unsheathed their swords and stood back-to-back as ten horsemen quickly surrounded them, pointing their glistening spears at the brothers.

"We are fools," Hunter grumbled.

"Caught like green boys." Archer agreed.

They were not sure who these men were and did not know what an Alahemwhey looked like, but they had expected them to be dressed in blue. These men were dressed in red and black leather armor although they had blue streaks in their hair, and many had blue tattoos. The boys waited, swords pointing down.

The riders that surrounded Hunter and Archer had spears tipped in shiny black stone pointed at them. They knew from Ulrik's description of their weapons that these were obsidian tips. That they were hard and sharp, the boys did not doubt because they looked lethal. Each warrior had a black knife under his belt and looked none too friendly.

One of the riders came forward gesturing and speaking in a tongue the twins did not understand. Hunter and Archer remained back-to-back and waited to see what the riders would do. One of them dismounted and then the others followed. Soon the boys were surrounded by spear-toting men.

"Well, this doesn't look good," Hunter said.

"Nope! Our father would be ashamed we let ourselves get surrounded and caught so easily," Archer replied.

Hunter said, "I'll try to talk to them, let them know we come in peace."

"I don't know if they are interested." Archer said and then added, "Maybe we shouldn't have drawn our swords so quickly?"

The rider who had dismounted first took a step toward them, speaking abruptly in their strange language, motioning toward their swords.

"Well, if you mean what I think you mean we're not dropping our swords," Hunter spoke almost cheerfully.

"Metal wins over stone any day!" Archer chuckled menacingly addressing the man.

The rider spoke more loudly and gestured sharply.

"Well, this is a fine situation." Archer offered, although he could not keep the grin from his face. They were each anxious to test their metal but did not want to misinterpret the situation.

The rider had enough of the delay and motioned for the men, spears raised, to advance toward the twins who raised their swords and took a fighting stance. They had trained sword against spear combat with their father and were good fighters, but they had never faced anyone but each other, nor so many at once. Neither one of them had ever killed a man. They stood ready to do whatever was necessary. Each of them instinctually knew it was time to grow up from being untried boys to become men who could kill if necessary.

Suddenly, the mounted men attacked all at once. Ten spears were stabbing at them all at one time from every direction. Archer took a shallow slice on his right arm and shook blood to the ground still smiling widely. Switching hands, he grinned at the spearman and sliced down and across breaking off two spearheads from the shafts at one time.

Hunter was laughing and making rude comments about fighting sticks against their superior swords when the leader pulled out a blue tube. He took a deep breath and shot an arrow into Hunter's sword arm. It went numb and his sword fell from his grasp.

"Now, that's not fighting fair!" he shouted as he reached behind him for his axe with his other hand. Both boys were equally skilled with their right and left hands. Just then the butt of a spear swooshed across and caught him just under the eye. Momentarily stunned, Hunter fell to one knee. As he swung out with the axe, he was smashed in the back of the head from behind.

Archer suffered a similar fate taking a dart in the neck. He staggered forward slashing down with his sword and then aiming a punch at the nearest man catching him square in the face and breaking his nose, which sprayed blood onto the dusty ground.

Hunter and Archer were quickly unarmed and grabbed by the riders. They tried to fight, but the darts worked quickly paralyzing them both. Their hands and feet were tied, and they were roughly slung over the back of two horses. The last thing Hunter heard was Archer saying in a slur, "We forgot about…"

"…the darts." Hunter finished and then fell unconscious.

#

Hunter awakened and turned his head slightly to see where they were being taken. He tried not to give away the fact that the effects of the dart had worn off. Hanging on the horse next to him, he could see Archer, his long blonde hair hanging down almost brushing the ground. He could also see from his upside-down view, what he guessed were buildings. Boots approached and Hunter's head was jerked up. The lead rider looked him in the face and gave a vicious grin. Someone spoke behind him and suddenly Hunter was yanked off the horse and dropped to the ground. He surveyed where he was, watching for any avenue of escape. He also saw that he and Archer had company. Another captive was bound, hand and foot slung over a horse and that person's long auburn hair swept the ground gathering grass and sticks. Next, the other captive was lifted off the horse and dropped to the ground next to Hunter. Archer followed still unconscious.

The three of them were hauled up and two men dragged Archer under his arms, and one tied Hunter's hands behind his back and prodded him along with a black stone pointed spear. The third prisoner was thrown over the shoulder of a large man and the three of them were left in a hut. The loud *"thunk"* sound of a heavy wooden bar, fell across the only door locking them in.

Archer had been dumped across the small room from Hunter. Their fellow prisoner was right next to Hunter but was still unconscious. He looked around noticing they were in a straw-strewn building with no windows and one door that was barred shut.

After laying there a short time assessing their situation, Hunter turned his head toward the other prisoner and found himself looking into the liquid gold eyes of a *girl*. She had been gagged and breathed heavily through the cloth. Hunter gingerly sat up. His hands were behind his back. Tied such, it was no difficult feat with some flexibility and stretching, to sit up and pull his hands under himself, down the back of his legs, and get them through his feet by bending his knees and bringing them tightly into his chest. Finally, he managed to get his hands in front. Working at the knots with his strong white teeth, Hunter managed to untie his hands.

When he was free, he moved toward the girl and carefully untied the gag from her mouth. She looked relieved but did not say a thing, just licked her parched lips watching him with intense golden eyes and she trembled with fear. Hunter moved over to Archer and untied his bindings. Checking him over for serious injury, he surmised that he was still under the effects of the dart, which Hunter pulled from Archer's neck and tossed aside. Leaving him to sleep it off, he moved back to the girl. Hunter spoke in low reassuring tones and hoped the girl knew he meant her no harm.

Although Hunter was a fierce and magnificent hunter, tracker, and woodsman, he also had a kind heart. He was the first to bring home a wounded animal or help with the birthing of farm animals. Hunter was always there to lend a helping hand. He watched his mother collect herbs and medicinal plants and prepare teas and healing poultices. He helped clean and stitch up wounds, had set Archer's broken arm once, and spent a lot of time reading many of the medical books found in the vast library of Dr. Jeremiah Tennbaum.

Without another thought, Hunter took it upon himself to see to the hurt girl. First, he untied her wrists, and she rubbed the feeling back into her hands and fingers. She was clearly in a lot of pain but made no sound. Hunter moved to unbind her feet. He saw that she had a badly hurt ankle. The ropes were cutting deeply into swollen blue and purple flesh. There was some caked blood, and the ropes would be painful when removed.

"This is going to hurt." He said to her although he guessed she did not understand his language. Then he went to work at the knots slowly untying them.

Hunter began to peel away the ropes, gently pulling them from where they cut deeply into the girl's skin. She let out a little cry of pain, her eyes glazed a little and she swayed a bit. After he finally got the ropes off of her, she pulled her good leg up, rubbing her ankle but left the other one outstretched because Hunter still held on to it, examining the terrible wound.

"Sorry, it couldn't be helped. They had to come off. The ropes were cutting off your circulation." Hunter said quietly as he continued to work. He looked into the girl's golden eyes again and was momentarily frozen by how beautiful she was. She was the first girl he had ever seen who was not his mother, or his sister. She fascinated him instantly.

Hunter looked around the room and spotted a bucket in the corner. Moving quickly, he went over to it and was relieved to find water, although he was not sure how clean it was, it was at least cool. He brought the bucket back over to the girl and tearing a sleeve from his shirt, soaked it in the water and cleaned the blood from the wounds on her ankle then wetted the sleeve again. He wrapped the ankle snuggly with his other shirt sleeve and then looked up at her.

The girl watched him with her liquid gold eyes. She had to be close to Emmer's age he guessed and despite the blood and dirt covering her, he thought she was very beautiful. He tore his eyes from her intent gaze and looked her over for other wounds. The strange tunic she wore was torn in many places and did little to hide the smooth lithe body beneath. Her pale skin was slightly tanned and smooth. Hunter told himself to keep his mind on the business at hand.

There was a long gash on the outside of the girl's thigh. He began to clean the wound and, as he was so intent on what he was doing, he had not noticed his left hand was holding the inside of her thigh. She noticed though and pushed his hand away none too gently. Hunter realized where his hand had been and blushed a deep shade of red. He shook his head and turned back to the water, dipped the cloth, and continued to clean the wound. He tore a long strip off and wrapped her thigh. Using what was left of his sleeve, he dipped it in the water and moved toward her face.

She flinched and hissed in pain. Someone had delivered a good blow to her mouth and her bottom lip was split, swollen, and bruised. Hunter slowly moved closer to her. He gently cupped her chin with one hand and cleaned the blood from her lip, and the dirt from her face.

The entire time Hunter administered to her the girl did not utter a word. The close contact with her made Hunter nervous and his hand shook a little as he cleaned her face, as his mother had cleaned his face when he was a little boy. He resisted the urge to kiss her on the forehead and make it better, also as his mother had done.

When he was finished, he leaned back and surveyed her once again. He cleaned any other minor cuts and scrapes just for a reason to touch her. She watched his every move.

Finally, he could find no more reasons to keep giving her medical care, so he rewetted and rewrapped the bandage around her bad ankle and had to call it good.

"It doesn't look like it is broken, just a bad sprain, I think. It is deeply cut and a little infected," Hunter said quietly to her. He placed his hand on his chest and said, "My name is Hunter." He patted his chest again "Hunter." Then he pointed to her, "You?"

The girl seemed to understand what he was asking and after a short hesitation said, "Soria" in a whispery, musical voice. "Soria." She pointed to her ankle and whispered something in a language Hunter did not understand. He just nodded his head, smiled, and continued to stare at her, not knowing what to say.

Then slowly Soria reached out and took a tendril of his white-blonde hair between her fingers examining it intently as if she had never seen hair of its kind before. Hunter remained very still until she dropped the lock. Then she turned her head away, a far-off look in her eyes.

Hunter stood and walked over to where Archer lay and checked on him. He sat next to his brother and leaned against the wall. He stared at the girl who had fallen asleep and soon his eyes became heavy and he drifted off to sleep as well.

As morning came, their prison hut lightened a little, and the scrape of the door being unbarred awakened Hunter. A warrior came in carrying a deep bowl and skin of water. He sat the items down just inside the door and then closed it roughly, barring it again behind him. Hunter rose and stretched walking to the bowl and saw that it was full of food. He glanced over to where Soria lay and saw that she was awake, watching him intently. He went to her and sitting beside her tried to get her to eat, but she refused. Holding the skin out to her he motioned for her to drink. She tried to raise her head but could not hold it up. Hunter could see sweat gleaming on her tanned skin. He put his hand to her forehead and found she was feverish. He scooted closer to her and gently lifted her in his arms. Sliding underneath her and propping her up, he held her against his chest and tried to get her to drink. She finally gulped greedily as he held the skin to her mouth then she fell back against him exhausted and slept.

That is how Archer found them when he woke a short time later. He sat up moaning and grabbing at his aching head. Looking around he spotted Hunter and arched a questioning brow at him.

"There's food here if you want and some water," Hunter told him quietly.

"Water, I could use some of that! Is that a *girl?*" Archer asked moving toward the food and water. "You don't waste any time do you!"

Hunter gave him a brief rundown of her wounds and said, "She needs more help. I think she has an infection. She definitely has a fever."

Archer nodded. "Have you eaten?"

"No. You go ahead. She is too weak but save her something for when she wakes again, and I can try to get her to eat."

"Where are we?" Archer asked.

"I don't know, but those who captured us were…"

"…red, I know." Archer finished his thought. "I can't tell if they are the Alahemwhey we seek. I thought they were supposed to be the blue people. It is so unreal to be seeing other humans." He paused and then grinned widely, "We gave those men…"

"…a good fight." Hunter finished Archer's sentence with an answering grin. "I just wish I knew why they took us captive."

"Good question," Archer said eating and then drinking a little water, handed the skin to Hunter.

"We need to get her a healer. Go bang on the door until they answer. Tell them she is sick."

"I'll take care of it." Archer rose and went to bang on the door. After a bit of shouting and pounding, the bar lifted, and two guards opened the door and pointed black obsidian-tipped spears at them. Archer gestured and shouted until one of the men stepped in prodding Archer back with his spear. He looked at the girl, then said in a voice full of contempt, "Solemeyha" and spit on the ground. He backed out the door slamming it and barring it.

"Well, I tried," Archer shrugged.

Hunter tried to wake the girl to get her to eat, she pushed food away but drank some more water, then her head fell back against Hunter's chest and she slept again. Sometime later the door opened and in walked a girl. She was about Hunter and Archer's age and had light golden blonde hair that was twisted and streaked with blue. She carried a basket and came confidently into the hut, the guards stepping in with her. She looked around the room, and then her eyes rested on the girl.

Then she stared wide-eyed in surprise at Hunter and Archer. "You are Ulrik's sons!"

Archer looked shocked that she had spoken his language "You speak our language?"

The girl looked at him and spoke as one would speak to a child. "Yes, I speak the Mohem tongue. All Ulrik's children do."

"This girl needs medical attention. She has a fever and a badly wounded ankle." Hunter said forcefully.

"She is Solemeyha." She said to Hunter and shrugged one shoulder.

Archer moved toward her. "Are you a healer?"

"Yes, but I can do nothing for *her*." She sneered.

Hunter gently laid Soria down and rose to his feet and walked over to the girl. He towered above her. Despite the guard's warning and the sharp spear pointed at him, he addressed her forcefully.

"I need hot water, bandages, medicine, some wine if possible. She has a fever and an infection. She needs a blanket, some decent food, and something clean to wear."

The girl scowled back at Hunter. "You speak some words I do not know. What is in-fec-tion?"

"Just get me what I need, and I will take care of her if you won't."

"Brother," the girl pleaded. "I cannot understand some of what you say."

"I am not your brother! I need hot water, medicine, bandages, a blanket, and some clean clothes for her. NOW!"

The girl just looked at him, rolled her eyes, and then stormed out.

A short time later, the girl returned with a couple of older women. They shooed Hunter away, knelt, and washed the girl. Hunter and Archer turned their backs as they changed her clothes, putting a clean blue tunic on her. They even combed her auburn hair and put it in a braid. Neither would answer any questions Hunter and Archer asked.

"I leave the rest to you, Brother." The girl who came earlier said, and the other women stared back and forth between the twin's identical faces, but eventually, they all turned and left.

Archer said, "They look like the Alahemwhey might. They have blue in their hair and some of them had the…"

"…Ohhem like Mother." Hunter grimly finished for him.

Hunter smelled each of the medicines the women left and selected a few, putting them in the hot water brought by the women, he let them steep. Then he unwrapped Soria's ankle and swore at the sight of it. It was even more swollen and infected. The rope cuts oozed yellow puss. He cleaned it with the hot water, made a poultice with some of the medicines the women left, and re-wrapped it with clean bandages. He moved to her thigh, and carefully unwound the old bandage. It was not as bad, but he cleaned it with hot water and put on a new bandage. With Archer's help, they carried her to a clean spot in the hay and laid her on a soft blanket. Soria went in and out of consciousness. He made her as comfortable as he could, and then again held her in a sitting position. Holding a cup to her lips he forced her to drink the tea he had made. She moaned and fought weakly, but Hunter persisted in getting her to drink the medicine. He carefully laid her down and she fell into a deep sleep.

Archer paced their prison. Both were unused to being caged up. They discussed possibilities of escape, the number of guards outside, and their weapons. Their swords, knives, bow, and arrows had been confiscated. Then they discussed Soria. She was too sick and wounded to be moved, and Hunter refused to leave her. Soria awoke later and seemed slightly better. She watched and listened as the two talked. Of course, she did not understand a word they said. Hunter gave her some food and touched her forehead again. Soria flinched back a little and had a puzzled look on her face. Hunter tilted his head to the side and gave her a stern look.

"I have to see if your fever broke." He said sternly.

Soria let him touch her forehead reluctantly. He looked pleased because she felt much cooler. Hunter got her some water and made her drink. Soria looked down at herself seeing she had been cleaned up and redressed. She narrowed her eyes giving him a suspicious look. As if sensing her thoughts, Hunter held up his hands in surrender and shook his head as if to say, "I didn't do it." She nodded once as if she understood.

Hunter went back to talking with Archer. Soria looked back and forth between the two of them confused by the fact that they looked almost exactly alike.

"Hunter?" she said and then pointed to Archer.

"Archer," Hunter said, placing his hand on his brother's shoulder, pleased that she remembered his name and could tell him apart from his twin. "Hunter, Archer," she said pointing back and forth between the two of them. Then the hut lit up as she gave them a beautiful smile, placed her hand on her chest, and said, "Soria."

Hunter held Soria's gaze for a long moment, while the smile played on her lips. Hunter's breath quickened in his chest as they stared at each other. Meeting the first people he had ever come across had not gone so well. Meeting the first girl he had ever seen went very well.

Chapter Sixteen – The Search

Ulrik, Tessa, and Emmer, despite being on horseback had not caught up to the boys. They stopped to catch a few hours of sleep during the night when it was too dangerous for the horses to travel in the dark. In many places going down the mountain, they had to dismount and walk the horses. Ulrik chaffed at their slow pace, frequently cursing in Old Norse and Tessa's brow was constantly creased with worry. It was at times like this when Ulrik's Viking heritage came out and he was prone to almost violent anger. This time she was not able to placate him. Their eyes constantly scanned the distance for signs of Hunter and Archer.

Emmer remained quiet during their journey. Guilt painted her lovely face, but when her parents were not looking her blue eyes sparkled with excitement at the adventure. She had always been the dutiful daughter but reading and hearing about other people made her feel restless in a way she could not describe to her mother.

They came to the open fields and after a tense search, Ulrik found the boys' trail. They followed quickly on horse for another day, sure that they would overtake them easily since they were mounted, and the boys were on foot. The following day they reached the spot where it looked like Hunter and Archer had stopped to eat and rest.

Ulrik cursed as he read the signs of their passing.

"There were many horses here. There was a scuffle. There is blood in the dirt."

Tessa gasped, "We must find them!"

Ulrik vaulted onto his horse and followed the path the horsemen had taken. Tessa and Emmer rode closely behind him. After another day and a half of riding over the gently swelling hills, they came to a valley. They dismounted and looked down. A huge settlement filled the valley floor. Smoke rose from the tops of many huts and small figures could be seen moving among the many buildings.

Ulrik swore again in his native Norse as he counted the number of men and estimated the size of the settlement. It was most probable that Hunter and Archer had come or been taken in this direction. Ulrik gripped his sword hilt, his knuckles turning white with anger. Tessa's face flushed with fear as she contemplated what could be happening to her sons.

Emmer's eyes grew wide with wonder at seeing the settlement. She had never in her life seen anything like it. The only people she had ever known were her family. She remained silent out of fear for her brothers, but her eyes sparkled with curiosity and she had to calm herself from wanting to dance with excitement.

Ulrik helped Tessa down from her horse and Emmer leaped lightly down from her own. He constantly searched the horizon to make sure no blue people would come upon them from behind.

"Tessa, you and Emmer are not safe here." He growled. "I should have never agreed to let you come. I do not know what I would do if you were taken too." He clasped her to him briefly then taking her shoulders in his hands he looked into her eyes.

"You must go back! Take Emmer and go home, ride swiftly, and do not look back. I will wait until night falls and then sneak into the settlement and find Hunter and Archer. If all goes well, we will be no more than a day or two behind you."

Tessa shook her head defiantly. "No! What if *you* get caught? We can help. You taught us both to use swords. Emmer is almost as good a hunter as the boys and I can hold my own with the bow. We will watch your back. I can't leave without knowing our sons are safe and I can't leave you alone to possibly get captured again."

Ulrik firmed his jaw, "No! I cannot risk you two as well. Practicing with wooden swords is nothing like taking on an actual foe that is bigger and stronger than you! I order you to go back!"

"We are not Thanes to be ordered around! We are your family and those are *my* sons too that are in danger! I am going with you and whatever happens, happens to us all!"

"Maybe we could just ride down there? Let's find Eleanor the Mohem maybe she will help us?" Tessa pleaded.

Trying to ignore Tessa's defiance, anger flushed Ulrik's face and he schooled his features trying to reason with her.

"That old woman was over two hundred and sixty years old! It has been almost twenty years since we last saw her. She is probably dead by now."

Tessa stood resolutely, "We are staying together. I *will* help get my sons back!"

Anger flashed in her eyes. This was the first time she had ever openly defied Ulrik and Emmer tried to hide a smile as she watched her normally calm and sweet mother, stand up to the imposing Ulrik.

"At the risk of our daughter as well?" Ulrik demanded angrily. "We do not even know if those are the blue people. The Alahemwhey are nomads and that is a permanent settlement. I do not know who is down there and I cannot risk you."

Tessa looked toward Emmer who stood staring down the valley. "I don't know what is best to do. I just know we should stay together, and I can't leave without my sons. Whoever lives down there, they make have taken our boys or they may have gone willingly. We can't know until we try!"

Emmer spoke for the first time. "Well, we can't stand here and argue. Let's just go down there and talk to them. Maybe they are friendly? Let's just ask them about my brothers."

Ulrik swore a streak of profanity. "I will go alone. If they do not release our sons, I will cut through them with this." He gripped his sword.

Tessa tilted her head to the side and placed her fists on her hips.

"Ulrik, men who live by the sword *die* by the sword. I will not have you die at all. Please, can't we all go down peacefully and assess the situation? Maybe they *are* friendly. If Emmer and I go, you won't be so threatening and perhaps we can bargain with them."

"Dying by the sword is every Norseman's wish. Then I will go to the halls of Valhalla and feast at Odin's table with my brother warriors."

He released his sword defeated, "but I cannot risk your lives. We will do as you suggest and hope for the best, but at the first sign of danger, I cut down as many as I can, and you and Emmer *will* escape. Is that understood?"

"Agreed!" The women chimed in unison.

"This is madness!" Ulrik cursing and shouting that he should never have allowed them to come.

The three of them mounted their horses, happy to be doing something.

Chapter Seventeen - The Blue People

After their capture by the Alahemwhey, the three prisoners spent the next day the same way. Soria improved greatly thanks to Hunter's care, but she could not walk. On the evening of their second day, the doors opened, and six guards came in. They motioned for the prisoners to follow them. They spoke harshly to Soria demanding she get up and follow, going so far as to point their spears menacingly at her.

Hunter stepped forward and yelled at them knocking the spears aside. "She has an injured ankle. She can't walk! Fool!"

One of the guards gestured and made it clear Hunter was to carry her. Hunter stooped down and cradled her gently. He easily lifted her in his strong arms. She felt as light as a feather. He pulled her close to his chest feeling her smooth skin under his fingers and her firm lithe body against his. Soria put her arms around Hunter's neck and looked down shyly refusing to meet his gaze. Then he led the way with Archer right beside him.

While walking through the village, Hunter and Archer looked around, taking in their surroundings. As they had heard their father describe in his adventures, they tried to pick out an escape route, counted the number of warriors, and noticed where the horses were kept. There were numerous houses and many of the blue people, a few women, and many very young children among them. They were taken to a large building with tall intricately carved doors that swung open and they entered.

The walls were lined with great flaming torches. Men and women dressed in various shades of blue and decorated heavily with blue beads and painted with blue tattoos milled around the lodge, and the twins caused a great deal of mumbled conversation. There were the smaller, dark brown-haired Alahemwhey and there were many entirely different-looking people who had to be Ulrik's *other* children.

Hunter and Archer were led to the center of the building. Soldiers surrounded them, pointing lethal-looking spears at them.

Archer leaned in to whisper excitedly to Hunter, "Look at all the…"

"…women, yes, I noticed." Hunter finished his sentence.

They walked forward until they stood before a beautiful young woman who lounged on a pillowed couch. She smiled widely and beckoned them forward with a slim hand. Hunter and Archer stopped just in front of her and could not help staring. This was the most exotic woman they had ever seen. Her long hair was so red it looked like rippling flames as it flowed down to her waist and her eyes flashed vibrant blue. She was richly dressed in a brilliant blue gown that was open to the waist and barely concealed her large white breasts, around her neck were multiple strands of brilliant blue beads and clear crystals. She had luscious full lips that smiled widely revealing perfect white teeth.

Behind her, arranged in a row were five large blonde men who unmistakably had to have been fathered by Ulrik as they had his height, blue eyes, and a strong facial resemblance. Dressed in red leather armor they stood at attention looking curiously at Hunter, Archer, and Soria in Hunter's arms. Hunter hugged her closer to his chest in a protective gesture as the men leered at her.

The red-haired woman sat up a little straighter as three old men dressed in heavily decorated blue robes, entered the building from a side door. They slowly lowered themselves into chairs arranged next to the red-headed girl and then sat looking expectantly at her.

"My brothers!" She finally turned to them and said in a rich musical voice. "I am Tahara, Mohem of the Alahemwhey. I am one of Ulrik's children and you must be Ulrik's sons as well. You are so beeeaauuutifulll!" She swept a long shapely white arm behind her dramatically. "These are some of our brothers you see!"

Archer stepped forward slightly and asked, "How is it you speak our language."

"Why have you taken us prisoner?" Hunter asked.

"Oh, patience my brothers." Her rich beautiful voice sang out loudly. She turned her beautiful blue eyes directly on Hunter.

"Why are you carrying the Solemeyha?" Frowning slightly, she seemed displeased.

"She is unwell and has an injured ankle. She has been badly beaten by your men and cannot walk." Hunter spoke up.

"She must be heavy. You can put her down over there until I am ready to deal with her." Tahara gestured to a dark corner.

"No," Hunter said simply, his deep voice reverberating in the room. Hunter had carried whole deer carcasses for a half a day-uphill-in the mountains when hunting. This slight girl was no drain on his strength and he secretly enjoyed the feel of her body against his chest, in his arms.

Tahara frowned slightly and stuck her bottom lip out in a pout. She clearly was not used to being told *"no."*

"Hmm," she said hesitantly, "to answer one of your questions, the one who was Mohem before me, has taught us her language so that we may speak to our Father Ulrik when he should return to us one day. It is said that the Father proclaimed he would return for his children. The Elders of our tribe, you see before us have seen the wisdom in learning his language so we may speak to him when he comes. We who are Ulrik's children have been lessoned in the Mohem speech. The other Alahemwhey do not know the Mohem language as it is considered the high speech. It is only for Ulrik's children to know."

As they spoke the doors at the end of the hall opened. Hunter and Archer stood straighter when they saw who entered.

They looked each other in the eye and said in unison, "Now we're really in trouble!"

In stormed in Ulrik, Tessa and Emmer followed Alahemwhey guards in deep blue and black armor.

Tahara turned to her Red Guard and issued an order. The guards surrounded Hunter and Archer, pointing their spears at them, as their parents approached.

"Ah, are you more of Ulrik's children?" asked Tahara smiling grandly.

Ulrik scowled and shouted, "*I AM Ulrik!*"

The crowd stirred and the men behind the Tahara's dais stood taller and looked with disbelief and awe written on their features. Finally, the day they all anticipated had come and the man who sired them all stood before them.

Tahara leaned forward and spoke to the elders who looked long and hard at Ulrik and then shook their heads affirming in Alahemwhey that he was, indeed, Ulrik.

"Father!" She joyfully proclaimed lifting her arms wide as if to display herself. "I am Tahara, daughter of your union with Tahala my mother who was the Chief's wife. *I* am now Mohem of the Alahemwhey. You have finally come and are most welcome!"

"*I AM NOT YOUR FATHER!*" Ulrik shouted. "You are the Meadwhey children, seed *stolen* from me," Ulrik yelled his face reddening with anger. "How do you know my language? Where is the other Mohem? She who was called Eleanor Tennbaum. Bring her here now!" Ulrik yelled impatiently demanding an answer.

Tahara spoke slowly and patiently, "Ulrik Father, the one of whom you speak is our Great Mohem. That one before me has taught us your language so that we may speak to you when you should come back one day. The Elders tell us you proclaimed you would return for your children. The other Alahemwhey do not know this high speech. It is only for those of us who are *your* children."

"You are not my children. You are abominations! Those two are my only true sons and this is my only true daughter." Ulrik continued to yell as he pointed to Hunter and Archer.

"Ulrik Father, these men, your *true* sons, are *my* prisoners." Gesturing expansively behind her, "These warriors, who are also your sons, are part of my personal Red Guard. These, your true sons, were captured on the great plain."

"Why are they prisoners?" Ulrik raged red-faced at Tahara.

Tahara paid no attention to his question. Instead, she looked at the twins and at Emmer, her eyes narrowing slightly as she looked Emmer up and down. Then they took on a calculating look as her eyes rested on Ulrik's sword. She turned and spoke to Soria in the Alahemwhey language. There ensued an argument between the two women.

"She says you can put her down now. She chooses to stand on her own two feet." Tahara commanded petulantly.

Soria began to wriggle and push away from Hunter's arms, so he gently lowered her to her feet setting her between Archer and himself. She could not put any weight on her foot. She made one attempt to stand on it but could not. She did not cry out, although she was clearly in pain. Hunter put his arm around her waist to steady her. Soria lifted her head in defiance and stood as proudly as she could muster under the circumstances.

Ulrik opened his mouth to speak again when the doors at the back of the lodge opened. Two columns of ten men in deep blue jerkins and black hardened leather armor, carrying black-tipped spears, entered in two disciplined lines. At the head of the column of men was a giant. He was as tall as Ulrik who easily was the tallest man in the room. He had raven black hair sweeping his broad shoulders, a heavily muscled chest, and massive arms. The women in the room gave a collective sigh as he led his men into the lodge.

With the huge warrior were some of Ulrik's *other* sons. They walked boldly through the crowd in two orderly columns. As he advanced toward the dais, the warrior observed everything looking hard at Ulrik, Tessa, and then at Emmer.

Only Ulrik saw as the giant man looked at Emmer, his deep emerald green eyes widened and his eyebrow rose ever so slightly, his mouth twitching just a bit. Ulrik growled, placed his hand on his sword hilt, and moved to block Emmer from the giant's sight. Emmer stared wide-eyed at the tall, dark, imposing figure as he stalked in.

Tahara sat up straight and leaned forward with her arms outstretched toward the tall warrior.

"Bondur! My beeeaauuutifulll Bondur! Come to me my beautiful Bondur!" Tahara said breathlessly, "Ulrik Father, this is Bondur! The Captain of all Alahemwhey warriors. He is the best and the bravest warrior we have, and he is completely loyal to *me!*" She said casting a narrow-eyed glare at Emmer.

Bondur mounted the dais and stood next to Tahara his spear at attention by his side, eyes forward. He cleared away a look of embarrassment and anger that colored his handsome features as Tahara lovingly caressed his arm seductively in front of the entire assembly, but he did not move a muscle.

"Captain Bondur does not speak the Mohem high speech because he is not one of your children."

Tahara spoke quickly to Captain Bondur in Alahemwhey and he looked from the twins to Ulrik and Tessa. Bondur's eyes rested on Emmer for a long moment then quickly snapped away.

Ulrik was running out of patience. "Tahara, I have no wish to be introduced to anyone in your tribe, just give me my true sons and we will leave peacefully."

A sly, cunning look crossed Tahara's beautiful features.

"I am sorry Ulrik Father, but these two men are under arrest for…for poaching. They were found by my Red Guard trespassing upon our land and poaching. They must pay for their crimes."

Ulrik quickly realized that these were false charges. He wondered, not for the first time during this meeting, why he had been allowed to keep his weapons. He took two steps toward Tahara, gripping the hilt of his sword until his knuckles whitened, and leaned in to say in a low angry voice, "You will release Hunter and Archer, or you will feel my wrath. Your puny stone spears cannot stand against my steel sword. I will kill many of your warriors, your Captain first, before you can cut me down. Release my sons and we will go without any bloodshed."

Captain Bondur took a step forward lowering his spear menacingly at Ulrik's chest. Ulrik drew his sword from its sheath.

The tension in the hall heightened and the only sound was the sound of the torch flames burning brightly. All eyes focused on the silvery gleam of Ulrik's Viking sword.

Tessa, not wanting any bloodshed, especially of any of her family, stepped forward.

"Tahara, I am Tessa Ulrik's wife and a friend to Eleanor Tennbaum, the Great Mohem before you. Can you tell me, what has happened to her? She is our friend and can speak for us."

Tahara leaned back on her divan and looked at Tessa with a curious smirk. Her eyes slowly wandered up and down her length taking in her dusty travel attire and resting upon her face.

"I had heard you were a great beauty Tessa, Ulrik's wife. These things are often *greatly* exaggerated. The Great Mohem of which you speak lies dying in her tent. You see, I and the other daughters Ulrik fathered, became her apprentices. We learned everything the Great Mohem had to teach us."

Tessa tilted her head in sorrow, but her eyes held a challenge, "I'm sorry to hear that she is dying. She was a great Mohem, the likes of which this tribe will never see again."

Tahara either did not catch the veiled insult or chose to ignore it because she turned toward Captain Bondur again and her face lit up with admiration. Smiling seductively, she spoke to him at length in Alahemwhey. Captain Bondur motioned to two of his men who brought forward a bulky bundle held between them. They bowed toward Tahara and the three Elders then placed the bundle on the floor and unrolled the cover. Out spilled about ten swords unlike Ulrik's in design and in various states of disrepair. Some were broken and many were rusted, dinged, or bent.

"We heard stories of your great sword, Ulrik Father, in the tale of when you were here so many years ago. The Alahemwhey have grown since then. Now we live in a village and no longer wander the plains living like beggars. We are more civilized now. Although, as with my mother and her husband, some of the older Alahemwhey still wander keeping to the old ways. Captain Bondur has recently been on a quest on behalf of the Alahemwhey, to find these metal swords for our warriors. These swords will make us a great people. We will raise an unstoppable army and our enemies will perish under our blades."

Unimpressed, Ulrik just looked at her.

"A fine speech, but what does that have to do with releasing my family?"

Tahara ran a hand down the swell of her hip, smoothing the scant cloth that covered her. She covertly looked toward Captain Bondur to see if he was watching her coy flirtation but noticed Bondur's eyes had once again rested on Emmer. As her gaze followed his, she narrowed her eyes and pursed her lips angrily. She leaned toward the three Elders, who had watched silently during this entire interview. In a sharp, angry tone she spoke with them for a long time.

"The Elders agree with me. We will set your *true* sons free, forgiving all their crimes, but you must pay a price."

"What do you want Tahara?" Ulrik growled.

"You will train Captain Bondur and my warriors to use metal swords. Then you will take many men and go to the Solemeyha and you will steal the secret magic to make swords and bring it back to me. Then you may all go free. If you fail or do not keep your part of the bargain in any way, we will put your *true* sons to death, for that is the punishment for poaching and trespassing."

Ulrik swore in Old Norse, then yelled at her, "You are an evil, conniving whore, just like your mother! You have no idea what you are talking about! There is no secret magic to making swords. You need a man who is trained and has the knowledge and skill to *make* the swords! You need a *Sword Smith!* There is no secret magic to steal."

Tahara took a deep breath as if she was controlling her patience with an errant child and said to Ulrik, "Yes, but we knew there was a man who knows the secret to sword magic," Tahara pointed a slender finger at Soria, "This is his daughter! My Red Guard took her from her father a few days ago in hopes that we could *persuade* him to come to the Alahemwhey. Upon their return, they found these two trespassing on our lands. You will teach our warriors to use the swords we have gathered and then you will go take the man who knows the secret to making more swords. Bring him back here or I will put your *true* sons to death." Tahara sat back looking very pleased with herself.

Ulrik swore some more in the Norse language no one in the room understood. Tessa stepped forward, "The Mohem before you was a great woman. She did everything to save your tribe from extinction, you have changed your entire culture and now you are trying to make your people into bloodthirsty thieves. You are placing false charges on my sons to manipulate my husband into helping you. You are no wise woman! No sensible Mohem would act this way."

Tahara grew red in the face and glared at Tessa, but spoke to Ulrik, "Father, you will do as I command or I will *kill* your sons, your wife, and your true daughter one at a time until you do as I bid. Am I making myself understood?" She raised her hand without waiting for his answer and spoke a shrill command in Alahemwhey. The Red Guard lowered their spears at the twins and the blue warriors stepped closer to Tessa and Emmer lowering their spears toward them. Tessa took a step toward Emmer as if she would protect her daughter with her own life. Emmer looked afraid but stared ahead with brave confidence.

Ulrik stood considering for a long moment looking at Tahara, fury coloring his face red and making his eyes blaze. Then he spoke through gritted teeth.

"I will do as you ask since you leave me no choice. But know this, harm anyone of my family, and I will split your spine open, pull your lungs from your back, and hang you from a tree! When I am done with you, you will beg me for death!"

"Excellent!" Tahara beamed with joy gesturing expansively. "This is wooonnderfuulll!"

Then she gave a long command to Captain Bondur who stepped down from the dais and looked straight into Ulrik's eyes. They assessed each other as if sizing up their next opponent for a fight.

"Captain Bondur will take you to the warrior's quarters. I am in a merciful mood so I will allow your wife to go tend the Great Mohem while she dies, but she will be guarded at all times. My little sister can be one of my handmaidens. I will keep her by my side and she can serve me." She glanced out of the corner of her eye at Captain Bondur. "Because of the charges against them, your two sons will go back to their prison hut to wait until you pay their debt to the Alahemwhey. The Solemeyha may stay with him," she gestured to Hunter, "since he seems so fond of her. The other will be kept under guard separately from his brother. You will all be well cared for, but you may not stay together. I cannot have you trying to leave us." She smiled wickedly.

"No! You will show your good faith by letting my sons help me train your warriors. It will go faster with the three of us teaching. My wife and daughter will stay with me."

"How do I know you will not take your family and escape?" Tahara asked shaking her head.

"You have my word as a Viking! I swear it by Odin."

Tahara thought for a moment, and then said emphatically, "No! I will keep your wife and daughter as security. I will allow your sons to help you train the warriors. That is the end of my generosity."

Tahara snapped an order at Captain Bondur and then at her Red Guards who stepped back from Hunter and Archer gesturing for them to move toward the doors. The Elders rose, mumbling and gesturing, and shuffled from the room without a backward glance. Ulrik, Tessa, Emmer, Archer, and Hunter carrying Soria once again, were escorted out. They were flanked on both sides by Captain Bondur's men, four of whom carried torches. They pointed the way with their spears and Ulrik and his family, were led out into the dark.

Chapter Eighteen – Hunter's Story

Hunter watched as the Alahemwhey warriors separated his family. They led himself and Archer away and poked and prodded them apart with their spears. Hunter was once again carrying Soria because she still could not walk. They led them to a small hut. One of the warriors with a torch opened the door and led them in. He lit a brazier in the middle of the floor and left.

Hunter looked around. The hut was mostly bare except for what appeared to be a straw-filled mattress covered in blankets and furs, the stone brazier, and a low wooden table. There were a few dirty rugs on the floor and an empty bucket in the corner.

Hunter went to the bed and carefully lowered Soria down. She quickly scooted away from him and looked away, a miserable look on her face. Hunter walked around the hut. He tested the door and windows and went to stoke the fire higher in the brazier and lit a lamp he found. Then he sat down and contemplated his situation. He had never been separated from his family or his twin brother before. He shook his head at the indignity and injustice with which they had all been treated. He realized he had never met any other people before and turned over in his mind everything that had happened and what he had learned about Soria. She belonged to a rival tribe that had metal weapons. Even more interesting, she was the daughter of the Sword Smith and was valuable to the Alahemwhey.

As Hunter and Archer grew up, Ulrik had instructed them in the use and upkeep of their swords. Archer excelled in the use of the bow and arrows, but Hunter was an expert with the sword and axe. Even Tessa and Emmer practiced with wooden swords and were fairly proficient. Hunter did not doubt that given a sword and half a chance; he could cut his way through the stone-tipped weapons and escape.

Hunter glanced toward Soria where she sat watching him with her liquid gold eyes that caught the firelight. Something told him she did not stand a chance without as much protection as he could offer. After a short time of sitting and thinking, he rose and approached her. Soria looked up at him from the shadows of the bed. The firelight twinkled in the deep golden depths of her eyes and painted her auburn hair with golden highlights. Hunter leaned across her and grabbed a fur, she startled and leaned away as he covered her up. Taking up another fur, he walked over to the brazier, spread the fur out, and lay down. Stretching out, crossing his legs at the ankles he put his hands behind his head and tried to sleep. He heard Soria stir once and then the hut fell silent as the deep night closed in. His last thoughts before falling asleep were full of guilt that flooded his mind and heart. If he and Archer would not have sought out the Alahemwhey, as his father had wanted, then none of this would have happened and his whole family would not be in danger.

The next morning Hunter awoke to a strange panting sound. He looked over and saw Soria trying to walk on her hurt ankle. He got up and went over to help her. She hopped over to the bucket in the corner and then chastised him in her language pointing to the door. Hunter guessed she needed some private time to herself, so he stepped outside the hut and went out into the cold morning. He could not go far because of the Red Guards posted right outside the door. He made them understand by motioning his request for food and drink. After a while, Hunter went back into the hut and checked Soria's bandages. He lingered in his examination for an excuse to touch her. Soria did not protest but watched him closely with her liquid gold eyes.

Eventually, warriors came and took him from the hut and he had to leave Soria and join his father to train the Alahemwhey warriors. At an open field where they were all taken, he saw Emmer approach and happily embrace Ulrik and then witnessed Captain Bondur's cruelty as he tore her away from their father's arms, and sent her off, heavily guarded by his blue-garbed men.

They spent the day training, starting with the most basic of instruction. The swords they had to practice with were rusting, many were bent and pitted. It seems the Alahemwhey had been *gathering* these weapons from the Solemeyha for some time but did not know about their upkeep. Ulrik, instructing through one of the *Others* as an interpreter, put some of the Alahemwhey to work making wooden practice swords. Hunter and Archer showed them how to take a sharpening stone and sharpen the edges and how to scrape off the rust of the metal swords. Archer displayed his prowess with his bow and arrow, which had been added to the pile of weapons, and they quickly earned the respect of *"the Others"* which is how Ulrik, Hunter, and Archer referred to the other sons and daughters of the Alahemwhey that Ulrik had unwillingly sired.

After a long and frustrating day, Hunter was escorted back to the hut he was to share with Soria. She had spent a long day on her own and seemed happy to see him. Hunter cleaned up in a small basin of water he brought to the hut and then they ate a silent dinner together.

Hunter's days passed in a similar succession of sword training and caring for Soria. He immediately began teaching her his language and she proved to be a quick learner. He brought home a long pole and carved it into a crutch as he had seen in one of his medical books. Soria's eyes sparkled and she thanked him with a beautiful smile.

Eventually, he demanded that Soria be allowed to go to the Great Mohem's tent to stay with his mother during the day. He argued with Captain Bondur and the Red Guard over it until they begrudgingly allowed it. From that day forward, Soria was allowed to go to stay with Tessa during the day but was returned to their hut at night. She made much better headway learning his language and could manage halting sentences.

One morning as Hunter and Archer were preparing to train, Archer privately commented that Alahemwhey girls were coming to his hut at night.

"What do you mean?" Hunter asked shocked.

"The girls! A different one comes to my hut every night and they *lie* with me. It is the most amazing experience. Their breasts are my favorite part and the things they can do with their mouths!"

Hunter stared aghast at Archer, "You mean you have…"

"Yes, I have! I have been with three or four of them. Hunter, you have got to try it! But don't mention this to Father. I am sure I do not want him knowing."

Archer spent the rest of the day regaling Hunter with stories of his prowess with women, about their naked bodies, and about the various things he was learning to do with them and how to do it to them.

Hunter listened silently, fuming inside. As the firstborn, he felt that he should have been the first to experience lying with a woman. Suddenly, some strange events began to make sense, like why so many of the dark-haired Alahemwhey girls watched the practices and why they giggled and waved at Archer every time he walked by. Being his twin, some of the girls waved and giggled at Hunter mistaking him for Archer, but he just scowled oblivious to the reason for their attention. Until now, he had not known what it meant.

After hearing what Archer had been up to, it all made sense and Hunter fell into a foul mood. He left the practice field as early as he was allowed to and went back to his hut where Soria waited for him. The Alahemwhey brought them small stores of food. Now that Soria was able to walk on her ankle, she was able to move around better and prepared meals for the two of them every day. Hunter entered the hut and watched her while she prepared their dinner.

Restless and irritable, he watched as she bent over the small table working. She wore a pale blue summer tunic of the kind the Alahemwhey women usually wore where her arms were bare and her legs were revealed by the short, slit skirt. Her tanned skin glowed with her efforts over the brazier and her long, thick auburn hair hung down her back in waves tied back with a strip of leather. As she bent over, Hunter caught a glimpse down the front of her tunic and saw the swell of her breasts which made him begin to harden painfully. He looked away and moved over to sit far away from her. Her every move, the smell of her, and her deep golden eyes frustrated him almost to the breaking point.

Soria was an enticement that had plagued him every night since they had been put in the same hut together. They lived jointly as a man and wife would, but she slept in the bed and he on the cold hard floor. There was no privacy and often he glimpsed her partially naked, her auburn locks cascading down her bare back. The memory of holding her against his chest and carrying her when her leg was injured, tortured him. He burned to touch her again and to do more than touch.

Hunter sat lost in his thoughts remembering what Archer had told him about lying with women and trying to control his body. He was hot, tired, and short-tempered. Soria seemed to sense that something was wrong. She tried to entice him out of his bad mood with food and drink, but he turned his back to her so that the sight of her would not torment him.

Soria brought a basin of clean clear water for bathing in and sat it down next to him. She tried to get his attention, but Hunter was lost in his thoughts. Clearly, he was angry at something.

"Hunter, wash?" she asked, but received no response. "Hunter?"

He still did not acknowledge he heard her. A playful gleam sparked in her golden eyes and she splashed him with some of the water, smiling. Hunter turned toward her, water dripping from the side of his angry face. He gave her a look that said he was in no mood to play. When he saw the mischievous gleam in her eyes and the beautiful smile on her face, he lost a little of his bad mood. He reached into the pail and splashed her back, raising his eyebrows as if to ask, *"What are you going to do now?"* Soria gasped as the cool water splashed down the front of her and she narrowed her eyes and splashed him back again.

A playful water fight ensued and soon they were both wet and laughing. Hunter tackled her to the floor straddling her hips, pinning her arms over her head with his large hands. He shook his wet hair over her, drops sprinkling everywhere. Soria laughed tossing her head back and forth uselessly trying to avoid the spray. Hunter laughed so hard he had to stop and catch his breath, but when he did, he saw that her tunic was completely soaked, and her round heaving breasts were outlined where the wet material clung to her. He could see straight through the wet fabric and stared at her large brown nipples that rose tantalizingly. Hunter longed to touch one even if it was through the wet fabric.

Slowly, he reached out a hand and cupped one of her heavy breasts rubbing his thumb across the nipple. Soria's laughs slowly stilled, and she held his gaze as his face grew serious. He released her wrists and cupped the other breast with his other hand and was soon massaging both her nipples with his thumbs, fascinated with the weight and feel of her soft breasts. Soria remained still, her eyelids lowering slightly as his rubbing made her nipples stand erect. She slightly arched under him and gave a soft hum.

Hunter's mind whirled. He wondered what it would be like to taste one. Since she was not protesting or pushing him away, Hunter leaned in closer, reached up slowly, slid one side of her tunic off her shoulder, and looked at her bare breast. Then he did the same with the other side and she was naked to the waist. Soria's eyes glowed with passion now instead of mischief as he kneaded and smoothed his hands over her breasts. As he bent down to take one into his mouth and taste the nipple with his tongue, she bit her bottom lip in a highly seductive manner, and she began to breathe a little harder.

Hunter kissed and tasted her breasts, rubbing his face against them, and then he kissed his way up her neck to nuzzle her soft throat. Soria's hands slowly smoothed up his arms and she squeezed his firm muscles as she allowed him to kiss her. As their lips met, Hunter gave a low growl and pulled her tightly against him. His wet shirt clung to his muscular chest and Soria pushed away the material pressing her breasts against his firm skin. Her fingers left warm trails across his flesh and he was lost in the feel of her and of being felt by her as her hands roamed over him.

They kissed passionately for a long time rubbing, caressing, and tasting each other, exploring each other. When Soria guided his hand between her legs, he thought he would explode. He rubbed her warm moist flesh astonished at how wonderful it felt. His huge erection stuck out of the top of his trousers and Archer's words describing what to do next, echoed in his mind.

Reaching the point of no turning back he, and Soria too seemed lost as she moved against his hand. He made a quick decision and picked her up, carrying her to the bed. They hurriedly pulled at each other's clothes, kissing passionately, until they were naked. Soria pulled him against her spreading her legs so that Hunter could lie between them. She grabbed his erection and rubbed him up and down causing Hunter to hiss with the greatest pleasure he had ever felt. Then reaching around and grabbing his bottom she pulled him to her guiding his shaft into her warm and inviting opening. She kissed him hard as he entered her, and she pulled him in as he pushed his hips forward. Hunter briefly encountered a barrier, but he burned to be deeper, so he plunged. Soria stifled a sob of pain as he broke through her maidenhead and then she sighed as he continued to move.

Hunter was lost in the feel of her. He wanted to touch her, to taste her everywhere at once. Weeks of frustration and the physical denial of her body all came to end as he finally was able to seek this new satisfaction he had longed for. Soria gasped and moaned in ecstasy as they moved, searching for their climax together. Hunter moved slowly lost in the feeling of sliding in and out of her warmth. Then, as the building tension reached its height of fullness, he began to move harder and faster. Hunter groaned as he felt her inner warmth clench around him tightly and she cried out pulling him in deeper. She pressed her hands to his bottom and gasped loudly. Hunter could not hold the explosion that threatened to erupt from his shaft, and he let go.

Soria pulled him in deep as she felt his seed pulsing into her. She moaned with pleasure as he pressed her lips against his and kissed her deeply. He lay atop her easily holding the majority of his weight off of her though they were still joined. He kept kissing her until he could not help but laugh with the pleasure of being with her.

Soria smiled at him and then reached a hand up to caress his cheek. They moved together and then lay side by side, looking deep into each other's eyes.

"I've wanted to do that to you since the first moment I saw you," Hunter said in a serious tone.

"And I have wanted you to do that since you bandaged my leg that first day." Soria's knowledge of his language had improved greatly since she had been spending her days with Tessa and Emmer, and her evenings with him. Then she whispered with a sad look, "You took so long to touch me."

Hunter blushed. Propped up on his elbow he ran his hand down her chest to cup her breast.

"I, well, I've never…I didn't know if you wanted me like I wanted you."

"I never have lain with a man. I wanted you, but you were far away in your head. I did not think you wanted a Solemeyha." She looked down not able to meet his eyes.

Hunter gently pulled her chin up to look at him. "I didn't want an Alahemwhey. *You,* I wanted more than anything I've ever wanted."

"Why were you angry when you came to the hut tonight?" She asked, smoothing a lock of his white gold hair back from his forehead.

He hesitated, and then revealed, "Archer said the Alahemwhey girls have been going to his bed every night and I was..."

"You were angry because you thought I did not want you?" Soria asked in a sad whisper.

"Yes, and I was jealous of Archer that he had all those women, but I just kept thinking, I only wanted you! I thought I couldn't have you."

Soria said no more. She just looked at him, her liquid gold eyes boring into his heart. "I only want *you,* Hunter. I never wanted a man before I saw you. I will never want another man, but you in all my days."

He kissed her, smoothing his hands down her naked side and along her hip. She rolled into him and soon was lying on top of him. Hunter began to grow hard, and they joined again. Soria was a passionate woman and Hunter perfectly matched her fervor. They explored each other, kissing, touching, and tasting each other until they lay spent and fell into a deep sleep. Hunter would no longer sleep on the cold floor.

Chapter Nineteen – Emmer's Story

On the night of her family's capture by the Alahemwhey, Emmer was more terrified than she had ever been in her life. At spear point, Captain Bondur took Ulrik's sword and long knife from him, then he and his men escorted Ulrik and his family out of the lodge. Following Tahara's order, his warriors with sharp, wicked-looking stone spears, surrounded them as they walked through the village. The imposing Captain of the Guard gave an order and Tessa and Emmer were separated from Ulrik, Hunter, Archer, and the Solemeyha girl.

"No!" Ulrik shouted at Captain Bondur when he tried to separate them. He lunged forward fists raised but stopped when he saw the spears pointed at the hearts of his wife and daughter. He held his hands up hoping to somehow renegotiate with the Captain, but it was useless.

Four warriors closed in and took Tessa in one direction and three took Emmer in another. Archer tried to fight, but Ulrik convinced him they were no use to the women dead and reluctantly gave in.

"We will have our chance," Ulrik whispered urgently to his son. "I promise you!"

The warriors pointed their spears menacingly at the captives and then led them in the direction they were to go. The other group of warriors took Emmer who walked away looking back at her mother with fear and worry in her eyes. She painted on a brave smile and shouted at her family.

"I'll be alright, don't fight them just do as they say. I'll be fine!"

Captain Bondur gave an order to his men and then waited as each group was led away in separate directions. Before Ulrik got more than three steps, he turned and stormed back where Bondur stood, batting away the threatening spears.

He walked up to Captain Bondur and stood face to face with the man who was separating him from his family.

Looking deep into the Captain's eyes he growled quietly, "If anything happens to them, I will gut you!"

A strange look passed Captain Bondur's face. He seemed to understand, and he said in a deep quiet voice. "Little One safe with Bondur." He pointed at Emmer. "She," pointing at Tessa, "go to Great Mohem." Bondur gestured at each of the warriors surrounding Emmer, "Bondur's men, Little One safe with Bondur."

With those final words, he turned and followed the warriors escorting Emmer. Ulrik was surprised that Captain Bondur had spoken to him in his language but was promptly prodded away by the wicked-looking spears and was not given time for more reflection on the matter. Deciding he had no choice, he reluctantly followed where he was led. The fury at being captured by the Alahemwhey again was etched plainly on his face.

Captain Bondur and three of his warriors led Emmer to a large hut. Unsmiling, he opened the door and motioned with his head, not unkindly, for her to enter. Emmer did as she was bid and slowly took a few steps into the dark building, arms hugging herself for comfort. She shivered with fear and fought back tears. Inwardly, she cursed herself for suggesting that they just walk right into the village and ask for the Great Mohem. Never in her life had she been separated from her family and she felt naive and more alone than she had ever known was possible.

Captain Bondur entered behind her and lit a candle. With a stony unreadable look on his face, he walked through the room lighting lamps and then lit a stone brazier in the middle of the room. Soon he had dispelled the darkness completely with warmth and light. Emmer's eyes slowly adjusted to the light of the room. With a final, contemplating glance at her, Captain Bondur left. Emmer could hear him speaking in Alahemwhey to two warriors outside the door. He briefly opened the door and she whirled around staring with wide frightened blue eyes. He pointed at the two men outside his door and grunted. His meaning was clear. She was well guarded and could not leave. Swallowing hard she took a deep shuddering breath as the door closed again.

Emmer surveyed her surroundings. The hut was strangely and luxuriously decorated, and she saw a large bed that was sumptuously heaped with furs, pillows, and blankets of deep blue. There was a low wooden table next to the crackling brazier, sacks, horse tack, many odds, and ends, and a small pile of dented and bent swords. Emmer sat down on the floor next to the brazier, gladdened a little by its warmth and light, and hugged her knees. She was hungry, weary, scared, and had no idea what to expect in the captivity of the Alahemwey. She thought about the story her father had told their family and shuddered. Bewildered, she did not know why she was left alone in this hut. Perhaps this was where Tahara's handmaidens were kept and she wondered where the other girls were if there were other girls. Emmer assumed that later, someone would come to instruct her on how to do Tahara's bidding. She was sure she would find out soon enough.

A very short time later the door opened again and in stepped Captain Bondur. He had come from bathing because his long black hair hung damply about his shoulders. He had removed his hard, black leather armor and now wore a loose, deep blue shirt with black leather trousers tucked into Alahemwhey boots. Entering the hut, after a few terse words to the guards, he closed the door behind him.

Captain Bondur turned toward Emmer holding his hands out, palms up, speaking in a soft quiet tone as if he was trying to calm a frightened animal. Emmer was terrified and sat paralyzed, her eyes going wide with fear and her breaths coming in short gasps. At eighteen years old, she had never been alone with a man who was not her father or brothers. Her breath came quickly, and her heart pounded loudly in her chest. Fear froze her body to the spot.

Captain Bondur moved forward very slowly until he stood just in front of Emmer. Then he eased himself down and sat beside her. Emmer hid her face in her hands and so did not notice as he sat patiently watching her, waiting for her to look at him. She trembled.

"Bondur have little Mohem words." Bondur finally spoke quietly in a deep heavily accented voice.

Emmer's head shot up. She felt great surprise that he had spoken to her in her language and she breathed a sigh of relief.

"Oh!" was all she could squeak out.

"No Ulrik's son." He placed his hand on his chest indicating himself and said again, "Bondur no Ulrik's son." He continued to try to catch her gaze, "Little One safe with Bondur."

"Oh," her breathing calmed a little, "Well, thank you."

Emmer looked into the large, handsome man's emerald green eyes. She felt lost in their depths as they stared silently at each other for a few moments. He spoke again.

"Bondur have little Mohem words. What name this?" He pointed at her, after a moment she gleaned his meaning.

"Emmer, my name is Emmer." Speaking slowly, she smiled shyly at him.

A huge smile crept over Bondur's handsome face showing straight white teeth, "Ehh-mer, Emmer," he breathed deeply. Then, gesturing all around him, "What name this?"

Emmer looked around and thought for a moment trying to glean his meaning, "Um, this is a hut." She gestured around copying his movements.

"Hut." Bondur repeated and looking around pointed at the brazier, "What name this?"

"Fire." She stated.

"Fire." Bondur frowned having trouble with the "f" sound but kept rolling the word around his tongue until he got it. "What name this?" He pointed down.

"Floor!" Emmer almost shouted, elated that he was trying to communicate and somehow that made her feel less lonely and afraid with the huge Captain of the Alahemwhey guard.

The two played the, "What name this?" game for about an hour. Emmer followed Bondur around the hut naming things. His stony demeanor dropped as they tried to communicate, and she found him easy to laugh with and childishly curious. She would laugh when he butchered the pronunciation of a word and soon the two were laughing and getting along very well considering their limited understanding. Bondur used every opportunity to touch her with light strokes on her arm, hand, or back. He gently picked up a lock of her long hair and examined it. Emmer forgot that she was his captive until their playtime was interrupted by a knock at the door.

Bondur's face fell back into an angry stony mask, eyes narrowed, he moved past Emmer to answer the door. An old woman came in carrying a tray of food and a clay pitcher of drink. She sat the tray on the low table by the brazier and silently, without looking at Emmer, left the hut.

Bondur gestured at the food. It was not until the smell of cooked meat reached Emmer that she was reminded of how hungry she was. She sat on a cushion Bondur placed for her on the floor near the low table and waited until Bondur came over to her. He lowered himself down and sat *very* close to her, his long legs stretching out beside her, crossed at the ankles, and hemming her in between the table and his muscular legs. Emmer could smell the clean masculine scent of him and was momentarily distracted from the other smells emanating from the food. Bondur uncovered the dishes and motioned to Emmer to help herself.

Emmer took a small bowl and filled it with some meat, fruit, and cheese. They ate in silence not knowing what next to say to each other. Bondur's eyes never left her, but he watched intently as she daintily ate. He ate slowly as well and Emmer had the stray thought that Captain Bondur had excellent manners, far different from those of her twin brothers. Her face fell a little as she thought about how much she missed them.

Bondur watched Emmer's face turn sad and broke the silence by pointing to the meat and chewing, "What name this?" He smiled slightly at Emmer.

"Meat!" Emmer proclaimed, "And it is very good!" she said smiling and rubbing her belly, "Mmmm, very good."

"Mmmm, very good." He repeated. "What name this?" Bondur pointed.

"Cheese," she said and then pointing to the other dishes in succession, quickly named each, "Strawberries and bread."

Bondur repeated each name and then went over the name of each item again. He was a fast learner. He picked up a cup and poured some dark red liquid into it.

"What name this?" He handed her the cup, and she took a tentative sip.

"Wine." She smiled delighted, closing her eyes, relishing the deep sweet flavor.

"Wine!" he repeated and emptied the cup in one gulp then poured more handing her the cup again. Gesturing that she should drink again. She drank deeply of the sweet red liquid.

Emmer giggled and said, "Good! You are doing very well. We will understand each other better in no time."

The wine went down easily as she drained the cup and Emmer's head swam a little with the potent draft. Bondur smiled at her praise and then took the lid off of a jar, stuck his finger into a thick golden liquid, and held his finger up.

"What name this?"

Emmer, a little tipsy, entirely relaxed, and lost in the joy of the game, leaned forward. A new feeling of boldness from drinking the heady wine filled her. Without thinking, she took the tip of his finger into her mouth and sucked the golden liquid from it. Bondur's breath stuck in his throat, his eyes going wide, and his face slightly flushed. He swallowed hard.

Emmer, realizing too late what an intimate thing she had just done, froze in fear and held his gaze for a long moment. Then breaking the tension that hung thick in the air, she spoke in a small wispy voice, "Hhhoney that is honey."

Staring intently at Emmer's lips, Bondur finally remembered to breathe. He took a deep breath and then slowly reached forward and cupped her cheek. He gently ran his thumb over Emmer's bottom lip, rubbing at some honey that glistened there. His voice came out quiet and husky. He asked, as he very slowly rubbed back and forth over her bottom lip, "What name this?"

Emmer could barely move. "Lllllips," she stuttered.

She was sure he could hear how her heart was thundering in her chest. Sure that he could see the frantic flutter of the pulse at her throat. The feel of his thumb on her lips made her feel strange sensations like she had never felt before, all warm and tingly. All she could do was gaze into his large green eyes, and her breathing quickened.

"Lips," she managed to gasp out again in a whisper. She stared down at his mouth and swallowed.

"Lips," Bondur repeated as he moved his hand to her cheek. Then he leaned very close to her and whispered, "What name this?"

His lips gently met hers and slowly rubbed back and forth then his tongue eased out and lightly licked the honey from her bottom lip before he withdrew.

"Kiss," Closing her eyes she let the warm feeling he caused, spread through her, and settle in the pit of her stomach. She stammered, "that is a kiss. My very *first* kiss." She gave him an amazed smile. Her eyes sparkled sapphire in the lamplight.

Bondur moved a little closer and leaned forward again, "Kisssss," he said, drawing out the "sssss" as his mouth descended upon hers again. His hand caressed her soft cheek, down to her neck, and he kissed her deeper. Then carefully his hands went to her waist and he pulled her onto his lap. Emmer went limp in his arms and warmth spread through her veins as he kissed her. Small tickles of excitement shot through her belly as she melted into his arms. She could feel his strength enclose her, his chest pressed against hers, and the smooth muscles of his arms rippled pulling her closer, holding her. Emmer was more afraid at that moment than she had been all night in this situation she was in.

In the back of her mind, Emmer thought it wicked that she had only just met this man a few hours before, he had taken her family away from her at spear point, and here she was kissing a man she did not even know…an *enemy*. She shuddered but was not sure if it was from his kisses or from fear. Admittedly, she did not want the pleasant feelings he was causing to stop.

Bondur kissed her deeper, his tongue coaxed hers into a dance when her mouth parted as she gasped for breath. He tasted like wine. The honey in her mouth mixed with his and it was a heady, intoxicating flavor assailing her senses. The taste of him and the feel of his strong arms around her were like nothing she had ever experienced before. Emmer's eyes closed and her arms went around his neck as they continued to drown in each other's kisses. She wondered if she was doing it right and tried to copy the way his lips and tongue moved with hers. Bondur broke the kiss breathing heavily, his forehead pressed against hers, his eyes closed.

"Honey kiss," his voice was husky with the passion from their embrace and the nearness of her body. "Emmer honey kiss. Emmer good honey kiss."

Emmer looked back at him her blue eyes dark with her first passion. She smiled shyly at him, waiting to see what he would do next. Fearing what he would do next.

Bondur placed the palm of his hand between her breasts momentarily feeling her heart skip and beat wildly. Emmer's breaths came fast in short gasps as the warmth from his hand spread across her breasts, flushed up to her neck, and spread through her body. Bondur swallowed and asked, "What name this?"

"Heart," Emmer said, her voice shaking.

"Emmer little bird *heart*." He smiled mischievously and his eyes twinkled. Emmer looked back at him raising her eyebrows suspiciously. She was not sure if he was as ignorant of her language as he had been letting on. Then Bondur bent his head and kissed her again, brushing her breast once lightly with his large warm hand. Emmer leaned away suddenly uncomfortable with his nearness and afraid.

Eventually, they resumed their game, him pointing to various body parts of hers and she quietly told him the names. He committed each word to memory quoting them back to her, hand, arm, leg, thigh, stomach, and so on down her entire body. He laced his fingers in her long hair and twined a lock around his finger enjoying its silkiness.

Bondur ended the game by giving her a long gentle kiss and Emmer kissed him back without hesitation. Her hand traveled up to rest on his smooth hairless chest where she could feel his strong heart beating fiercely.

Reluctantly, Bondur pulled away and gently withdrew his arms from around her. He stood, pulling her up with him. She was quite a bit shorter only just coming up to his chest and she looked up at him, her blue eyes sparkling. Bondur took her hand and led her across the room.

"What name this?" he spoke slowly pointing to the bed.

Emmer swallowed looking at the huge thick mattress, covered in lush gauze sheets, thick pillows, and furs, a strangely luxurious bed for a warrior she momentarily mused.

She quietly answered, "bed."

A serious look crossed Bondur's face and his chest heaved with unspent passion. He bent over and picked her up, carried her closer to the bed, gently laid her down, and removed her boots. He pulled a large soft blanket over her then turned and walked away. Emmer watched as he moved around the hut extinguishing the lamps until they were cast in almost complete darkness, but for the dying brazier's flames.

Emmer's eyes grew wide as they became accustomed to the dark. She could feel Bondur's weight as he lowered himself onto the bed beside her. He made some quick movements as he took off his boots and then slid under the blanket next to her. They were fully clothed, but her mind still whirled with a combination of fear and excitement about the unknown. She had read books about love and romance. She had questioned her mother about some things she had read in those books, and about what a man and woman did when they were alone in bed. Things that happened in some of the stories made her blush. At this moment, those stories were reeling quickly through her mind. She was frozen to the spot where he had placed her, afraid to move or even breathe loudly. All she could think about was the kisses and touches they had just shared and how strange it was that he had *wanted* to kiss *her*.

Bondur rolled over and caressed her face. His arm went around her, and he pulled her closer to him. Emmer's breathing quickened with fear and exhilaration. Dread and desire battled within her breast. Then Bondur gently turned her over onto her side, pulling her against him, spooning his body around hers. All that separated them were their clothes and Emmer could feel the length of his muscular body pressing against her. He tucked her in to fit perfectly against his body and then he kissed her hair, breathing deep to take in her scent.

He whispered, "Emmer safe with Bondur" and they lay silent and still in the darkness, his large, warm presence bringing her a sense of security and serenity.

Emmer had never slept with anyone before and the feel of Bondur's warm muscular body pressing against her was the most deliciously disturbing thing she had ever felt. Strangely, the weight of his arm over her made her feel peaceful and safe. Soon, she fell into an exhausted sleep.

Bondur stared into the darkness for a long time. When he heard Emmer's breathing slow and deepen into sleep, he caressed her white-blonde hair and let his hand wander down her tiny body and over the gentle swell of her hip. His hand was resting there when he too finally drifted off into a restless sleep.

The next morning Emmer woke buried in gauze sheets, soft blankets, and furs. The early light barely showed through cracks in the hut roof and through a shuddered window in the far wall. Very carefully she rolled over to see if Bondur was still there. He was, but he was not asleep, he just lay next to her staring intently at her. A fierce, unreadable look passed through his eyes and Emmer was momentarily afraid as his deep green gaze seemed to burn her. She was finding out that, when in an unknown situation, not knowing what to do or expect, made her uncomfortably fearful and she felt a little cowardly without knowing exactly why. It was hard to be brave when he was looking at her this way.

Bondur lifted a hand and gently caressed her cheek. Then he reached for her and pulled her into his arms. He held her that way for a few minutes and then gently disengaged from the embrace. He rolled away, leaned over, and grabbed his boots slipping into them quickly. Emmer slowly sat up in the bed, hugging her knees to her chest and resting her chin there, watching Bondur stride around the hut, slipping into his shirt and a leather vest, preparing to leave. He took a long pull from a skin of water and then just stood for a long moment, not moving nor looking at her.

Then he turned and stalked purposefully back to the bed. He sat down next to Emmer and gently grabbed her by the shoulders.

"Emmer," he pulled her close, his voice full of emotion, "this face," he made a circular gesture indicating his face.

"This face in hut-not Bondur outside." He pointed to the door using some of the words he had learned last night. He repeated himself and looked at her, his eyes asking for her understanding. He spoke a long string of words in Alahemwhey sounding frustrated.

Emmer did not understand what he was trying to say, but she shook her head "yes" and smiled warmly at him as if she did. Bondur leaned forward and kissed her gently on the lips one last time. Then he laid her back, tucked her in the furs, and left the hut without a backward glance.

Emmer stared up at the hut roof contemplating everything that happened last night and what Bondur said this morning. She finally gave up trying to figure it all out and fell back asleep with a slight smile on her face.

Later that morning Emmer was escorted out of the hut by two guards. She was taken past a large field where many warriors stood in a circle. As they drew near, she saw her father standing with his arms crossed over his great chest staring crossly down at something on the ground. The something turned out to be a rusty pile of swords. When she saw him, she could not help herself, she ran to him.

"Father!" She cried and threw herself into his arms. Ulrik clutched her to him in a fatherly hug that squeezed the breath out of her. A shout brought her to her senses, and they turned to see Captain Bondur striding toward them and glaring.

Emmer's eyes alit with joy at seeing him again, but he refused to look at her. His face was a mask of stone as he yelled a stream of commands at her guards, gesturing sharply. Then one of the guards roughly pulled her away from Ulrik's embrace. Emmer's heart sank at the cruelty with which she was treated by Bondur, as she was pulled away from her father's arms and the group.

Ulrik gritted his teeth and said, "Go with them, Emmer. Hopefully, they will take you to your mother." He turned and fixed his eyes back on the rusty pile of swords. Captain

Bondur's eyes narrowed, and Emmer blanched at the sight. His stony face held none of the tenderness it had earlier that morning. Her heart fell a little and she stared at him in disbelief. Captain Bondur looked away from her and just flicked a hand at her guards, gave a short barking order, and turned back to Ulrik. The two of them faced each other with stony faces and angry, glaring eyes.

Emmer turned away, her eyes swimming with tears. She willed herself not to cry with frustration and lack of understanding. She was not sure if she wanted to cry because she was taken from her father again or because of the cold way Bondur acted toward her. She thought they were friends but truly had not understood anything since coming here. The guards led her across the village to a large blue tent. The tent flap opened and out stepped her mother who ran to her and threw her arms around Emmer. Tessa held her while she cried like a little girl.

Chapter Twenty – The Story of the Alahemwhey

Emmer wiped her eyes and followed her mother into the hut. She needed her mother's comfort after Bondur had treated her so strangely. Inside the hut it was gloomy, and herbs burned in a small brazier giving off a strong flowery scent. Tessa led Emmer over to a low table just like the one in Bondur's hut.

"Emmer are you alright? I've been so worried. After they took you away, I didn't know what could be happening to you. Where did they take you?" Tessa held Emmer's hands and looked at her daughter with great relief that she appeared safe and well.

"I'm fine Mother. I was taken to a hut. I was given food and treated very well. Please don't worry."

Her hands were folded in her lap and Emmer could not meet her mother's eyes, but then she gained some courage and looked around the tent. Strangely, she did not want to mention what happened with Captain Bondur.

"This is where the Great Mohem lives?" Emmer asked.

"Yes, she is asleep in the bed over there. She hasn't woken all night. I haven't gotten a chance to talk to her at all."

Tessa offered Emmer some food and they ate together talking of everything that had happened to them and what might unfold. Emmer told her what happened with Ulrik that morning but left out the part about Captain Bondur. Tessa was greatly relieved that Ulrik and her sons were alive and safe for now.

While they ate Emmer ran over the events of the night in her mind. She was terrified for her brothers and very worried about her father and mother. Inside, she felt quite a bit of shame over kissing Bondur and did not completely know why, well, not *exactly* at least. She rationalized; Bondur was Captain of the Alahemwhey guard and Tahara's man, he had split their family apart on her orders and he might eventually put Emmer's brothers to death. She shivered thinking about it. Then she shivered again as she remembered how he had kissed her and touched her. Bondur had been gentle and kind when she was so terrified and alone. He held her in his powerful arms while she slept giving her a sense of security and peace. She thought long and hard about the last thing he said to her that morning *"This face in hut-not Bondur outside."* Bondur had looked at her with patience and kindness which signified much.

As they finished their breakfast, they heard a cough and stirring from the figure in the bed. They both hurried over. In the bed was the oldest woman they had ever seen. Her thin gray hair had been painted blue and twisted in elaborate ropes and her face was deeply lined with age. It was the Great Mohem. As she slowly awoke, she shifted on the bed and looked up at the two women at her bedside. Her eyes rose in surprise and recognition when she looked at Tessa.

"Eleanor it's me Tessa, Ulrik's wife. Do you remember me?"

"Of course, I remember you, my Dear. I may be ancient and dying, but I still have my eyes." She smiled and looked at Emmer curiously.

"This is my daughter, Emmer. She was born a year after Hunter and Archer."

"Emmer, this is Eleanor Tennbaum, the Great Mohem."

Emmer smiled shyly at her.

"Emmer is it? A woman blessed with many virtues, beauty, voice, speech, wisdom, and chastity. That is what your name means child. Did you know that?" Eleanor nodded her head.

"No, I did not know that. Thank you for telling me." Emmer smiled a little and blushed at the last virtue, chastity.

"Yes, but your mother pronounces it differently, instead of the long 'e' as in ee-mer she shortens it as eh-mer. Very interesting, very beautiful, just like you." Then she stopped her rambling and looked around and seemed to wake up again.

"Tessa? What are you doing here?" She seemed to grow a little agitated and then asked, "Ulrik? Is he here? I did him a great…" she stopped and swallowed, "all those years ago, a great wrong, a great, great wrong." She shook her head sadly.

"Yes, he is here, and he holds no resentment against you. Would you like to see him?" Tessa asked calmly.

"I would like to see him and your sons, Hunter and Archer Ulriksson, are they with you too?"

"Yes, we are all here. I have a long story to tell you, my friend, but first, let me get you some food and drink."

"Wonderful!" Eleanor smiled widely and her face wrinkled with a huge smile. Then she launched into a long dissertation about the benefits of various herbs and plants. They listened politely to her educational ranting. Eleanor could not stop teaching it seemed.

Tessa and Emmer helped Eleanor sit, propping her up with pillows. They brought food and drink for her and while she ate Tessa told her how they had come back to the Alahemwhey, what happened with Hunter and Archer, and of Tahara's death sentence.

Eleanor sat in silence so long that they were afraid she had fallen asleep until she suddenly spoke up.

"Tahara is a good girl. She is just young and foolish, and very ambitious." Eleanor said. "I will try and intervene if I can but I'm afraid it wouldn't do much good. The Alahemwhey have not heeded my advice as much since Tahara took over." Eleanor stopped and then coughed a little but didn't seem in much pain. "How's that little mountain house of mine?"

"It has grown. We had to add some rooms for all the children." Tessa laughed and Eleanor seemed not to hear but stared off into the distance.

"Eleanor," Tessa took her hand and held it. "What happened here? What has happened to the Alahemwhey?"

"Eleanor? No one has called me Eleanor for over a hundred years. They call me the *Great Mohem!*" She gave a self-deprecating chuckle. "You know they call her the Red Mohem-Tahara that is." She laughed again and coughed a bit. "You may call me Eleanor though. I miss hearing the sound of it."

"Eleanor, what has happened here? The Alahemwhey have *changed.*" Tessa went on.

"Oh, well, I'm afraid that was my fault. After what I did to Ulrik, bringing in all his children to add new blood to save the people, well the whole culture changed, everything changed. At first, the Alahemwhey would not breed with other tribes, so I had to do it for them, through Ulrik. My people practically worship Ulrik's children and then they grew arrogant but also fearful the children would not be enough to bring the Alahemwhey back from extinction, back to greatness. Ulrik's children became the ruling class. The Alahemwhey stopped roaming the steppes and built permanent huts. They feared extinction so much they forgot the long tradition of keeping the Alahemwhey blood pure. They joined with their brother tribe, raided other tribes and stole their children, and made them Alahemwhey upon pain of death. Their numbers swiftly grew, and their traditions changed drastically. I couldn't stop it. I was getting too old and Ulrik became a legend. I tried to fix things, to make things better, the people stronger, but everything I did turned back on me."

The Great Mohem stopped, took a sip of water, and then continued her tale.

"The girls, Ulrik's daughters, they wanted to start breeding them at too young an age, so I took them in, protected them, and taught them everything I could. I tried to make healers of them and taught them to be wise, to be rational, and intelligent but instead, they became conceited and vain, and empowered by their knowledge. The male children became fierce warriors as you would expect with their father being a Viking." She laughed and coughed, drank more water, and then continued. "The Alahemwhey treated Ulrik's children like little kings and queens. The one, the red one, Tahara, was just like her mother, spoiled, selfish, and stubborn when she wanted something, and she wanted *everything*. I trained her to be a Mohem, a wise woman, but she wanted more-always more. Tahara wanted to rule everyone. Because of her flaming red hair, the Alahemwhey held her in more esteem than the others and they made her Mohem after me and now, they follow her as if she were a Queen."

Tessa and Emmer tried to follow the story, but she jumped around a lot. Occasionally Eleanor drifted into speaking Alahemwhey and so it took a long time to get the entire story from her.

"With Tahara leading the Alahemwhey," she paused sadly, but took a deep breath and went on. "Well, let's just say that everything changed even more. She became obsessed with growing stronger, taking more and more land, more people. She made laws and rules and the people blindly follow her like the only flame in the dark."

"What about the Elders? Have they no influence on the people or with Tahara?" Tessa asked.

"Oh, they do. They wield more power than Tahara likes to admit. Ultimately, they have the final say if they choose to interfere. They try to keep the old traditions alive and they make nice in front of Tahara because the people love her *and* are afraid of her, but the Elders will intervene when it suits them. That's when the real fireworks fly." Eleanor paused and launched into a stream of Alahemwhey.

Emmer leaned over and whispered to her mother, "What are fireworks?"

Tessa just smiled and patted her hand. She filled Eleanor's cup and waited until the old woman noticed they waited. She looked at Emmer and her eyes seem to tear up.

"What I did to your father. What I did to your father! There is no forgiving it, so many people have suffered over my bad decisions, but I had good intentions. There is an ancient saying about the way to Hell being paved with good intentions. I forget who said that…" Eleanor stopped to think.

Emmer leaned over and asked, "What is Hell?"

"Oh, you know I read to you about it from the Bible," Tessa spoke distractedly, without looking at Emmer.

"Oh!" Emmer's eyes grew wide as she suddenly understood.

"Eleanor, can you help us? We knew there could be some danger when we came here, but Tahara wants to put my sons to death. She has made false charges against them and is demanding Ulrik go and kidnap some man who makes swords from another tribe. She is making Emmer work as her personal slave. Can you do anything to help us?"

Emmer blushed as Tessa related that last bit of information, but then Tessa's voice dropped, and she said, "We just want to go home."

Eleanor sat up straighter in the bed and thought for a long time.

"I will see what I can do. I may have some influence with the Elders. Hopefully, they will step in at the right moment and stop Tahara. Let me think on it, but now I need my rest." With that, she slumped down in her bed and closed her eyes. Tessa covered her with the blanket.

Eleanor grabbed her hand suddenly and said, "I miss ice cream. Do you remember ice cream? And chocolate chip cookies, Captain Crunch, Lady Fingers, and…" Eleanor's eyes closed, but her voice droned on with a long list of sweets Tessa had not thought of in over twenty years. She and Emmer crept away to let the old woman sleep.

#

Emmer spent the rest of the long day talking quietly with her mother. She was overwhelmed with happiness being reunited with Tessa and helped tend to the dying woman, but she was also distracted. She worried that at any minute Tahara might send for her and who knows when she would see her mother again.

Tessa looked at her daughter suspiciously. She knew when Emmer was upset. A stab of fear and uncertainty hit Tessa in the chest, but Emmer assured her that she was fine. Tessa let the subject go, for now.

As the evening started to descend guards came to take Emmer away and she feared she would finally be taken to do Tahara's bidding. Emmer clung to her mother not wanting to leave, but they roughly separated mother and daughter and led her back the way she had come that morning. They returned Emmer to Bondur's hut where she was relieved and disappointed to find he was not there.

Emmer was terribly conflicted inside. She dreaded seeing Bondur after the way he treated her that morning, but also could not wait to see him. She feared he would kiss her again and then feared he would not. She had spent the better part of that day trying to figure out what Bondur was trying to tell her that morning. *"This face in hut, not Bondur outside."* She remembered the hard, stony, uncaring look on his face when she ran to her father that morning.

Emmer rubbed slowly at her arms pacing anxiously about the hut as she contemplated what all this meant. Assuming he meant he had to treat her differently in front of the people outside, show her a different face than he did in the hut. It baffled her. Why would he not show her kindness in front of the other Alahemwhey? Still, it was with great trepidation that she contemplated seeing him again. This was his hut, and he would return, but it was not even full nightfall yet and something told her not to expect him until late if he came at all. She again relived the moment in the great lodge when Tahara had called him, *"her beautiful Bondur."*

There was a knock on the door and some men carried in a large wooden basin and filled it with many buckets of steaming water and turned and left without a word. Emmer was thrilled to be given a cloth, a sweet-smelling bowl of something she guessed was soap, and a soft blue robe. Also, they left her an ornate comb and a soft brush for her hair. Emmer had been in the same clothes for days now and her hair and skin felt dirty and gritty. She quickly undressed and stepped into the large basin sighing with ecstasy at the feel of the warm water on her skin as she washed for the first time in days. She submerged her head and scrubbed herself furiously with the soap. As she came up for air, she smoothed her hair back, wiped the water from her face, and stood. The water ran down her slim body.

Just then the door to the hut suddenly opened and Captain Bondur stepped in. Upon seeing her standing naked in the water, they both stood shocked for a moment, his mouth hanging open, his green eyes flaring. While Emmer stood frozen, his stare wandered over her wet body, he gulped loudly, then turned sharply on his heel and left.

Emmer, horrified that Bondur had seen her naked, quickly dried herself off with a cloth, and put on the soft blue robe. Then, trying hard not to think of him, *seeing her naked*, washed her clothes, and hung them to dry. She marveled at her presence of mind to do these mundane things when any moment now she would be faced with seeing Bondur again. However, she could think of nothing better to do to get her mind off that eventuality. Combing through her hair with the beautiful comb that had been left for her, she sat next to the brazier drying her long white-gold hair.

Finally, what felt like hours later, Bondur returned. He hesitantly entered the hut and quietly shut the door. He approached her warily, a stony look on his face.

Emmer stood trying to keep her face placid as he approached her. Then, she could not help it, a huge smile broke across her lovely face and she beamed up at him. He suddenly smiled back at her, took a step forward holding open his arms and she threw all caution to the wind and threw herself into his embrace. Bondur clasped her tightly against his body, molding her slight figure against his as he lifted her off her feet, kissing her passionately. He flooded her face, neck, and hair with kisses, his deep voice speaking an unintelligible stream of Alahemwhey. Emmer glowed with happiness knowing this was really what she had waited for all day.

Finally, he set her down gently and looked into her face. He raised his eyebrows at her, tilted his head to the side, and looked her up and down. She wore the deep blue Alahemwhey robe, circled by a wide belt around her tiny waist, her arms were bare, but the rest of her was mostly covered, and his eyes sparked at the sight. He smiled widely showing his approval with a shake of his head.

"This face in hut, not Bondur outside." She said smiling and nodded her head, "I understand."

Chapter Twenty-one – Little Bird Heart

Emmer spent the evening teaching Bondur more words and they were moving further on to better sentences. He had completely mastered, "I like Emmer's honey kisses," and the nickname he made up for her, "Emmer little bird heart." Although, she did not know where he learned the word 'bird,' he had learned other words from Ulrik that day; words like, "thrust," "parry," "hack," "backswing" and some curse words that made Emmer's face burn red.

"What is *'Skraeling'*?" He asked.

At which Emmer laughed and explained her father was calling him a heathen, although she was not sure he understood 'heathen' either, and she finally gave up trying to explain.

They ate dinner together and enjoyed each other's company late into the evening. When Emmer could not stifle her yawns any longer, Bondur rose and pulled her to her feet a serious look crossing his face.

"Emmer little bird heart, go Bondur's bed." His voice was deep and husky, and he motioned toward the bed with a single nod.

At the thought, Emmer's heart skipped a beat, and little tickles of pleasure and fear coursed through her chest to land in her stomach and between her legs, causing her to warm and moisten. She blushed, thinking she knew what that meant, but she was too nervous to think too deeply about it or make any assumptions. Dropping her eyes and smiling shyly she walked to the bed, removed her belt, and hesitated. Did she have a choice in this, sleeping with him again? Was it right? She shook her head slightly and climbed under the gauze sheets and furs.

Bondur turned toward a pitcher of water and poured some into a basin. He pulled the deep blue shirt off over his head and washed. Emmer discretely watched him from across the room. He was so handsome and masculine that it made her ache, and her breasts tighten. Long sleek muscles rippled under his tanned smooth skin as he moved, and his long black hair hung down his broad back. He performed his ablutions and then turned toward the bed. A stern look was frozen on his face and he would not meet her eyes.

Emmer was not sure, but he seemed to be waging some internal war because his jaw clenched and the muscles in his smooth chest twitched, his fists clasped and unclasped as he took halting steps around the hut extinguishing all but the fire in the brazier which provided ample light for her to see him cast in its warm glow. Finally, he stalked slowly toward the bed. Emmer stayed completely still, watching him with her large blue eyes as he sat down and pulled his boots off. Not knowing what else to do she laid down on her side, fully expecting him to pull her up against his body as he had the night before. She held her breath in fear and anticipation, in dread and wanting. What it was she wanted she was not sure.

Bondur eased himself into the bed and pulled the blanket up to his waist. He breathed in a deep heavy inhalation and Emmer could do nothing but lay frozen to her spot. Bondur reached under the covers and after some fumbling, he pulled his trousers off and tossed them to the floor, sighing deeply with relief.

Emmer's eyes grew round as she realized he was now possibly completely naked under the covers, only inches away from her. She was not sure how she felt about that, but her heart was fluttering like a bird emulating the nickname he had given her, *"Emmer little bird heart."* Truly, she felt like panicking, like bolting up from the bed and running away. She felt like rolling over, pulling away the blanket, and looking at all of him. Wide awake now, she was sure she would not be able to sleep next to his large, muscular, *naked* body. What if he pressed against her in his nakedness? She had no idea what to do next. So, she just lay still for several minutes and tried not to breathe too loudly, working on calming her racing pulse.

After a few more tense moments, Bondur gave a low quiet groan where he lay staring at the ceiling, as still as she was. Emmer had no idea what that could mean, but suddenly she came to a quick decision. She reached under the gauzy sheet and grasping the blue robe she wore, drew it up and over her head and dropped it to the floor. Turning slowly toward Bondur she found his deep green eyes burning hungrily into hers. Slowly, she inched closer to him.

Bondur reached toward her and gently pulled her into his arms, drawing her naked body slowly up against his. The firelight painted him with gold. He was warm and firm all over and very enticing. Emmer shivered with fear and anticipation as his mouth came down upon hers in a slow caressing kiss. His hands stroked her skin, moving over her soft back and smooth hips. As she responded his kisses grew more urgent and he clutched her bottom kneading gently and pulling her hard against him. Emmer could feel his hard arousal pressing against her thigh. Bondur continued caressing her hips, her thighs and then moved his hands up to cup her small, soft breast. He practically growled as she gasped with each new caress and touch.

Emmer's mind and body were flooded with new sensations. Not knowing what to do with her hands, not being able to help herself, she touched him too, rubbing her hands over his smooth skin. Then her hands seem to gain a will of their own as they moved across his chest, feeling his powerful arms, ribs, and down to linger a moment on his lean hip, and then between them where she boldly brushed his hard, erect shaft. Bondur broke their kiss and shuddered as she lightly explored him with her fingertips and palm, while his mouth dipped back down and sucked her lips and tongue harder. She had never touched a man before and she was awed and surprised at the smooth, warm, powerful feel of him.

It was apparent Bondur wanted her as he rose over her, pressing her back with fervent kisses over her face and neck. He moved lower kissing her breasts and took one of her nipples between his lips and suckled her, causing sparks of pleasure to shoot within her body. Stopping to admire her beauty, he worshiped her with his eyes, hands, and mouth. Then he settled his hips between her legs. Kissing her passionately, he moved gently against her. He whispered soft words in the musical Alahemwhey language. Emmer's hands slid along Bondur's sides and up along his broad muscular back as she lost herself in the feel of his luscious male body and what his mouth was again doing to each breast. Looking up and holding her gaze, he said something, a worried tone entering his voice then he guided his huge erection into her moist opening.

"Emmer," he let out a deep, whispered hum as he gently slid inside her holding her eyes with his emerald gaze the entire time.

Emmer slowly, deeply inhaled with surprise at the feel and size of him as he carefully joined them. He was warm and hard and very large. It was wonderful and frightening. She felt elation and apprehension, then a sudden blinding pain as he spoke her name again and gave a smooth, deep thrust. She cried out as stars of pain streaked through her vision. Arching up, pressing her breasts against his chest, she panted hard through the pain. Bondur stilled, waiting. He kissed her reverently until the moment passed and her body relaxed. All she could feel was him, deeply embedded inside her, connected and one with her. Spreading her legs wider she slid her arms up his back. He began to move gently, giving her body time to adjust to him as he slowly pushed deeper then withdrew almost completely, only to move in deep again. He rose over her, his arms supporting himself as he slowly undulated in and out. His head flew back, and his eyes closed enraptured, as he repeated over and over, "Little, Emmer little." Then he began to move faster and then slower again as if savoring every thrust.

Emmer's sheath grew wetter, her breath came in short gasps and she could think of nothing else, but the junction where his body connected to hers, making them one. Her hands went to his backside and smoothed over the tight, warm muscles feeling them flex and release. A strange tension began to build and built higher within her body where he plunged between her legs. She pulled his hips in deep and finally that tension burst inside her. Eyes wide with surprise and passion, she cried out again as her body pulsed and squeezed him within her sheath.

Bondur collapsed to one elbow, and gently pulled one of her legs higher over his hip, caressing her thigh as he continued to move with her. He plunged deep, bucking his hips then throwing his head back, green eyes flying open, his entire body flexed hard as he let out a deep breathy, "Huh!"

His shaft seemed to grow larger and then burst inside her. Emmer drew in a sharp breath feeling the pulsing inside her tender sheath causing her to explode with pulsing yet again.

As Bondur spent his seed within her, he slowly leaned over her, breathing hard. His long black hair made a curtain around his sweat-shined face. Emmer lay still under him as their hearts slowed, and they caught their breath. Looking into her blue eyes he just stared at her for a long moment as she lay beneath him. He caressed her cheek with one hand. She glowed, smiling up at him. Then he withdrew from her and slid next to her, pulling her into his arms and placing gentle kisses on her cheeks and lips.

Emmer's heart still beat furiously as she lay with her breasts pressed tightly against him. She tried to catch her breath and slow her racing heartbeat as she clung tightly to him. Resting her head there she heard his deep chuckle and quietly he said, almost in a whisper, "Emmer, little bird heart."

The next morning Emmer awoke to Bondur kissing her breasts. His lips and tongue teased her nipples as she slowly awakened murmuring with pleasure. Bondur rubbed her other breast with his thumb and slowly caressed down her stomach to between her thighs. He moved his body closer to hers and cupped her between the legs. She moaned aloud as he rubbed, and the pleasure built and swept through her. Bondur moved over her and guiding his morning erection into her, moaned low with pleasure, as he entered her tight sheath. He moved slowly at first and then more forcefully. He put his hand under her and pushed deeply in and out of her. Emmer moved with him until their pleasure in each other burst forth at the joined juncture of their bodies. Pulsing and squeezing deep within her, their climax erupted sweeping through them, they shuddered together.

Bondur kissed her deeply, rubbed his stubbly cheek against hers for a moment, and then reluctantly, he left the bed. Emmer stretched languidly, her muscles were sore, but she sighed with contentment as she watched him dress. Soon he left the hut and Emmer was lonely without him. She rose, washed some blood from between her legs, frowning slightly at it, and dressed in her leather traveling pants and shirt, she laced up her vest and then waited for her guards to retrieve her and begin her day.

Later, the guards led her past the field where the men were now practicing with wooden swords. She waved and smiled at her father and saw Hunter and Archer swinging wooden swords at a couple of the Others, but she kept moving, her face calm as she walked past Bondur, half hiding a secret smile but not looking at him. She lowered her head a little and noticed out of the corner of her eye, his face was stone, but his hungry green eyes followed her as she walked past.

After another day spent with her mother avoiding talking about what had happened between her and Bondur, Emmer's guards came and returned her to his hut. She waited straightening, cleaning, and organizing wherever she thought it needed it, just to pass the time and give her hands something to do. She folded Bondur's clothes that lay in a disorderly mound and also stacked the numerous rusty swords into a neat pile sorting them by size and level of damage. Then, taking up a sharpening stone, she began to draw the stone against one of the better swords as she had seen her father do a hundred times before.

Night fell. The door opened and in stepped Bondur. He had bathed and carried dinner with him. At the sight of Emmer, his stony demeanor fell, his lips curled into a slow smile and his emerald eyes glimmered with hunger. He looked around at the straightened hut and gave a nod of approval. He watched intently as she drew the stone over the sword and for the next few minutes memorized her movements. He took the implements from her, setting them down, and then pulled her up against him, lowering his mouth to hers into a deep kiss. He effortlessly lifted her off the floor and she wrapped her legs around his waist. He kissed her passionately as her arms reached around his neck. Smoothing his hands under the short tunic she wore, up over her hips and bare bottom, crushing her against him. After a few moments, he held her with one hand and unlaced his pants with the other, freed his erection, and impaled her. Emmer gasped as he took her standing and plunged into her, his powerful legs held her joined with him. He watched her face fill with wonder as she rose and settled down hard on his shaft. More passionate moments in this position passed until he finally carried her, still linked with him, to the bed and finished burying his passion within her receiving warmth. Emmer moaned as her pleasure pulsed through her body and she ran her fingers through his long hair as he trailed kisses down her neck and over her breasts. The scent of his body overwhelmed her and the slide of his skin against hers made her bite her lip seductively as he thrust hard, bucking deeply until he gritted his teeth, cursed, and found his completion.

"*In-ohloo-my. In-ohloo-my.*" He whispered over and over in Alahemwhey, but she did not understand his words. She smiled at him and pulled his face into another kiss.

Later, they ate their dinner and Bondur surprised Emmer by telling her some new words and sentences he had learned earlier that day. His knowledge of her language was improving very quickly showing he was very intelligent as well as physically powerful. While they ate and talked, a short rap on the door sounded. Bondur's brow furrowed, his eyes narrowed warily, he rose and stalked swiftly to the door. Cracking it open a short way he spoke tersely with the guard outside the door. Closing it firmly, he turned back to Emmer, anger narrowing in his eyes. Quickly he motioned for her to come to him. She rose swiftly and obediently went to him. He gave her a quick kiss on the lips and then spoke very quickly in Alahemwhey. She only understood one word, "*Tahara!*" Grabbing her hand, he led her to an empty corner of the hut. He stripped her blue robe off in short swift movements, grabbed an old shirt of his, and put it on her. Then he messed up her hair, quickly smeared some soot from the fire over her cheeks, and then gently placed her in the corner. Whispering forcefully, he patted the air in front of her and ordered her to, "*Stay!*"

He went back to the low table where the remains of their dinner sat cold, grabbed the sword and stone Emmer had been sharpening, and with a last warning look at her, began to calmly draw the stone over the sword. Emmer waited to see what was making Bondur act so strangely, but he had told her to stay put and stay put she would.

They did not have to wait long. Suddenly, the door burst open, and in walked Tahara, the Red Mohem. She checked her pace and then sauntered in slowly, swinging her hips seductively. Her smooth shapely legs could be seen through the long slits of her richly dyed dress and her ample breasts were barely covered by the plunging neckline. Her slim waist was accented by a wide richly embroidered belt.

Tahara smiled and tossed her long red hair. She gave a confident laugh and moved a step closer to him.

"Bondur! My beautiful Bondur!" She spoke loudly reaching her arms out toward him, an invitation. Bondur remained seated and continued to scrape the stone across his sword blade as if there were nothing else in the room to hold his interest.

Tahara dropped her arms undaunted and turned around in a slow circle as if looking for something. As her eyes fell on Emmer huddling dirty and seemingly miserable in the corner, a wicked smile slowly crossed her lips and a satisfied gleam twinkled in her blue eyes.

"Ah, I see Ulrik's daughter is *here*. Why is she not with my serving maidens as I commanded?" She asked Bondur, turning toward him with a flirtatious flip of her hair.

"Em Alahemwhey Tahara," Bondur grumbled not taking his eyes off his sword sharpening.

Tahara launched into a string of Alahemwhey that Emmer could not understand. Although, she did hear Ulrik and her mother's name mentioned. Bondur gruffly answered her, gestured around the hut, and resumed his sword sharpening. Tahara's voice got louder and her tone became angrier the more he seemed not to comply with her demands.

Bondur finally rose to his feet towering above her. Crossing his arms over his chest he spoke calmly to Tahara which only seemed to make matters worse. Emmer heard Bondur speak her father's name again. Tahara began yelling.

When yelling did not work, Tahara decided to change tactics. With a huff and a pouting lower lip, she stopped screaming at him and smiled demurely. Stepping closer to Bondur she lazily ran one finger up and down his arm speaking in a more serene but teasing tone. Her voice grew more pleasant and her eyes sparkled with promises. She stepped closer and ran a bare leg up against his.

Emmer did not want to watch Bondur's response to Tahara's blatant seduction, so she buried her face in her hands and tried not to watch through her slit fingers. Tahara watched Emmer out of the corner of her eye and her actions seemed to have the desired effect. She spoke more softly to Bondur and continued to rub her leg against him while her hands moved up his chest. Bondur gave a short curt reply to her flirtations and took one step away from her.

Tahara's eyes narrowed and she struck him smartly across the face. At the sound of the slap, Emmer gasped, head coming up and her hands flying to cover her mouth in shock.

Bondur did not move, he just answered Tahara calmly. When she made to slap him again, he caught her wrist and stopped her, growling something low and menacing.

Tahara wrenched her arm away and stalked from the hut slamming the door. Bondur stood where he had been and waited, watching the door, arms still crossed over his muscular chest. He did not look at Emmer but stood calmly watching the door. Emmer did not move, but waited, wide-eyed, and frightened. A moment later the door burst open again and Tahara stormed back in.

She pointed to Emmer and said something low and threatening to Bondur.

Bondur's eyes narrowed angrily, but he did not say anything. He watched as Tahara turned around and stormed out again. Bondur waited a long minute then strode to the door pulling it open, gave the guards some instructions, and closed the door again sliding a bar down to lock it from the inside. In a few strides, he was at Emmer's side. He pulled her up and hugged her tightly, almost painfully, against him. Smoothing her hair and wiping her face with his sleeve, he pulled the ragged shirt off her body and then dressed her once again in the soft blue robe. Then he just stood silently and held her against him, eventually taking her hand, he pulled Emmer across the room, gently sitting her down next to him at the low table.

"Emmer," he began his voice deep with a stern look on his handsome features, "Tahara very angry."

Emmer nodded her head that she understood, and he continued.

"She angry Emmer not her...her...what is name?"

"Serving maiden?" Emmer quietly supplied.

"Serving maiden, yes, Tahara very angry Emmer not her serving maiden. Emmer in Bondur hut. Bondur say, Ulrik not teach warriors sword skill if Emmer not safe, and Bondur keep her safe. Tahara very angry." Bondur stopped and ran his hands through his hair. He looked very angry himself as he spoke.

He shook his head as if he really did not want to say what he had to say next. Taking Emmer's hand, he said, "Tahara want in Bondur's bed." He said firmly but more quietly.

"Oh, I understand." Emmer paled then slowly withdrew her hand from his leaning away from him, and said again, "I understand," although, she did not quite understand fully, and it made her feel angry and hurt and sick all at once.

Bondur grabbed her by the arms fiercely and looked into her eyes.

"No, Emmer not understand." He hesitated and then said heatedly, "First night Bondur see Emmer, Bondur's heart stop." He laid his hand on his chest and then he moved it between his legs and said quietly, "Make Bondur burn here. Bondur want *Emmer* in Bondur's bed. Understand?"

"I understand." She gave him a slight smile and relaxed a little. "The first night I saw Bondur, my heart stopped too, and Emmer burned here." She placed her hand between her legs. She gave another weak smile and waited, "Understand?"

Bondur reached over and lightly slid his hand behind her neck and he pulled her mouth to his. He kissed her gently and then more fiercely. Emmer's arms flew around his neck and she pressed herself tightly against him. When they broke the kiss to catch their breath Bondur pressed his forehead to hers, and closed his eyes, taking in a deep breath, he let it out slowly. A moment later he said quietly, "Bondur want Emmer in Bondur's bed." He looked into her blue eyes his green eyes burning with passionate hunger and longing.

Emmer gave him her most winning smile and gave a small giggle, "Emmer want in Bondur's bed too."

He lifted her in his arms and carried her to the bed. Slowly drawing the robe over her head, he gazed appreciatively down at her naked body. He caressed her breasts and she arched into him. She looked at him with all the emotions and fears burning in her heart and said, "Kiss me Bondur, make all the fear go away. Hold me tight."

Emmer lowered herself to the bed, her long white-gold hair fanning across the pillows. Bondur quickly took off his jerkin, pulled his shirt over his head, bent to pull off his boots, and then slid his trousers down over his lean hips, and stepped out of them. He stood completely naked before her for a few minutes just watching her, the anticipation building between them, his green eyes burning with desire and his hunger for her erect and hard. Then he slowly bent and moved over her, tenderly kissing her hips and her stomach, planting kisses and small licks up her body as he moved over her. Emmer inhaled sharply with pleasure as his lips caressed her warming skin. He took one breast into his mouth, plucking the nipple until it stood erect. As he reached her mouth, he caressed her lips with the tip of his tongue and then closed over her mouth, his lips warm and inviting. Her lips were eager and hungry, feeding his desire.

Emmer arched against him and pulled him to her, spreading her legs and sliding them up to his hips, settling him against her warm heat. As their bodies met, she guided him into her with a caress and he finally plunged deeply, again and again.

"Emmer so tight!" He growled and plunged until she cried out caught in the pleasure of her release. Emmer's inner walls pulsed, squeezed and clenched Bondur's hard shaft as he moved in and out of her until he could hold off no longer and he pressed deep and released within her. As their heartbeats slowed, and they caught their breath, he looked into her eyes, caressed her cheek, and whispered very slowly, very reverently, *"In-ohloo-my."*

The next morning Bondur awoke early and dressed. Emmer opened her eyes sleepily and smiled up at him. She stretched languorously, naked beneath the soft gauze sheets and furs. He came to the bed and sat down beside her. A stern, hard look crossed his face, and his brows drew down.

"Emmer," he began slowly. "Tahara says she come to Bondur's bed tonight. She says, she takes Emmer away if Bondur not," he growled with frustration and said a stream of what sounded like curses in Alahemwhey. "She very angry, want in Bondur's bed." He hesitated and shook his head. Taking a deep breath, he said quickly, "Bondur not say *'no'* to Tahara. Bondur *must* keep Emmer safe but Bondur Captain of all Alahemwhey warriors. Have duty."

Emmer realized Bondur was telling her that Tahara wanted him to bed her or else she would harm Emmer and worse, take her away from Bondur permanently. Tahara was not afraid of what Ulrik would do and was giving Bondur an ultimatum. Either he takes Tahara to bed that very night or Tahara would take her vengeance out on Emmer. Was he also saying he kept Emmer with him because he felt it was his duty? She steeled herself to ask the question that came next to her mind, but she had to put words to her fears.

"Bondur have you..." she faltered not knowing how to ask her question, "Did Bondur take Tahara to bed before Emmer? Did you kiss her and touch her and?" Emmer's eyes filled with tears and her voice caught. Bondur closed his eyes and turned his head away. After a long pause, he stood and gave her a long searching look. Large tears fell down Emmer's cheeks and she could not stop them. Bondur did not answer, but he did not have to. The answer was written plainly on his face. He turned away from her without a word and left the hut. Emmer slowly sat up, stunned at his quiet departure then she slumped down, rolled over, and cried.

The guards did not come to take Emmer to the Great Mohem's hut that day as they had every day before. She waited and waited, apprehensive about all that had happened last night, Tahara's ultimatum, and about all that would happen later in the coming evening. A woman came and brought her food to break her fast and then brought more food at noontime. Emmer had a hard time eating any of it and spent most of the day pacing or mindlessly tidying the already clean hut. She stood for a long time staring at the bed. It now dawned on her why a warrior had such a fine luxurious bed because the warrior did not always sleep alone. She had an overwhelming urge to burn the sheets but refrained. Nothing would be accomplished by that. She felt stunned and embarrassed over the naivety she had displayed the past few days. No wonder Bondur gained a quick command of her language. Tahara must have taught him.

Questions kept circling her mind. Was Bondur only keeping her out of a sense of duty? Why had Tahara not sent for Emmer days before? Had Tahara simply forgotten she ordered Emmer be her serving maiden? Why was she coming for her now? Maybe Tahara learned Emmer was staying in Bondur's hut? With no experience with men or jealousy, Emmer felt lost, like an ignorant child.

Finally, overcome by the need to get the coming evening's events off her mind, she set to vigorously cleaning and sharpening the rest of the pile of swords. She rubbed and shinned and honed until each had a fine edge on it. As she worked, the lushness of Bondur's bed mocked her. The thought suddenly came to her, would Tahara make Emmer watch as Bondur took her to his bed? Emmer shook with dread and disgust at the thought and decided she would tell Bondur not to do it, no matter the threat to herself. Emmer was surprised to find herself angry and defiant when it came to Tahara's demands on Bondur. She would endure anything rather than have Bondur touch Tahara the way he had touched Emmer, even if it meant leaving him.

As nighttime fell, Emmer waited in breathless anticipation and defiance. Finally, the door opened and Bondur came in. Emmer watched him enter, arms folded across her chest, everything she wanted to say was ready in her mind, but before she could speak to him about the subject that had been burning on her conscience all day. She noticed he held his hand to his side. Blood seeped from between his fingers. Suddenly, forgetting all the other worries, she ran to him exclaiming, "You're hurt!"

She pulled him into the room, anger and worry forgotten, and sat him down. He let her lift his fingers away and she cried out as she surveyed the deep bloody gash in his ribs.

"Emmer's father not like Bondur!" He grinned, apparently delighted, and chuckled. "Work Bondur very hard during sword practice. Bondur step in too close. Take sword in side."

"Oh, Bondur! You could have been killed! Let me clean that wound. You need that stitched up! It could get infected!" She hurried away and grabbed a bowl, filled it with clean water, helped Bondur remove his shirt, and began to gently clean the wound. His side trickled fresh blood as she worked but Bondur just grinned ear to ear, leaning in and pressing his nose against her temple drawing in the scent of Emmer's hair. Emmer tried not to look at him and just continued to clean the wound. A suspicious thought crossed her mind that Bondur had become too good of a swordsman to be so easily wounded. She finally looked up at him with mistrustful eyes.

"You need this stitched up!" She chastised angrily. "My mother, Tessa, is good at stitching wounds. You must have her brought here to tend to you or send for Hunter. He is very good at stitching wounds too!" Emmer's eyes pleaded with him.

"No! Emmer do stitched." He spoke with calm finality.

"Me? I've never! Well, I couldn't. I don't have a needle or thread and I don't know for sure what all is needed." She gasped and then said more quietly, "I could hurt you."

Bondur laughed and then yelled loudly for a guard to come in. He gave instructions in Alahemwhey and the man ran off. A few minutes later the man returned with a fine bone needle and thread, some bandages, and a large skin of wine. Another man followed with a bucket of fresh water.

"Emmer do," Bondur ordered gently.

Emmer looked terrified, but dutifully set some of the water to boil as she had seen her mother do many times, laid out the implements, and tore some bandage strips, trying desperately to remember the times she had watched her mother sew wounds.

Bondur waited, strangely still, but his eyes sparkled with mischief and occasionally he looked toward the door. He cast knowing glances over Emmer's shoulder. Taking long pulls from the wineskin, he seemed to be waiting. As Emmer prepared to stitch the wound and double-checked her supplies, the door suddenly flew open. In strutted Tahara dressed in her finest blue gown and dowsed in so much scent, it wafted around her like a sickeningly sweet fog. It was obvious how she had expected the evening to be spent. She came to a shocked standstill as she took in the blood-stained shirt and the bandages. The seductive smile fell from her face and she scowled, and then paled, her eyes growing wide.

Not stepping any closer she swiftly questioned Bondur in Alahemwhey. Bondur answered her calmly and shrugged his shoulders. Tahara scowled again and pointed an accusing finger at Emmer, after several more minutes of arguing, Tahara turned and left, slamming the door behind her in a fury. It was obvious that Tahara would not be sharing Bondur's bed that night. Bondur chuckled low in his chest and grinned a knowing half-smile.

Turning his head back, Bondur smiled more widely at Emmer, nodded his head and she began to sew his wound with shaking fingers. He took long pulls from the wineskin watching her, stealing a kiss here and there. He did not move or flinch as Emmer stitched the sword gash in his side. She finished, cut off the extra thread with his small knife, and then bound his ribs in clean bandages.

There was a gentle knock on the door and a woman brought in food. She placed it on the low table and left. Emmer and Bondur ate in silence. Bondur grinned looking very pleased with himself and ate hardily. Emmer could hardly eat wondering what had passed between him and Tahara. She avoided meeting Bondur's eyes.

As if reading her mind, Bondur spoke up.

"Bondur tell Tahara he too wounded to take her to bed. Need Emmer to do stitched up wound. Tahara hate see blood. Ha! She *very* angry now. Not share Bondur's bed for many days till wound healed! HA!" He tossed his head back and laughed loudly.

Emmer gave him a frown. "What happens when you've healed and she comes back? She will expect you to..." Emmer's eyes flashed, and she spoke defiantly. "I do not want you to do *that* to protect me!"

Bondur leaned toward her and pulled her onto his lap. "Wound worth getting to keep Emmer in Bondur's bed."

"I knew it!" Pursing her lips, she almost growled at him, "You *let* my father wound you so you would not have to bed

Tahara?" Bondur just smiled and shrugged a shoulder as if to say it was nothing. He pulled her closer and kissed her, chuckling at his cleverness, he trailed kisses down her neck. Emmer tried to remain angry but eventually relaxed into his embrace, not too disappointed in how things had turned out.

Later that evening when it was time to rest for the night, Bondur lay back in the bed propped up on pillows amongst the sheets and furs, watching as Emmer undressed. The lamp light caressed her nude body and painted her smooth skin with a golden glow. He caught his breath, wondering at how beautiful she was. He barely resisted licking his lips. Her curving hips and small perky breasts intoxicated him. He reached his hands up to her grasping the air impatiently, beckoning, wanting, and itching to touch her. Getting carefully into bed next to him, Emmer took care not to lie on the side of his wound. He made to pull her to him, and she leaned back, glancing at his large erection.

She asked in a worried tone, "Your wound?"

He just smiled wider and pulled her on top of him. He eased her legs up until she straddled him and then drew her in to kiss him. Lifting her hips and guiding her, he impaled her on his hard shaft. Emmer's eyes widened taking in this new position. She arched back and gasped as he ran his hands over her hips moving her. She continued the movement, learning the rhythm. As she loved him, Bondur leaned back, folded his hands behind his head, and smiled with pleasure.

Chapter Twenty-two – Ohhem

As Bondur's wound healed, the days were blissfully free from any more visits from Tahara but then the Great Mohem died. Tessa and Emmer mourned her death along with the people of the Alahemwhey. Emmer had gotten to know Eleanor during her visits, and she had learned many things from her.

The Alahemwhey held a ceremony at which they burned her remains with great reverence in a grand ritual. Afterward, a feast was held to celebrate her life. A long period of mourning followed where no one did any work beyond the barest necessities and none of the warriors trained with the sword. It was meant to be a time spent with family and loved ones so that the living could more fully appreciate what they had in this life. There was feasting along with the mourning and much happiness mixed with tears. Bondur spent every moment with Emmer. He took her riding, leaving in the early morning hours before dawn and returning after dark. He gave her strands of cobalt beads and a beautiful blonde-colored horse to ride. They became friends as well as lovers as his knowledge of her language improved.

Bondur covertly allowed Ulrik to stay with Tessa in the Great Mohem's hut. Hunter and Archer were confined to their huts which did not prove to be too much of a burden as they each had company. Hunter had Soria. Archer had visits from various Alahemwhey girls. As soon as the mourning period ended the warriors would return to training.

#

One night, Bondur went out and came back an hour later followed by four old women. They carried bowls and strange implements. Emmer had no idea why the women were there. Each one smiled at her and giggled behind their hands and spoke to her briefly in Alahemwhey, which she did not fully understand though she had picked up a few words here and there.

The women lit the brazier and also many lamps casting the hut in bright light. They set up their implements talking and laughing with each other. Emmer smiled and watched them with growing interest, watching as they mixed a thick deep blue liquid in bowls.

After a while, a knock came on the door and Bondur answered it. In walked Tessa and Ulrik who were escorted by Bondur's blue guardsmen. The guards waited outside. Ulrik scowled at Bondur but smiled gently when Emmer leaped into his arms, hugging him tightly. Tessa beamed at Emmer, embracing her and kissing her on the cheeks, and then embracing her again with excitement. It was a happy reunion.

Emmer blushed a deep red realizing that her parents might figure out she had been spending her nights alone with Bondur. Bondur respectfully invited Ulrik and Tessa to sit and then sat next to Emmer, back straight and hands grasping his knees. He seemed nervous and distracted but braced himself as if for a serious discussion.

Before Bondur could speak and explain what was happening, Emmer spoke up.

"Father, Mother, what are you doing here? What's going on?" Emmer asked looking back and forth between them. The women continued to bustle around the brazier and prepare their tools.

It was Bondur who answered. He cleared his throat. "Bondur wishes Emmer to take the Ohhem with him. This is markings like Mother Tessa and many Alahemwhey woman have. This means Emmer belong to Bondur only and have protection from all other man. Live together as mates and have children. No other man can have Emmer," he paused and said pointedly, "and no other woman can have Bondur." He smiled widely and watched her with an intense burning emerald gaze.

Placing his hand over his heart he bowed to her and said, *"In-ohloo-my."*

"Emmer, he is asking you to marry him, in the Alahemwhey tradition, to be his wife." Tessa beamed with joy. "He said, 'I love you' in his language."

Emmer, sat stunned realizing all this time he had been telling her he loved her, *"In-ohloo-my."* She looked at her father when he grumbled.

"Bondur is a good warrior. He is the best among the Alahemwhey. He has asked me for you, and I have consented as long as you are willing." Turning a hard stare at Bondur and narrowing his eyes, he added. "I have told him if he ever mistreats you or harms you in any way, I will gut him." Ulrik's eyes bored into Bondur. Bondur held Ulrik's eyes in return, a stony, unyielding look on his face. Bondur turned to Emmer and took her hand.

"Will Emmer take Bondur as mate, as wife?" His green eyes sparked as he waited for her answer.

Emmer looked at Bondur, her face full of love and happiness, and said, "Yes, yes! I am yours!"

She threw her arms around his neck and kissed him on the mouth. Ulrik grunted and Tessa clasped her hands together, a joyful smile on her face and happy tears filling her eyes.

The Ohhem ceremony that followed took up most of the night. They all feasted while the women painted the Ohhem on Emmer's arms and down her hips at her outer thighs to just above the top of her knees. They heated the newly painted areas and the blue color intensified sinking in and staining her ivory skin. When they were done the delicate scrolling swirls, flowers, leaves and a picture of three spears closely placed, down the center gleamed with a beautiful deep cobalt blue against Emmer's pale skin. Emmer shined and wore them proudly. Bondur too was marked with two rings of cobalt blue designs circling his biceps in matching patterns to Emmer's, with the same three spears centered in the pictures, except without the flowers it was a masculine version. Then without further ceremony, the two were mated for life.

Tessa and Ulrik left after kissing Emmer goodbye, holding her tightly they expressed their congratulations and happy wishes. Ulrik had a hard time letting Emmer go but after a few moments turned to grasp Bondur's arm firmly and stared meaningfully into his eyes. Silently, an unspoken message passed between them.

Bondur gave a slight nod saying, "Little One safe with Bondur."

"That's what you said before and now look at her," Ulrik grumbled then he and Tessa were escorted back to their tent.

Within the next few days Tahara found out Emmer was now Bondur's mate and she threw a royal temper tantrum, but what was done was done, and try as she may, she could not go against Alahemwhey tradition and law in this instance. The three tribe Elders upheld Bondur's choice saying the union between Ulrik's daughter and the Alahemwhey Captain was a great benefit to the tribe. The marriage was sanctified by the Elders as a demonstration to Tahara and the tribe's people that the real power was with the three Elders and not the Red Mohem.

Emmer and Bondur spent the next days in happy bliss. After the mourning period for the Great Mohem passed, he returned to attend to his duties as Captain of the Alahemwhey warriors, trained with his men, and continued to learn the sword skill from Ulrik. He was a fast learner and quickly excelled at the sword skill.

Their happiness was short-lived though. Soon it came time for the men would leave to go against the Solemeyha tribe and steal the man who knew the secret of making swords. Bondur came to the hut earlier than usual on their last evening together and packed his saddlebags in moody silence, his face was stone cold, his brow furrowed in anger. Emmer just sat and watched as he moved around the hut, her eyes glistening with unshed tears. Bondur finally spoke as he packed, but he did not turn to look at his mate.

"It is three days to the Solemeyha village." His usage of her language had greatly improved over their weeks together, but he spoke with frustration. "I hope to be in and out in one night then three days ride back if all is done well."

Emmer nodded, not trusting herself to speak.

When Bondur had nothing left to prepare for his journey, he turned toward Emmer. He swiftly went to her in three long strides and pulled her into his arms. He held her for a long moment and then smoothed his hand over her cheek and hair as he looked deep into her sky-blue eyes.

"I would take you if it were possible, but there will be danger and it is not allowed."

"I know," Emmer said quietly and tried her best to smile at him. She could not help it and a tear got loose and slid down her cheek.

"Emmer understand, we must get the man who knows the secret of making swords or your brothers will be put to death by Tahara. Bondur does not wish for that to happen. They are good men."

"I know. You do what you have to do, just come back to me safe and unharmed. Keep my father and my brothers safe as well."

"Emmer will be protected here. Many of Bondur's warriors will stay to keep you from Tahara."

"Just come back to me, my Love."

Bondur looked at her with his eyes going dark and said very firmly, "Emmer *nothing* can keep me from you."

Emmer smiled a sad smile. Bondur's eyes darkened with ardor and a fierce look crossed his handsome features. He pulled her close, feeling her body pressed to his. He kissed her passionately. Emmer sighed into his mouth and clung to him as their tongues danced. He slid his hands over her and gently pushed the robe from her shoulders, easing her down onto the bed. Her small perky breasts lay revealed, tantalizing him. He knelt above her and ran his hands over her soft flesh, his eyes traveling over her curves. He bent his head and licked one nipple, plucking it between his lips, and then did the same to the other. Emmer shuddered beneath him and ran her hands through his hair, holding him against her breasts. She hummed with pleasure as he moved down her body planting kisses along her sensitive curves. Her blood burned in her veins and she wanted more of him, all of him.

Bondur kissed her stomach, lingered his kisses along her hips, and then rubbed his cheek over her belly marveling at the softness against his face. He kissed her ivory skin working his way down then rose over her and rammed his hard shaft firmly into her sheath, anxious to join with her. Rearing up he knelt and pulled her legs around his hips and they bucked together until he arched back, and pushing deeper into her, spilled his seed in a forceful climax. Bondur collapsed over her breathing hard with spent passion.

Emmer clung to him and pulled him deeper, glorifying in the feel of him inside her, his weight on top of her and their sweat mingling. Wanting to memorize every inch of his body, she ran her hands over his broad back and then down over his firm, muscular bottom.

Bondur moved beside her and pulled her into his arms. He nuzzled her hair and took a deep breath smoothing his hand over her belly and hips. They fell asleep in each other's arms, bodies entwined.

A few hours later Bondur awoke in the dark of the night. The embers in the brazier cast a red glow in the darkness. Emmer had rolled to her side and he spooned her body with his just as they had their first night together. He caressed her hip and Emmer smiled, moaning with sleepy pleasure parting her legs a little and giving him better access to that which he sought. Bondur gently pushed her forward a bit, pulling her hips back and up, and guided himself inside her sheath from behind. Silently he moved, undulated inside her until he spent within her once again. Emmer's climax overtook her she arched against him pressing her bottom into his hips, her body clenched around him with satisfaction.

Bondur gently disengaged and Emmer rolled over and she clung to him. They slept again until the early glow that signaled morning's approach began to lighten the hut. Bondur once again rose and moved between Emmer's legs, kissing her awake. Emmer slid her hands to his backside and rubbed his smooth taut muscles feeling them ripple and firm as he plunged inside her, more loving, more desperate. She pulled him in deeper as if she never wanted to let him go.

Then it was time for Bondur to dress and leave to begin his mission. Emmer helped him with the straps of his hardened leather armor, a metal sword, and a knife, while he laced his boots, she packed some fresh food for the road, and then it was done. She dressed in her finest Alahemwhey tunic, wore the necklace of blue beads he had given her, brushed her hair, and briefly clung to him, eyes brimming with tears. Bondur bent and gave her one last kiss taking her taste with him on his journey. Head held high, she bravely handed him his spear and pack, smiled brightly, and walked beside him, out into the morning light.

Chapter Twenty-three – Soria's Story

Life was full of joy for Hunter and Soria while he trained the Alahemwhey warriors to fight with swords. If it were not for the Red Guard following them around constantly and the fact that they were prisoners of the Alahemwhey, they would have been happy, but that lack of freedom began to weigh on Soria.

As they sat together eating dinner one night, Hunter told her of his home in the mountains. He made her laugh with stories about his exploits with Archer and she gasped in wonder when he told her of the house and the huge underground cellar area with all its treasures from another world. Soria could not comprehend much of what he was describing, but listened intently, a look of longing in her eyes. Deep inside her heart she longed for a home of her own and to be a part of the family that Hunter described.

Hunter told her what he knew of Ulrik's first capture by the Alahemwhey and about the *Others* who were the result of Ulrik's stolen seed. This was not new information to Soria because the legend of Ulrik had spread even among the Solemeyha.

One night, Soria revealed her biggest fear to Hunter.

"Hunter, I know you teach the sword skill to the Alahemwhey warriors so they can go to my village of the Solemeyha and take my father. I know the Red Mohem wants him to teach them sword making, and they think they can use me to force him."

"Yes, Tahara says she will put me and Archer to death if Ulrik does not help her get the sword maker. I am not afraid. The Alahemwhey warriors are doing well, but they are no threat to us. Bondur has become almost as good a swordsman as Ulrik, Archer, and I, but I do not fear him. I have seen the way he looks at Emmer. Father said Bondur wants Emmer to take the Ohhem with him. I think Bondur respects my father, but I question if his loyalty is greater to Emmer or Tahara and the Alahemwhey. I do not trust Bondur or Tahara and her Red Guard."

A look of longing stung Soria's eyes, *"They*-take-the-Ohhem?" She spoke haltingly.

Soria shook her head as if to chase away some hidden yearning of her own. The ceremony of the Ohhem and its meaning was the same in her tribe and the desire for such a union was strong in her heart.

Then fear shown in Soria's eyes, "Hunter, my father will not help the Alahemwhey even if they threaten to kill me. You see, he is not my blood father. My mother was his second wife. She died when I was little child. He cared for me after her death but has no love for me. He kept me to cook and clean. Ulrik can bring him to Tahara, but Tureck will not help them to save me."

Hunter thought long and hard about this and then he pulled her close. "Ulrik will find a way. He is a Viking warrior and greater than any of the Alahemwhey. He is smarter too. I will speak to my father. He will know what to do." He smoothed her hair calming her and kissed her on the forehead.

"I will protect you with my life."

Soria's arms went around him, and she held him tightly.

"What is a Viking warrior?" Breaking a long silence Soria asked, her mind whirling with all they had discussed.

Hunter chuckled and told her Ulrik's story as best he could. Soria told Hunter of her life and capture by the Alahemwhey. They talked long into the night until it was time to go to bed. Hunter held Soria close to him and caressed her naked body. They embraced until their mutual passion was spent and then Soria slept in Hunter's arms. Hunter stared for a long time into the darkness contemplating their circumstances before he managed to drift off to sleep.

The following day, Hunter managed to get Ulrik alone. While Archer kept the Alahemwhey warriors busy with sword practice, Hunter divulged what Soria told him. Ulrik looked none too pleased and swore under his breath. They discussed some plans of action but were interrupted when Bondur approached them. The stone-faced giant looked Ulrik in the eyes narrowing his own suspiciously at the two and then motioned them over. Ulrik wondered for the hundredth time if Bondur treated Emmer with the same cold roughness. She looked well treated and happy since taking the Ohhem with Bondur, but Ulrik still wondered.

Bondur wiped the sweat from his muscular chest with a cloth and looked back and forth between Hunter and Ulrik. They stood in silence, catching their breath after a long and vigorous bout of sword training. The tension lay thick between them.

"How is my daughter?" Ulrik asked abruptly.

"Emmer is well," Bondur said his eyes softening and a smile almost breaking his rocky countenance.

"See that she stays that way." Ulrik snapped and turned to walk away.

"Ulrik," Bondur called after him. "Bondur must speak to you about the sword maker."

Hunter worried that Bondur had overheard his conversation with Ulrik about Soria. He took a menacing step toward the giant. He was almost the same height as Bondur but was not as thickly muscled. Still, Hunter was not afraid of the bigger man and stood ready to defend Soria if necessary.

"Come and sit." They followed Bondur to a place under a large tree and the three sat down in the shade on large wood logs. Before they could begin their conversation, Tahara approached, flanked by her Red Guard. She was clearly not in a happy mood.

"Bondur!" She snapped at him and launched into an angry stream of Alahemwhey.

Bondur stood and acknowledged her words with a sharp nod of his head. His voice took on a placating but firm tone toward her. She seemed slightly mollified and spat loudly, "See that you do!"

Tahara cast a haughty look at Ulrik and Hunter. Her nostrils flared as if she smelled something bad. After a long tense moment, she turned to stomp away, hips swaying seductively.

Bondur sat down with Ulrik again and closing his eyes, took a deep breath. For a few more moments he sought to control the anger he let show after the fiery Red Mohem left.

"Ulrik, Bondur will...*I* will speak plain. Tahara is very angry we are taking so long to sword train. She wants us to go soon to take the sword maker. I want..." He again tried to control the anger that reddened his face. He momentarily closed his eyes again to calm himself. "What I want makes no matter. We leave in three days."

Ulrik looked at Bondur suspiciously.

"What are you not telling us?" Ulrik fairly growled narrowing eyes and muscles tensing.

Bondur sat up straighter and said, "Tahara badly wants the sword maker to make Alahemwhey people great warrior tribe. I wanted the same thing once." He lowered his voice. "No more. I want only Emmer."

"You have Emmer! She has taken the Ohhem with you." Hunter snapped.

"Yes, but Emmer is not safe here. Tahara is very jealous. She threatens Emmer with death if Ulrik fails. We must go in three days and bring back the sword maker." He lowered his voice and spoke quickly and more quietly. "Then Tahara has ordered you all put to death regardless if we succeed or fail. All of you, Ulrik, Tessa, Hunter, and Archer she says must die. She keeps the Solemeyha woman to force the sword maker to teach the Alahemwhey the secret of sword making."

Hunter tensed, swearing under his breath, but Ulrik remained strangely calm.

Eyes narrowed thoughtfully he asked, "What is your plan?" Unsmiling, he placed his hands on his knees and looked Bondur in the eyes.

"We will go and get the sword maker, bring him here to make swords. Tahara is beautiful woman she will persuade him, and she has the Solemeyha woman. We take Emmer, Tessa, and your sons and go before Tahara can order your deaths at the hands of her Red Guard."

"Soria is mine!" Hunter said between gritted teeth. "She is the Solemeyha and she goes with me!"

Bondur looked at him a long time, searched Hunter's angry face, and quickly assessed the situation between him and the Solemeyha.

"Done! We get the sword maker and then he is Tahara's problem. We all go! But we must go as soon after we return. In three days, I will leave my most trusted warriors to guard Emmer, Tessa, and the Solemeyha."

"Her name is Soria!" Hunter snarled through his teeth.

Ulrik narrowed his eyes, "Why? You are Alahemwhey, Captain of all the Alahemwhey warriors, why would you do this for us? I thought you were loyal to Tahara and your people. Why would you leave here?"

"I was not always Alahemwhey. I was taken by the Alahemwhey when just a small boy." He said quietly. "Grow very tired of Tahara ruling my life. Emmer..." he stopped to collect his anger. "Emmer is everything I want now. Tahara threatens Emmer's life and everything Emmer loves."

Ulrik looked at Hunter and gave a short nod. A look of begrudging respect passed over his features and Ulrik said, "Then we are agreed. I do not think Tahara will allow us to take the women with us on this raid, so you must keep our women safe while we are gone. Let Tahara think she still leads you around by the balls. You must do what it takes to convince her that you are still *her* man. My sons and I will do the rest."

The three stood to return to the practice field, but Hunter grabbed Bondur's arm and stopped him.

"Wait a moment. I need you to do something for me."

He took Bondur aside and spoke to him in a few quiet words. Bondur nodded once, then grasped Hunter's arm in a brotherly clasp, sealing the deal they just made.

Later that night, Hunter returned to his hut where he lived with Soria and he took her in his arms and held her tightly. He quietly told her of their conversation with Bondur and their escape plans. A short time later a knock on the door revealed four old women waiting outside the hut. They came in smiling and carrying strange implements, strange to Hunter, but not to Soria. When she saw the old women and the implements, she threw herself into Hunter's arms flooding his face with kisses. He grinned widely at her and kissed her back. Soon, they were joined by Ulrik and Tessa, Bondur and Emmer, and even Archer.

Archer roared with laughter when the ceremony was explained to him and he made fun of Hunter for limiting himself to one woman. Hunter grinned back at his twin knowing that his twin would someday understand.

The family feasted while the old women painted Soria and Hunter with the Ohhem, bonding them together for life. Down through the middle of their arm designs, they drew a two-bladed axe, like the one Hunter had when he was captured, connecting it with the swirls with leaves and the flowers of the Alahemwhey. The two-bladed axe would signify them as man and wife. Hunter grinned widely and his deep blue eyes sparkled as they similarly drew the axe and swirls on his biceps, then heated them to bring out the deep cobalt color and seal the designs permanently into their skin. The family celebrated late into the night and when the ceremony was complete Hunter took Soria to their bed and made passionate love to his wife.

Chapter Twenty-four – The Raid

The day came when it was time to leave and go to the Solemeyha village and take the sword maker. Bondur's men escorted them to where Ulrik and the rest of the raiding party prepared to leave. Bondur and Emmer had said their goodbyes within the hut where he had kissed her gently, one last time. Emmer ran to Ulrik and hugged him and then hugged Hunter.

Tessa came escorted by the Red Guard and she hugged Ulrik. She held tightly to him until he gently disengaged her arms. Ulrik took her aside and they spoke in quiet voices saying their goodbyes.

Soria approached with Hunter and she clung to him as well, kissing him deeply, before he mounted atop a dark golden-colored horse.

"Where is Archer? Isn't he going with you?" Emmer asked looking around.

"No, Tahara commanded he stay here as security so we come back as if we would leave you." Hunter scoffed, but then his forehead creased. "I guess he was too angry to come to see us off."

Tahara, surrounded by her Red Guard and accompanied by the three Elders, gathered to watch the warriors go. She stood insolently, one hand on her hip, and glared at Bondur standing with Emmer.

"Bondur!" Tahara snapped in a shrewish tone. Bondur immediately turned to go speak to her. She was dressed in her finest, rich blue gown and the sunlight sparkled on the many necklaces of blue beads she wore. She gave him a wicked and cunning smile and took a deep breath, her large breasts heaving just enough to draw the eye. She spoke in a low seductive voice and reached out to caress Bondur's chest with one long delicate finger. Bondur gritted his teeth and endured her touch as he always had.

Ulrik and the others waited a few feet away from where Tahara stood shamelessly flirting with Bondur. Eventually, a look of disbelief stunned his face and he argued with her and even raised his voice, but she crossed her arms under her ample breasts and made her demands. The village Elders looked sad but nodded their consent to whatever Tahara's command had been. Bondur finally relented and nodded his head sharply and turned to go. He did not look Ulrik in the eye, just strode away.

Bondur mounted a large black horse looking splendid in his black leather armor and gleaming sword. Ulrik and the other men were similarly armed and armored. Emmer thought it strange to see her father and brother looking so much a part of the Alahemwhey. Together the women watched as the horses moved off to begin their quest.

As Ulrik led the mounted men through the village, Bondur moved his black horse to the side of the column of men and watched as they moved past in an orderly fashion. He called out orders and looked every inch the leader he was. As the last of the riders fell into place, he turned his horse and took a long last look at Emmer. Holding her gaze, he briefly placed an open hand on his chest, a secret message to her that she has his heart. Turning toward the mounted men, Bondur galloped to the head of the column with Ulrik. He did not look back again. Tessa, Emmer, and Soria stood, watching until the column of men was completely lost in the distance.

As soon as the warriors were out of sight Tahara spoke a sharp command and the Red Guard moved to try and surround the three women. Bondur's men, who were charged with protecting them, moved forward and took a protective stance around them. It became a tense standoff as Tahara spoke to Bondur's men in a commanding tone. The village Elders tried to interfere, but it was not clear whose side they were on.

Soria translated in a quiet voice for Tessa and Emmer.

"The Red Mohem is ordering Bondur's men to hand us over to her Red Guard. Bondur's men are refusing. They say that they are under orders from Captain Bondur to guard us until he returns."

Soria listened as the argument continued, her eyes darting back and forth. Tahara was loudly demanding, but the leader of Bondur's men remained stubborn in the face of her commands.

Soria's face fell as the argument ended and a worried look crossed her lovely features.

"Tahara has won." She whispered. "We are to be taken to Bondur's hut and kept there until Ulrik returns, but Bondur's men are allowed to be the ones guarding us."

Emmer and Tessa stood proudly waiting while their fate was discussed, while Soria stared at Tahara with defiance of her own.

As Bondur's men spoke, directing them toward the hut, they took their eyes off the Red Guard, just as they turned to surround Tessa, Emmer, and Soria and lead them off, the Red Guard fell upon them. They disarmed Bondur's men after a long fight, and then beat them down to the dirt. Some of the Red Guardsmen hauled the girl's would-be protectors away and the others held the three women at spearpoint.

"As *I* commanded, you will be held under *my* guard until Ulrik comes back and all has been done to *my* satisfaction."

Tahara sneered and approached Emmer looking her up and down contemptuously. Then she motioned with a quick cut of her arm for the Red Guard to take them away. They led the three women to the same small hut where Hunter, Archer, and Soria were imprisoned the first night of their capture. There they found Archer. He had been beaten unconscious and left face down, bleeding in the hay.

Chapter Twenty-five – The Sword Maker

Ulrik, Bondur, Hunter, and their company of Alahemwhey warriors rode toward the Solemeyha village. Bondur was strangely silent and angry. They rode through miles of tall grass and made camp that night under some sparse trees. Bondur estimated that it would be at least two more days before they reached the village. He pushed the men hard going as fast as was possible.

The first night they camped Ulrik approached Bondur as he sat alone in the moonlight.

"Bondur, what is it that you are not telling me?" Ulrik spoke knowingly.

Bondur stared out into the distance for a few minutes and then ran his hands through his long hair in a frustrated gesture.

"Tahara!" He growled through gritted teeth, then continued angrily, "She has ordered that we burn the entire village and put to death all of the Solemeyha. She says otherwise they will follow us and try and take back the sword maker. We are ordered to put them all to death, men, women, and children! I told her I could not, *would* not do it, but the Elders agree that it is too risky to leave the Solemeyha alive. No matter how I argued, they would not release this demand. I hate to admit it, but if the Alahemwhey are to keep the sword maker, I may not have a choice."

Ulrik sat silent for a long time. "Tahara has a lot of confidence in you with only twenty-three men to put a whole village to the torch."

"She knows nothing of fighting. She insists it can and will be done because it is what she wants." Bondur responded.

"We may be able to come up with another plan," Ulrik spoke slowly. "Let us sleep on this tonight and we will think of a way to get around Tahara's orders."

Ulrik hesitated then continued, "I worry about the women. Will she harm them while we are away? I hated leaving them, but we had no choice." Bondur did not answer for a long time he just continued to stare out at the night.

Then finally he answered, "Hunter's Soria is safe because Tahara needs her. Tessa should be safe until we can get there with the sword maker because she is no threat to Tahara. I have left my most trusted men to guard them and Archer remains there. I hope it will be enough."

Ulrik noticed Bondur did not mention Emmer's safety but chose not to bring that up.

They continued to talk for a short time, and he and Bondur agreed to think of a way around the slaughter of the entire Solemeyha village. Ulrik went to speak to Hunter about the new developments and they all bedded down with the problem forefront of their thoughts.

The next day as Ulrik, Hunter, and Bondur rode, they privately discussed plans to avoid slaughtering the entire Solemeyha village. Hunter worried that unless they completely met the demands Tahara had set for them that their women's safety would be at risk. He shared what Soria had told him about Tureck, the sword maker and Bondur swore under his breath and looked thunderous. As they came within a few miles of the village, they stopped and Ulrik commanded the men to conceal themselves within the forest that was outside the boundary of the Solemeyha territory. Scouts were sent out to look for any Solemeyha warriors guarding the land around the village. They disappeared like the morning mist and returned with the news that no guards were around.

In his previous life, Ulrik had raided many villages with a small number of warriors and had put many men to death, but in this new life, he had left that kind of brutality behind. The desperate struggle to survive had not, until their stay with the Alahemwhey, required that he raid and kill men who would not hesitate to kill him.

Ulrik, Hunter, and Bondur came to a consensus, albeit they all admitted it was a weak strategy about how to proceed.

Whether or not their actions would please Tahara, was a matter for later.

The men waited together until nightfall. As darkness covered the land, the three of them rode out with one of the *Other* warriors named Emparo. He had infiltrated the Solemeyha for months and was involved in the raid when Soria had been taken. Because of his familiarity with the Solemeyha, he knew the hut where the sword maker lived and acted as a guide. Luckily, it was the furthest and most secluded hut on the outskirts of the village. Together the men skirted around the village border toward the sword maker's hut. They tethered the horses within the trees and waited until deep into the night. They watched the sword maker's house for hours and then saw a huge man staggering and swaying, drunkenly approaching the hut. As the moon began to set, they drew their swords and jogged swiftly among the trees toward the house. Inside, it was silent. The black of the night waited in heavy anticipation of the coming dawn.

Bondur looked in an open window and motioned to Ulrik beckoning him forward. Ulrik nodded to Hunter who lithely leaped up and eased noiselessly in through an open window. A few tense moments later Hunter opened the door of the hut from the inside. Bondur and Ulrik entered silently. Inside, the hut was littered with pieces of swords, rickety furniture, dirty plates scattered on the table, with filthy clothing randomly strewn about. In the corner was a bed where the occupant snored loudly.

The smell of spirits and rotting food was strong. Ulrik drew his sword and approached the bed. Hunter lit a candle and Bondur drew a small tube from the pouch at his waist and approached the bed, ready. The light cast the dirty hut with dancing shadows and Ulrik nudged the occupant of the bed with the tip of his sword. He continued to poke the man, but he would not awaken and only mumbled in his drunken sleep.

The sword maker was a huge man. Years of pounding metal into swords had built massive chest and arm muscles. Ulrik guessed he was in his late thirties and life working with metal and fire was etched into his face. Ulrik, whose poking gained no response, ran completely out of patience. Looking around and finding a pitcher of water, he poured it over the head of the sleeping man. The man sputtered and gasped roaring with anger at being awakened so rudely. He tried to stand, but he was clearly very drunk and Ulrik easily pushed him down with one hand. He placed the tip of his sword against the man's throat. Bondur addressed him in his language.

"Are you the sword maker?" Bondur asked.

The man sputtered more and wiped his face with a hand squinting blearily at the three, armed men in his hut. Bondur repeated his question.

"What is the meaning of this?" The man demanded angrily.

"Are you the sword maker?" Bondur repeated his question impatiently.

"I am Tureck the Smith. What of it? Why have you woken an honest man asleep in his own bed? It is the middle of the night!" His words were slurred from drinking and he swayed a little where he sat.

"You will come with us," Bondur spoke gesturing with his sword.

"Come with you? HA! What is all this?" The big man tried to rise. Ulrik kept his sword at the man's throat so he sat back down eyeing the point.

"That's not one of mine." He said curiously eyeing Ulrik's Viking sword with great interest.

Hunter spoke up impatiently, "Ask him if he is the father of Soria?"

The man started at the mention of Soria and asked Bondur, "Soria? Do you know where she is? The worthless wench left me months ago to fend for myself. What has she to do with all this?" He demanded, but began again, "I am an honest man, what…"

Bondur broke in calmly and quietly. "If you are the sword maker you will come with us. We will take you to Soria. She is a captive of the Alahemwhey, as of this night, you also are our captive."

The man crossed his large, muscled arms over his chest stubbornly and glared.

"I may be the swordsmith, but I am not going with any Alahemwhey." He sneered. "I do not care if you have Soria or not. I am not leaving my forge."

Bondur swore and told Ulrik in one short sentence that the man refused to leave willingly. He spoke to the large man who sat stubbornly on the bed, "You will come." With those words, he quickly put the tube to his lips and blew. The blue Alahemwhey dart streaked out and took the man in the neck. He was so large the dart had little immediate effect, but to make him grunt and surge to his feet pulling out the dart. He struck out clumsily at Ulrik trying to land a blow to his chin. Ulrik deftly dodged the first hap-hazard blow. The large man moved surprisingly fast and Ulrik failed to miss the second blow which landed squarely on his chin. Ulrik rocked back with the force of the blow.

Bondur and Hunter both flew into action jumping on the large man. The three of them crashed back to the bed which could not take the weight of three large men and collapsed noisily to the floor. They rolled around punches flying, curses roaring.

A wrestling match ensued. Ulrik stood watching, rubbing his chin while Bondur and Hunter tried to hold the large powerful man down. Soon they were successful and Bondur stabbed the man in the backside with another dart. Tureck finally fell back totally incapacitated.

Ulrik and Bondur began to work gagging him and tying him up. Hunter jumped up to begin his designated job. Grabbing a dirty sheet off the bed he began throwing everything he could get his hands on, into the sheet. He took a few of the sword maker's clothes, some food, a wineskin, and a few of the completed swords that were lying on the table. When he had everything he could carry, they set the hut to rights, as much as they could. There was nothing that could be done about the broken bed. The hut looked as if Tureck packed up his implements and moved away from the Solemeyha.

Ulrik and Bondur each took an arm and dragged the big man out the door. A low whistle brought Emparo with the horses and they heaved the sleeping Tureck over the saddle of his horse they took from the barn. Bondur and Hunter led the burdened horse away and Ulrik and Emparo went into the building where the swords were made. They quickly bundled up every tool and instrument they could find and joined Bondur and Hunter. They made their escape quietly into the night.

During the return trip, they kept Tureck securely tied in the Alahemwhey manner, with a rope around his neck and hands bound tightly in front of him, ankles likewise bound. They explained to him he was now the Alahemwhey sword maker. The big man shouted and had to be gagged, but eventually, he subsided his struggling and admitted defeat. Just before they arrived back at the Alahemwhey village, they took Tureck to the river and dunked him, fully clothed in the river, washing away some of the last few days' travel stink. When some of the black grime washed off, he did not look half bad. He proved to be somewhat of a challenge due to his strong muscular upper body and stout legs from working the forge. Four men had to hold him tightly bound as he kept trying to escape. His unkempt auburn hair fell thickly about his shoulders and if it were not for the constant scowl he wore, he might be considered almost handsome or at least not ugly. Tureck was sly and had bronze-gold Solemeyha eyes, so similar to Soria's, that held a shrewd cunning glimmer. He attempted to fight and escape given the slightest opportunity but was never successful. He also tried bribing his way free but had no takers as his only value was in his skill.

They returned to the Alahemwhey village just as evening began to fall on the seventh day. They entered the quiet streets of the village, travel-worn and dusty from the road. Earlier in the day they had seen an Alahemwhey scout in the distance and knew that their arrival had been reported. None of them were surprised to see the streets empty of people as they headed straight for the large meeting hall in the center of the village. There they found everyone gathered waiting for the party's arrival.

Before reaching the meeting hall, each one of them, Ulrik, Bondur, and Hunter was lost in his thoughts of who they expected to find awaiting them upon their return. Hunter's horse danced with agitated excitement in response to his rider's anticipation. He pranced and tossed his blonde mane and Hunter did nothing to stop his liveliness. Bondur was silent as stone on the back of his black horse and his green eyes flashed everywhere watching, searching, and expecting. He gave sharp explicit orders to his men all who had been armed with stolen Solemeyha swords.

Ulrik looked on with grim determination making an immense effort to cloak his anticipation. His face rippled with emotion as he tried to hide the feelings of hope that another nightmare with the Alahemwhey would soon be over. The distant look in his eyes said his thoughts were on going home, but under that same deep blue gaze, wariness crouched ready for anything. He expected betrayal before this was all over.

They approached the large meeting hall and dismounted. Immediately, Bondur gave a quick sharp order to his men and they fell into two lines, one each flanking the party. Ulrik moved swiftly to Tureck's side as he dismounted awkwardly with his hands bound. Taking a firm hold on the rope around the man's neck, Ulrik drew his long dagger and held it against Tureck's throat. Ulrik nodded to Hunter and he drew his sword taking a stance in front of the prisoner. Bondur gave Ulrik a calculating look as if with an unspoken signal. He stepped forward to take the lead. As one, the company moved into the hall and the crowd of people parted to let them pass.

Moving forward through the villagers crowding the hall, Ulrik heard Bondur curse and then heard Hunter's swift intake of breath and growl of anger. Then he saw what garnered their attention. To the side of the hall next to the raised dais where Tahara lounged, were their wives and Archer. The four of them had been bound by the hands and hung by long ropes looped around the high rafters of the hall. Tessa and Soria did not look too bad although their clothes hung dirty on them as if they had not changed or bathed for days. Archer looked as if he had been badly beaten as his hair was caked with blood and the greenish-purple bruises on his face appeared to be about a week old. His blue eyes looked wild with pain as his gaze came to rest on Hunter. A small smile flickered across his split lip as he noticed Ulrik and his prisoner. Emmer was a different story.

Bondur's face smoldered red and his eyes sparked with fury as he stared at Emmer hanging by her wrists. She was pale, with deep circles under her closed eyes, and looked ill swaying on her feet. He could only spare her a glance realizing the more attention he spent on her the more vengeful it would make Tahara.

Emmer managed to turn her head, tried to open her eyes, and looked directly into his handsome face. Bondur raised his right hand bringing his company of men to a halt in front of the dais where Tahara waited.

A wicked defiant smile crossed Tahara's red lips and she licked her bottom lip as if hungry. Bondur's left hand gripped his sword hilt tightly, and he had to struggle not to draw his weapon.

"Aaahhh, my *Father* and the Captain of my guard have returned." Tahara purred with delight. "I see you have a prisoner with you! Is this truly the sword maker?"

She raised herself slightly to examine the prisoner with a greedy victorious gleam sparkling in her vibrant blue eyes. Beside her, sitting regally on their chairs the three Elders mumbled heatedly to each other, gesturing, and discussing excitedly.

Tension hung heavily in the air. Bondur stopped in front of the Red Mohem. Schooling his features, he spoke sharply, "Mohem, we have brought the sword maker." Fury gleaming from his green eyes he pointed at his wife

"Why?" He did not finish his sentence, but let it hang in the air, his meaning unmistakable.

Before Tahara could answer Ulrik stepped forward prodding his prisoner with his long knife.

"Release them all or I will slit the sword maker's throat, right here and now!" Ulrik yelled. Hunter stood sworn drawn, slowly inching his way closer to his brother and the women.

Tahara's eye narrowed at Ulrik and then her eyes traveled slowly to Hunter. She was clearly not pleased, and neither was she in any hurry to comply. With an arrogant tilt of her head, she ignored him and spoke to Bondur.

"This is truly the sword maker? I am greatly pleased with you, my Captain! You shall be rewarded. I will release my *other* prisoners as soon as I am satisfied that *all* my demands have been met."

Leaning a little closer, she beckoned to the sword maker, "Come closer and let me look at you."

Ulrik allowed Tureck a step nearer and stopped just in front of Tahara. He could feel Tureck's breathing quicken and noticed the man grew red in the face, his gaze riveted on the beautiful Red Mohem. His mouth hung open stunned by her beauty. Ulrik had to hold him up from going down on his knees in front of her.

Tahara gave him her most winning smile and leaning closer so that her breasts pushed against her fine gown half peeking out, she cooed at Tureck.

"Aaahhhhh, he is handsome and strong." She paused meaningfully, her eyes playing over him then darting at Bondur to gauge his reaction to her flattery. She continued, "You will make many swords for the Alahemwhey. You will be flooded with riches, have the finest lodgings, and as many women as you wish. What say you? Will you be sword maker for the Alahemwhey?"

Tureck opened his mouth to speak, but before he could utter more than a gurgle, Ulrik pushed the tip of his dagger into the man's flesh so that a slow trickle of blood ran down his neck.

"Release my family or I *will kill him*, right here, then you will be next Tahara. I am in no mood for your games. Release them or he dies, *now!*" Ulrik hissed through clenched teeth.

Waiving a hand lazily she purred, "They are merely my assurance that my orders have been carried out. Did you put the Solemeyha village to the torch as I ordered, so they will not come looking for the sword maker? I must know that there will be no retaliation before we can be armed and ready. If you have taken this man and the Solemeyha come, it will all be for nothing! If you have *not* done as ordered, I will kill you and your family." Her composure began to slip, and she grew angrier.

"Do you think you can get past my Red Guard with just two swords? Your women will be dead before the sword maker hits the ground." Pointing at Emmer she raised her voice to all the people in the hall trying to gain their attention. "She will die first. I do what I have to do to make the

Alahemwhey a great people! We must be stronger than any other tribe! That cannot be unless we have swords and metal and that cannot happen if the Solemeyha come and take him back, slaughtering us all in the night!" She turned to Bondur and yelled, "Did you put the village to the torch?"

Bondur stepped closer to her, his hand on his sword, and quietly spoke in Alahemwhey so that only Tahara and the Elders could hear, "Mohem, this is Tureck, the sword maker. He will make swords for you as one of the Alahemwhey or as your prisoner. I did not have enough soldiers to kill every man, woman, and child of the Solemeyha. The village was too large to burn. We took everything from his hut and forge and made it look as if he had moved away on his own. They will think he left to find his daughter. You can safely release Ulrik's family. I do not think the Solemeyha will have cause to think he has come here. We covered our tracks very well and there has been no sign of pursuit. The Solemeyha cannot know *we* took him. Now, my Mohem, release them. We have done as you commanded, the Alahemwhey are safe, and the sword maker will do *your* bidding."

Tahara turned and spoke to Tureck, "You will be the Alahemwhey sword maker and show us the sword magic? Live among us and do as I command, or I will *kill* your daughter."

Tureck looked at Soria and spoke to Tahara with reverence, "Oh, most beautiful Red Mohem. I am an honest man, and she is not my daughter! She was the daughter of my second wife and not of my blood. I let her cook and clean for me to earn the roof over her head. Kill her I do not care! You offer me very little in return for what power I can bring to your tribe."

The Elders all began to speak at once and the crowd mumbled. Tahara's face reddened upon learning that Soria was not his true daughter and she glared with deadly rage at Soria. The Elders appeared reasonably happy, Ulrik and

Bondur had returned with the sword maker and their solution to potential Solemeyha retaliation seemed reasonable. They quickly stood to pronounce that Ulrik and his family should be free to go.

Tahara's face blazed nearly as red as her hair. She stood abruptly and motioned for her Red Guard to surround Tessa, Emmer, Soria, and Archer. The Red Guards leveled their spears at them, ready to strike. The Elders began to argue, and she silenced them with a quick motion of her hand. Bondur spoke to the Red Guard and ordered them to stand down, then he motioned to his men and they began to close in drawing their stolen swords. Those guards who were Ulrik's other sons hesitated and were slow to react, but the Alahemwhey men were eager to fight. It was obvious there would be a battle between Bondur's Alahemwhey men and Tahara's Red Guard.

Tahara screamed in rage. "Bondur! You are Captain of the Alahemwhey! You do as *I* command. I say that my demands have not been met! The village was not burned, and they have put all the Alahemwhey in danger." She screamed pointing at Ulrik and his sons. "Ulrik and his family must die! *All* of his family, including that pathetic little creature you call your mate."

Bondur shouted and, raising his sword, leaped toward Tahara, who was instantly surrounded by more of her Red Guard. She looked momentarily shocked that Bondur would attack her, but she quickly regained her composure, her proud head coming up, eyelids lowering to disguise her hurt.

Ulrik likewise roared. He had not understood all of the argument as it was held in Alahemwhey. He had enough of this farce and yelled thrusting Tureck to his knees grabbing him by the hair and wrenching his head back to expose his neck.

"*HOLD!* I will cut his head off if anyone takes another step toward my family. Release them all now or he dies!"

Tahara momentarily hesitated. It was clear by the look on his face that Ulrik meant to do it. She looked for a long time into Bondur's eyes and then waved a hand for her Red Guard to lower their weapons and stand down. Everyone in the hall watched holding their breath, waiting to see which side would prevail. Tension in the room was high as each side waited for the other to concede, but neither did and they all remained tense and ready to fight.

Tessa watched with apprehension for her husband and children. Emmer swayed sick and pale on her feet barely able to stand, and Soria stood head held up-defiant. Archer twisted and pulled at the ropes binding his wrists and swore under his breath, aching to be free to fight.

"My blade grows impatient Tahara. Release my family!" Ulrik shouted.

Bondur sheathed his sword and turned. He shoved aside the spears and moved toward the women. He reached Tessa first and drawing his dagger, he swiftly cut her free, then he moved to Archer who was the next closest, and then Soria. As he moved to cut down Emmer Tahara yelled out to stop him.

"Cut her down and I will have my men slaughter them all. I do not care if Ulrik slays the sword maker! They must all die!" Tahara screamed!

Then a desperate, seductive smile crossed her lips as she smoothed the deep blue gown over her hips collecting her composure. She had the attention of everyone and looked hungrily at Bondur. An idea seemed to strike her and a look of triumph crossed her lovely features. Speaking in Alahemwhey so that Ulrik and his family could not understand she cried out in a sweet pleading voice, "Bondur, *My* Captain. I will set them all free, including that one," she said pointing at Emmer who had swooned and hung listless in her bonds. "I will free them all if you will set her aside and take the Ohhem with me. Stay by my side and they will all go free. Together, with the sword maker, *we* will rule over all! *We* will make the

Alahemwhey great! Be with *me* and they all go free or else they all die."

Silence and stillness hung in the stifling air of the hall. No one moved as they waited for Bondur's choice. As Tessa and the others had just been released, they quickly stumbled toward Ulrik and Hunter. Ulrik did not release his hold on the sword maker though. Soria, who had fled to Hunter's side, spoke to them quickly translating Tahara's words loud enough that Ulrik could hear. Ulrik's eye narrowed at Bondur as he stood contemplating what he would do.

Before Bondur could answer though Tureck yelled out, "Wait!" Wrenching one arm free of Ulrik's grasp and risking the sharp knife at his neck, he staggered to his feet stepping forward and bellowing out, "I know not what goes on here, but I am tired of this. I am a free man, and I will agree to stay with the Alahemwhey and teach the swordcraft, but I will not be anyone's prisoner."

Despite Ulrik's dagger at his throat he struggled to shove him away and took another step pulling Ulrik toward Tahara. "I will give you the sword magic and I will tell the Solemeyha that I left willingly to come here should they come to find me." He swallowed, visibly shaken, "Even among the Solemeyha we have heard of the great Red Mohem."

Distracted by his flattery, a look of curiosity painted Tahara's face and she gazed at the sword maker intrigued.

Tureck went on, "Free this man and his family and I will do as you want and make the swords, but my price is that you, oh fire-haired Mohem, you must take the Ohhem with *me* and be my mate! *I* will rule by your side or I will not help the Alahemwhey. You will give me the sons my first two wives could not, and I will make your warriors unstoppable with my swords! That is my price! Or I will let this white-haired giant take my life. I will not live as a slave!" He stepped back as Ulrik's captive and Ulrik replaced his knife at Tureck's throat.

While Tureck was speaking and everyone's attention was distracted, Bondur moved quickly and cut Emmer's bonds. She fell unconscious into his arms, and he picked her up cradling her close to his chest. In the time it took to free her, Tureck was done making his demands. Soria translated for Ulrik and his family.

When Tureck's speech was done, Tahara's eyes flew to Bondur and saw he had freed Emmer. She screamed in rage, but before she could issue any commands Ulrik released Tureck and leaped forward. He grabbed Tahara by the arm and wrenched her against him. Her scream of outrage was cut short as Ulrik's hand went around her throat cutting off her protests. His other hand pressed his knife against her ribs. Everyone in the room was on their feet yelling and gesturing wildly. Chaos filled the hall.

Chapter Twenty-six – Ulrik's Proclamation

"Quiet!" Ulrik roared above the din and the hall stilled all but for Bondur who carried the unconscious Emmer to where Tessa and the others stood within the safety ring of his blue guard. Tahara's angry eyes never left Bondur's face.

"I am Ulrik Wolfgarsson! I am a Viking warrior and by Odin! I will no longer be ordered around by this little girl!" Turning to Bondur, he narrowed his eyes and spoke directly to him, "Tell the Elders my words." Bondur gave a sharp nod and addressed the Elders who stood erect waiting for Ulrik to speak.

Ulrik ground his teeth and with a look of disgust on his face, spat the distasteful words out, "The Red Mohem made a bargain with me and you agreed. I was to train your warriors and bring the sword maker to the Alahemwhey. Then my family and I were all to go free. There were no other conditions at the time the bargain was made. I was told my family would be kept hale and whole while I was gone. I have returned to find my wife mistreated, my son beaten, and my daughter sick." Ulrik hesitated while Bondur finished translating. Then he tightened his grip on Tahara. She made a small choking sound but remained still.

Ulrik continued, "You Alahemwhey act without honor or reason, you are driven by greed and envy over what you do not have. You allow this spoiled little girl to rule you without questioning her wisdom and ability to rule. Now, I have kept my side of the bargain and we will leave." He held Bondur's eyes for a moment as he translated before continuing.

"The sword maker has made an offer for," here he faltered a little before spitting out words that felt distasteful in his mouth, "*my daughter* Tahara. As her *father,* I accept on her behalf! Tahara will take the Ohhem with Tureck and he will stay with the Alahemwhey as he has said." He spoke louder centering his stormy gaze on each of the Elders. "I have kept my side of the bargain! Do you agree? Or do I snap her neck right here and the bloodshed will begin?"

Tahara's eyes grew wide as she realized Ulrik had as much as given her to Tureck or he would kill her. She tried to struggle and protest, but Ulrik growled low in her ear. "You did call him handsome when you first met. I think you will be happy with this match. He will make the Alahemwhey great and you will give him sons. Sounds like a fair trade to me."

Tahara stopped struggling in his tight grip. Just then the Elders turned to deliberate and then spoke to Ulrik. Bondur translated as one of the Elders gave them their decision. Ulrik's *other* sons stirred and gathered together in a confused group, red and blue guard alike. They understood everything that was being said also many of them looked at Ulrik with admiration in their eyes.

"The Red Mohem commanded Ulrik and his family would go free if he trained our warriors and brought the sword maker. We, the Elders of the Alahemwhey, proclaim Ulrik has done as agreed and may now go free with all of his family. As Tahara's father, he can declare the match between the sword maker and the Red Mohem. We agree. This match will make the sword maker one of the Alahemwhey and his magic will make the Alahemwhey greater than any other people. As the Elders of the Alahemwhey, we make this proclamation, but she is still our Mohem. Release her now and you all go free."

Hunter moved toward Tureck and cut his bonds. Tureck stood taller, smoothing his clothes and grinning ear to ear, his glazed eyes beheld Tahara as he realized he had just been given the beautiful Red Mohem as his mate. Bondur turned and commanded his men who formed two lines around Ulrik's family. The Red Guard moved back, lowered their weapons and the crowd parted to let them go. All eyes turned toward Ulrik who still had a death grip on Tahara's neck.

Ulrik slightly tightened his grip on her neck and whispered in Tahara's ear, "You are a disgrace and no true leader of your people. You shame me more than any of the other Meadwhey children of the Alahemwhey. Now you will have the power of a mate over the sword maker. I suggest you use this marriage to make your people great. If you can."

Ulrik released Tahara none too gently and she fell back to the wide seat she sat on earlier. Then Ulrik strode away, following his family down the length of the long hall and out into the night.

Tahara, her hand at her throat, gasped for air. Humiliation, fear, and grief welled up inside her as she tried to speak. A tear threatened to fall from her eye as she raised a hand toward Bondur's retreating back.

"Bondur!" She rasped pleading, *"In-ohloo-my!"* reaching out for him as he left.

Bondur did not turn or acknowledge that he even heard her but kept walking out of the hall carrying Emmer tightly in his arms. The last thing any of them heard was one of the Elders crying out for the Ohhem women and ordering a celebration feast.

Bondur hurried from the hall, carrying the unconscious Emmer. His Blue Guard followed protectively surrounding Bondur, Ulrik, and his family. Emparo followed last to leave the hall, watching their backs. Bondur briefly turned to Tessa but kept walking while he spoke to her.

"What happened?"

"After you left Tahara had your men beaten and we were taken to a prison hut and treated very badly. Emmer grew ill with the lack of food and water. We gave her what care we could but there was not much we could do. I think I know what is wrong," Tessa smiled hopefully, "Food, water, and rest should quickly restore her."

Bondur led them to his hut, ordered his men to stand guard, and then went inside placing Emmer on the large bed.

Returning to the door he commanded food and water be brought to the hut and placed a heavy guard outside the door. Ulrik went to embrace Tessa. Hunter, who had gone to check over Archer and finding him in fairly good shape, turned to embrace Soria. She flung her arms around his neck and kissed him wildly.

After greeting their respective husbands and assuring them they were well, Tessa and Soria went to Emmer's side. Her eyes fluttered open and she looked around wildly, searching.

"Bondur," she whispered. A small, tired smile spread across her lips. He went to her side and took her hand.

"I am here." He spoke gently.

"Bondur, I think we are going to have a baby." She smiled up at him. "I have what mother calls morning sickness. I'm so happy to see you."

Bondur stared at her speechless, smiling widely, "Emmer little bird heart! You have made me the happiest man!" He bent over and kissed her on the lips. Then he turned to Tessa, "What does she need to get better?"

Tessa shook her head, "I think food, water, and rest will help immensely."

Bondur looked to where Ulrik sat with his sons talking quietly. Just then the food arrived. Bondur himself took food to Emmer, and Tessa and Soria helped her eat and drink. After so many days with very little to eat and now that Bondur had returned, she was looking better in no time.

Bondur crossed the hut taking food to Ulrik and his sons. He handed it to them and then sat down with them. "Ulrik, we must leave as soon as possible. I am convinced we are still not safe. We must leave before morning comes as soon as Emmer can travel."

"Agreed. We need horses and provisions. We will head east away from our home then double back as soon as we are satisfied that we are not followed and then backtrack to the mountains. Does anyone of the Alahemwhey know the location of our home in the mountains?"

"No," assured Bondur. "The Alahemwhey stay on the plains and do not go into the mountains."

Ulrik turned to Archer, "Can you ride."

Archer shrugged one shoulder and stated confidently, "Aye, I will."

"You stay here and guard the women. I must free my men Tahara imprisoned. I will get the horses and return as soon as I can." Bondur rose, turned, and quickly explained to Emmer what they needed to do. He took her in his arms and held her briefly, kissing her gently, and then he left.

Ulrik looked around the large hut. He saw a stack of weapons in the corner and retrieved arms for Archer and took a couple extra of the best ones. He gave Tessa and Soria light short swords from the pile. Tessa and Soria packed any clothes they could find which were mostly Bondur's it turned out. They gathered the comb and brush set Bondur had given Emmer their second night together, and the pack she brought from home. They prepared as much as they could, bundling blankets and furs from the bed and anything else they thought they might need for the long trip home. Then, they waited.

An hour trickled by, aggravatingly slow, and still, Bondur did not return. Off in the distance, they could faintly hear Tahara and Tureck's marriage celebration. Ulrik paced the floor cursing under his breath while Hunter stood taut and ready. Archer and the women ate and rested trying to gain strength for their flight into the night.

Suddenly, the door swung open and Bondur entered, he gestured for them to follow. Ulrik and the rest quickly grabbed what they could of the provisions they had packed, and the weapons, and left the hut. Bondur moved toward the bed. He kissed Emmer gently.

"Are you well enough to travel?"

"Yes, I'm feeling much better now you are here." She smiled bravely.

Wrapping a fur around Emmer's shoulders he easily lifted her into his arms, gave her another tender kiss on the lips, then carried her toward the door. Ulrik and Archer had mounted as did Tessa. Hunter mounted with Soria behind him. Emparo stood holding the reins of Bondur's black horse and the gold horse Bondur had given Emmer was tied behind. Placing Emmer in the saddle, he turned to Emparo.

"You are Captain of the Alahemwhey warriors now. Do not follow us. This is my last command to you, hold off Tahara for as long as you can. Do not follow us or I will have to kill you. We will never return to the Alahemwhey."

Emparo did not respond except with a tentative smile and to offer Bondur his hand and they grasped arms for a moment before Bondur vaulted up into the saddle behind Emmer. She leaned against his chest and sighed with contentment.

Emparo moved to Ulrik's horse and stood looking at him. "Father?" Emparo offered Ulrik his arm.

Ulrik stared at it for a long moment, the muscles in his jaw tensing, then he reached down and grasped Emparo's arm and looked into his face, so much like his own. Before he could turn his horse to go, Emparo grasped Ulrik's horse's reins, halting him, and spoke up.

"My mother, she was from the brother tribe to the Alahemwhey. She spoke of my making and how it was done. I am sorry you were so dishonored, but I would have you know she was not given a choice either. She had no other after you." He looked as if he had more to say but did not.

Ulrik looked at him for a long moment, mixed emotions warred in his eyes. He realized he had never given much thought to those girls who participated in the ceremony which was his great shame.

"Emparo, you are a good man," was all Ulrik could manage to say.

"We must go!" Bondur whispered hurriedly.

Bondur nudged his horse and they took off into the night. Luck was with them and a full moon illuminated their path. They headed east deeper into the grasslands and eventually turned south as they planned. There was no way to hide their trail completely, so they relied upon speed to put as much distance as possible between them and the Alahemwhey. With no way of telling whether or not they were going to be followed, they assumed the worst and escaped. After a few hours of travel, Bondur called a halt. Sliding off his tired horse, he swiftly lifted Emmer from the saddle he lent her the strength of his arm as she staggered a few steps. Pulling away, she heaved the contents of her stomach into the tall grasses.

Bondur strongly suggested they camp for the night so that Emmer could rest. The thick grasses grew so tall above their heads that they could press down the wide stalks and make comfortable enough grass beds to lie upon and even cut out semi-private spaces within the thick, towering grass. Bondur's love for Emmer was apparent as he swiftly prepared a bed of grasses and covered her with as many furs and blankets as they had to spare. The other women bedded down a short distance away giving them some privacy.

Bondur kissed Emmer and made her drink as much water as she could hold.

"I missed you." She whispered as she fell asleep.

Bondur stared at her for a long moment and smoothed away a white-gold lock of her hair from over her face before rising and going to stand guard.

A short while into his watch Ulrik approached him. "You should get some sleep you have not rested for a couple days now."

"Neither have you," Bondur said dispassionately, standing immobile only the wind wrestling through his long raven hair.

"Do you think they will follow?" Ulrik asked.

"I am not sure. Tahara is relentless in her desires. I am hoping the new mate you have given her this eve will keep her busy."

Ulrik peered at Bondur, his eyes piercing even in the moonlight. "Why do you do this? Why do you help us?"

Bondur checked himself and did not reveal his surprise at the question.

"Emmer is my mate. I protect her and our child."

"I understand, but you have given up everything and left your home. You could have protected her from the Alahemwhey and remained Captain. We live a spare and hard life in the mountains. We have one cabin that we will all have to share until we can build your own home. There are strange things you have never seen there, and the winters will be hard. You will have to hunt and live off the land, living every waking moment working for survival. Is this the life you chose?"

Bondur did not hesitate but took a step forward so that his green eyes bore into Ulrik's blue. Even in the dark Ulrik could see the conviction written on Bondur's face.

"Emmer is everything to me. I would die protecting her. Make no mistake, I go gladly just to be with her. It is all I want. My life with the Alahemwhey was empty until Emmer. I was Tahara's plaything. Until Emmer, I had no family. Now, I have what I truly want."

Ulrik stared at him for a long moment.

"You will do as I say. I am the head of this family and what I say stands. You are no longer Captain. As long as Emmer is happy, you are welcomed into our family."

Then without another word or glance, he turned and walked away into the night. Bondur turned his attention back to the watch and sighed with contentment, his thoughts on Emmer and the child they had made together. A slight, contented smile touched his lips as he stared out into the night.

Ulrik returned to the place where Tessa lay a little far off from the rest of their family. He could hear Archer snoring softly, and Soria and Hunter whispered together in the night. Soon they grew quiet too and Ulrik finally lay down next to his wife.

Tessa was awake watching for him. She reached her arms up to him invitingly. Ulrik did not hesitate but lowered himself next to her. Tessa clung to him whispering his name over and over flooding his face with kisses. Her voice caught as she told him how much she loved him and had worried about them and missed him. Ulrik was just as happy to see her. Exhausted, they quickly fell asleep, glad to have survived the Alahemwhey once again.

A couple of hours later in the grayness before dawn, he reluctantly rose to relieve Bondur from the watch.

Chapter Twenty-seven – Flight

After being released from the watch by Ulrik, Bondur picked his way slowly through the tall grasses back to where Emmer lay wrapped in blankets and furs. The tall grasses rose around her creating a private barrier and walling her in like a roofless grass room. The stars above twinkled over them. He removed his armor and shirt and eased himself down beside her, careful not to wake her. He closed his eyes and breathed in deeply. Just as he was about to drift off to sleep, Emmer's small hand reached out and clasped his, calmed that she was finally safe, and he immediately fell into an exhausted sleep. Too soon the morning came. Bondur and Emmer rose and joined the rest of the family.

Ulrik was already mounted and was watching intently back the way they had come the previous night.

"Our trail from last night is clear through these tall grasses."

Bondur considered for a few moments and then said, "Let us go toward a stream I know. The women can wash and eat while we backtrack making wrong trails. It will not slow them for long, but it might be enough to give us more time should they come. The wedding of the Red Mohem was a grand celebration and they are probably still drunk. I am almost convinced they will not follow if they have not caught up to us by now."

"Best to take measures to hide our trail. I am not convinced they have not followed." Ulrik stated flatly.

The party packed the horses and followed Bondur to a nearby stream. The women dismounted as did Hunter and Archer who were ordered to stand guard. Ulrik and Bondur led all the horses away creating false trails through the towering grasses.

Tessa, Soria, and Emmer took advantage of the cool water to wash up while Hunter and Archer stood watch. After their long imprisonment, it was greatly appreciated. They quickly finished up and stood quite refreshed and ready to resume their flight. As soon as Ulrik and Bondur returned, they mounted up and continued their circuitous way home winding through the tall grasses. They rode for a half-day more and then stopped for a quick meal and so that Emmer could rest.

The tall grasses had begun to thin and shorten and the ground grew rockier as they circled and made their way back toward the mountains. That is where the Red Guard caught up to them.

They were all Alahemwhey men and none of the *Others*. On horseback, they all were heavily armed and dangerous. All men of Tahara's Red Guard. Their orders could be detected easily as they were written clearly on their cruel faces as they rode forward to ambush them. As Ulrik's party drew toward the foothills of the mountains toward Ulrik and Tessa's home, the mounted men held in a line ready to move left or right and block their path.

Ulrik and his family drew to a stop a few hundred yards away. Bondur, with Emmer on the saddle before him, Hunter and Archer went to confer with Ulrik on how they should approach the situation.

"They have seen us," Ulrik spoke first and then swore under his breath.

"Yes," Bondur said staring off into the distance. "We could make a run for it, but they would come after us. It is clear Tahara is not going to let us go. I will go and talk to them. Perhaps I can convince them to let us pass."

"I will go as well." Ulrik said and then turned to his sons, "Hunter, you and Archer stay and guard the women. If it looks like things will go badly, take the women, and run. Emmer, can you mount your horse."

She nodded without hesitation.

"This is a…" began Archer.

"…bad plan. Let us go with you, if things go wrong, we will help cut them down if they don't let us go." Hunter spoke up.

"There are only ten of them." Archer finished shrugging.

"Bondur and I will go. You must be ready to take the women and escape if negotiations go badly. I will not risk the women again."

Ulrik spurred his horseback to Tessa and relayed the plan to her. After a brief argument, she reluctantly agreed. Ulrik looked for a long moment into her storm blue eyes and then turned his horse to return to Bondur.

Bondur had taken this time to move Emmer to her golden horse. He slid lithely to the ground and gently lifted her into her saddle. After a brief embrace during which she whispered to him, "I love you. Please be careful and come back unharmed."

Bondur stood for a brief moment memorizing her face then shook himself and gave her a confident grin.

"Keep her safe." He commanded Archer who nodded, his face turning grim.

Bondur turned and swiftly remounted. Archer turned his horse's head and Emmer reluctantly followed trotting back to the rest of the waiting women, Hunter followed close behind.

As Ulrik and Bondur approached the Red Guard, Ulrik spoke to Bondur. "Bondur, if it comes to a fight, we must kill them all. They cannot escape to return and give away our position to Tahara."

"As you wish. I hope it will not come to that as some of those men used to be my friends."

Approaching their enemies, Bondur held up empty hands while Ulrik meaningfully drew his sword. The Red Guard advanced in a line. Most of them were armed with stolen Solemeyha swords and all had the Alahemwhey deadly black spears. Bondur recognized the leader and approached him calling him by name.

"Mikan, you will let us pass." He spoke in Alahemwhey.

"We have orders to return you." Mikan spoke sullenly, "or we are to kill you and bring the bodies back."

Bondur translated for Ulrik who shifted his sword meaningfully but said nothing.

"Mikan, I have no wish to kill you. I was your Captain, I ask you, let us go in peace."

Mikan considered for a few moments, shifting in his saddle. He sneered turning to speak to his men.

"The deserter refuses to surrender." The Red Guards shifted in their saddles, angry looks crossing all of their faces, teeth bared, they drew their swords.

"Mikan!" Bondur spoke loudly. "Stand down!" He drew his sword and his horse pranced with anticipation.

"We are ten against two. You are no longer Captain you are a deserter and a traitor! You will die and I will personally take your golden-haired woman."

Bondur's face drew into a fury at the mention of Emmer. He had enough of negotiations and drove his heels into the horse's sides. They lunged forward. Ulrik was right next to him and he gave a great battle cry as they plunged toward the Red Guard. Bondur and Mikan clashed together swords ringing. After a few vicious swipes, Bondur's sword took Mikan in the side. He fell to the side, but before he could right himself on his horse, Bondur's sword cut through his neck. He fell. His head separated from his shoulders and he was dead before he hit the ground.

Ulrik had engaged two Alahemwhey warriors one to the right and one to the left of him. He quickly dispatched them both. He turned at the sound of thundering hooves to see another warrior galloping toward him with a spear raised to throw. Before it could leave his hand, an arrow struck him through the neck, and he tumbled from his saddle. Ulrik wheeled his horse to see that Archer had circled and was skillfully firing into the battle from horseback. He was swiftly gaining on them with Hunter on his heels brandishing his axe.

Ulrik cursed loudly at the approaching twins for disobeying, before clashing swords with another Alahemwhey which he swiftly killed.

Bondur had taken down two more and only three men remained. Two of them turned to face Hunter and Archer who had reached them by now and they engaged one man each. Quickly dispatching them after vicious swordplay, they turned to find Ulrik had finished the last.

As the last of the warriors fell, Soria, Tessa, and Emmer rode forward to join the men.

"BY ODIN! Does no one follow my orders!" Ulrik yelled at the women, his horse prancing beneath him.

"We came to help!" His twin sons answered in unison.

Emmer slid down from her horse and Bondur leaped from his. She flew into his arms and they stood embracing each other in a thankful reunion. Bondur, still holding Emmer's tiny form, turned his head toward Ulrik.

"We should put the bodies on the horses and send them home. The horses will return to their stables and it will be a final message to Tahara. They will never know where to find us."

Ulrik still red-faced with anger at being disobeyed saw the wisdom in this and leaped from his horse. Leading it over to Tessa, he handed her the reins, giving her a disapproving look, and then went to round up the dead guards' horses. Hunter and Archer did likewise, while Bondur helped Emmer mount her horse again and then went to help. They caught most of the loose horses and tied the bodies tightly to the saddles. They smacked the backsides of the Red Guard's mounts and the startled horses, spooked by the scent of blood and the dead weight of their riders, galloped off in the direction of the Alahemwhey village. Eventually, they would find their way home.

They were all about to remount when a lone rider slowly approached them from the woods. Although he held his hands up to show he was unarmed, Ulrik's hands flew to his sword hilt and Archer knocked an arrow in his bow as the rider came closer into view. It was Emparo approaching with a shy smile and a hopeful look in his eye.

Emparo kept his hands raised showing he was unarmed and wanted to talk. He approached Ulrik and slid from his horse. Ulrik sheathed his sword, crossed his arms over his large chest, and looked at him with a frown and wary eyes. The hard set of his mouth revealed his building anger, and a stubborn look crossed his face that indicated he was short of patience and tired of delays.

"Father," Emparo began carefully, going down to one knee in front of Ulrik, "I did not come with the Red Guard to kill you. I came because…" Emparo hesitated then looked down, "I came because I wish to go with *you*. I have left the Alahemwhey and I wish to be one of your true sons." He swallowed hard, but then looked up and bravely held Ulrik's gaze, "If you will have me."

Ulrik threw his hands up in frustration and swore vehemently in a stream of Old Norse no one could understand. Then he grabbed the reins of his horse and mounted swiftly.

"I am the head of this family. If you are to be one of us, I require your complete and unfailing loyalty. Are you willing to follow my orders without fail?"

"I am!" Emparo agreed quickly.

"Come along then if you will. No one will stop you!"

Satisfied with that, Emparo grinned widely and leaped back onto his horse. Finally, free from the Alahemwhey, the family headed toward their mountain home.

Chapter Twenty-eight – Archer's Story

Archer was overflowing with anger as he stomped through the woods. He swiped at branches in his way and kicked a stone in his path. He cursed the singing of the songbirds and even growled at the sun warming his back. He was that angry.

During the two years, since their escape from the Alahemwhey village, many changes had transpired. Upon their return, they immediately set to work building a house for Bondur and Emmer. Not long after their return, Emmer gave birth to Bowen. He was a strapping baby boy crowned with a head full of dark wavy curls and he had a strong set of lungs. Bondur was such a proud father he was almost unbearable to be around. Bowen had recently learned to walk, was constantly underfoot and he carried a tiny wooden sword around as if it was part of his arm. Ulrik had carved it for him and it was a delight to see the tiny boy swing at anything that got in his way. Now, Emmer was pregnant again.

Shortly after Bowen was born, Soria gave birth to a baby girl whom they named Azure because of her striking blue eyes. Archer had to admit to himself that the sweet, red-gold-haired baby girl was even-tempered and easy to be around. Work on a house for Hunter and Soria was underway. It was hard work, and the days were long. Archer congratulated himself on escaping early this morning on the pretense of hunting for food which was always a priority with so many mouths to feed.

Even Tessa, to the surprise of everyone, had just recently brought another daughter into the world. Archer's anger softened a little more as he pictured Luna's chubby pink cheeks, fuzzy white head, and the way she gave him a toothless smile when Archer held her. Still, with all these babies around it was hard to get any peace. There was always a crying child needing attention. Sometimes Archer had to escape to sleep up the mountain to avoid babies crying for a midnight feeding and waking everyone within a two-mile radius with their cries.

Archer knew he was being unreasonable and moody. He loved his new sister and his nephew and niece, but he surprised himself by longing for children of his own. That longing brought to mind the newest insult to injury that was so difficult to accept, forced him out that day and was the reason for his angry stomping. Six months past Emparo had disappeared. It was eventually revealed he had left with Ulrik's permission!

Emparo had been a surprisingly good fellow to have around. He was a relentless laborer, working hard on the new houses and contributing in every way. Archer found out Emparo had left to go to the Solemeyha village where, at some point when he was with the Alahemwhey, he had been secretly courting a young Solemeyhian girl. He returned a few weeks later with the shy little thing in tow. Genoa had a head full of dark auburn hair like Soria's, big brown eyes, large breasts, and a tiny waist over curving hips. The worst part was that Emparo had not taken Archer so that *he* could find a wife. Now, despite Archer's continual requests, Emparo refused to take Archer to the Solemeyha to find a wife. No matter how many times he pleaded and even demanded he show Archer the way to the Solemeyha village, Emparo refused to go against Ulrik's wishes. Ulrik flew into a rage the one time Archer even broached the subject.

Tessa wisely argued that kidnapping a wife, who would not know him and had never seen him before, was not a good plan for a happy marriage, and would ultimately bring the Solemeyha down upon them. She told Archer he would just have to be happy as a bachelor because they were not going through *that* again.

As Archer stomped through the woods, he recalled the nights he had spent in the Alahemwhey village. There he had enjoyed a different Alahemwhey woman practically every night. At the time he had no wish to commit to any one of the women. It was constantly on his mind now. Although he could not remember any of their names or faces, he remembered their soft, warm bodies and how it felt to take his pleasure with them. At night, his dreams were haunted by soft breasts, shapely hips, and hungry mouths. He awoke each morning hard and aching, unable to find release.

Adding to the list of the things that had made him most angry today, an hour past, he had unwittingly stumbled upon Hunter and Soria. They were laying naked in a meadow going at each other with passionate fervor. Azure lay next to them peacefully sleeping on a blanket in the shade with her thumb in her mouth. They were trying for a son. Archer had quickly and quietly backtracked to get away from the amorous pair. The sight of Soria's shapely tanned legs wrapped around his twin's naked backside had pushed Archer over the edge. He gave up his idea to hunt and now stormed toward the sacred lake to take a plunge in the crisp, cold waters and ease his hot temper. Hopefully, it would also cool his aching groin. Everywhere Archer turned his relatives were having sex and babies, and the happy couples painfully reminded him of his forced bachelorhood. Archer had seen too many full breasts suckling babies and he had enough. He wanted to escape it all even if it were just for the day.

Archer followed the path through the woods on the way to the lake, his customary arrow notched ready on his bow. His watchful eyes searched the lush forest for game and something, anything, to *kill*. As he neared the lake, he heard a strange noise. Along with the soft trickle of the nearby stream and the roaring of the waterfall, the soft delicate sound of a woman singing reached his ears. He slowed, stalking carefully forward, trying not to alert whoever it was, of his presence.

Archer inched forward mentally counting the women of his family and their whereabouts. He knew he had left his mother and sister at the big house. He knew where Soria was with Hunter so it could not be her. Emparo and his wife were together working on the beginnings of their future home, so all the women of his family were accounted for.

Archer's mouth went dry, his anger fell from him like rain from a cloud, and his heart began to race. Who could be singing beside the lake? He slung his bow onto his back, quietly placed the arrow back within the quiver, and crept forward through the bushes toward the beautiful voice. He covertly parted the lush greenery and stared toward the huge rock that protruded into the lake, offering a nice sunning spot.

There sitting peacefully in the sun singing, combing her fingers through her long curly tresses, was a beautiful, red-haired girl. Seeing the red hair, Archer was startled at first thinking somehow Tahara had found their sacred mountain lake. This girl, however, had deep rich red hair that hung in wet ringlets down her back. It was nothing like the bright brassy red locks crowning Tahara's head and was slightly more similar to Soria's auburn coloring.

The girl sang in an accent he did not recognize, and the tune was one Archer had never heard. As her song finished, she cocked her head to the side listening and spoke fearlessly into the sunny day.

"You can come out now, I know someone is there."

Archer, who was known for his stealth, wondered how she had heard him. He stood up and pushed his way out of the bushes. He slowly walked toward the rock where the girl sat drying in the sun. Before he could say anything, she spoke with awe.

"Are you a Fairy Prince?" She turned large, piercing green eyes on Archer, and stared at him brazenly, looking his tall form up and down. A wicked smile grew on her lovely full, red lips.

"A what?" Archer's brow furrowed, and he rubbed at the pale stubble on his chin. "Who are you?"

"Who am I? I am Alana Kathryn McMahon. Did *you* bring me here to your fairy realm?" She almost purred as she looked him up and down.

Archer's slow, crooked smile spread across his lips and he chuckled to himself. He suspected what had happened, but he enjoyed the sound of the girl's sweet voice and sing-song accent, so he decided to play dumb. Blue eyes sparkling with mischief, he spoke slowly.

"Well, Alana Kathryn McMahon. Why don't you start at the beginning and tell me where you came from and what you are talking about?"

He sat down on the rock next to her, furtively looking her up and down, his eyes coming to rest on her mouth. Leaning toward her he took a deep breath and smelled the faint scent of heather.

It was clear that she had come from the lake as the soft cream-colored chemise she wore hugged her rounded breasts. She was all over partially wet, slowly drying in the sun. Archer's mouth almost watered as he stared at the beautiful girl. She had removed her blue and yellow plaid bodice and skirts and spread them on the rock behind her to dry. Long shapely legs stretched out from under the cream undergarment, and her dainty feet were bare.

Archer smiled at the freckles that dotted the girl's shoulders, legs, and arms. She even had a dusting of freckles across her small perfectly shaped nose. Her chin came up and her eyebrow rose knowingly as she felt Archer's hungry perusal of her body. She smiled slowly feeling a sense of power rise from the eager look he was giving her.

"I was," she started again bringing Archer's eyes back to her heart-shaped face, "walkin through the woods of my home near Monaghan County. I'd just managed to get a peaceful moment for myself, away from all the work takin care of my sister."

She paused to take a deep breath and calm herself. Then began again, "As I walked along, I felt a great tearing in my chest like someone stabbed me right in the heart with a sharp knife and when I crumbled to the ground, I fell into a fairy ring."

"What's a fairy ring?" Archer interrupted, fascinated by the girl and her story. He reached forward and grabbed a lock of her red hair, twirled the curl with his fingers all the while holding her gaze with his.

"Why doesn't cha know being a fairy yourself? Although, you look more like an elf you're so big and tall. Do ya have pointed ears?" Her voice hushed and took on a dramatic tone. "A fairy ring is a ring of mushrooms that marks a gateway into the fairy realm. My Ma always warned us not to play around a fairy ring or we'd be whisked away to a far-off land and a fairy prince might keep us in his castle forever." Alana stopped and laughed a musical sound, and then she continued her tale. Archer watched her every move, fascinated.

"What is your name, my Fairy Prince?" Alana asked turning back toward him.

"Archer Ulriksson," he smiled grandly back at her, leaning so close he could feel the sun's warmth emanating from her attractive body.

Alana turned sparkling light green eyes on Archer, and they stared at each other for a long moment. Archer broke the silence wanting to hear her sweet voice again.

"Well Alana Kathryn, did you leave anyone behind? A husband? Children?"

Alana's smile fell from her face and her eyes grew hard.

"No, Prince Archer. I did not leave anyone behind. Just my sister, who never had a kind word for anyone. I helped care for her four brats till they were all grown. I worked my hands to the bare bones, gave up my chance for a family to help her when her husband deserted her and left them all ta' starve! I never had a husband or a family of my own."

Her voice fell to a sad whisper and she dropped her eyes to her hands in her lap.

"I'm sorry Alana. And I'm not a Prince." He said gently, again reaching to smooth back a lock of her hair.

"Would you like a second chance?"

Alana looked up quickly, alert green eyes sparkling with hope.

"A second chance? At what, a new life? Is it possible? Here in the Fairy Realm?"

She held his gaze intently and then smiled shyly. He just grinned back at her.

"I wouldn't want to go back. Yes, I think I'd like that very much, Prince Archer." She smiled radiantly.

For Alana it was simple, she had fallen into the Land of Fairy and was rescued by a handsome Fairy Prince. Just like in the romantic tales she had grown up with. She smiled wider at the realization of it all and her eyes twinkled with laughter. Archer noticed she had dimples and he had to shake himself back from where his mind began to wander which was somewhere beneath her shift. He reached up and gently touched her cool cheek. She half-closed her eyes and leaned into his warm hand.

"Well, up then and get dressed. I'll take you to my mother and father and they can explain it all to you as best they can." Archer rose to his feet and offered her his hand.

Without hesitation, she reached up and took it, her small cool fingers wrapped around his large warm hand. He helped her up and then back into her skirts. She finished dressing, slipped on a pair of stockings and worn slippers, and turned to him, eyes expectant and enthusiastic.

Archer laughed inwardly because he really just wanted to get her *out* of her clothes, but surprisingly, despite his earlier protestations to himself. He was willing to be patient. His eyes had roamed over her willowy body as she dressed. She was almost as tall as he was, coming up to his nose. Her rich red hair was turning into a riot of springy curls as it dried in the sun. The freckles on her face, neck, and creamy white shoulders, begged to be connected by tracing his tongue along them. He inwardly vowed he would do that *and soon.* It was her eyes that drew him the most. They held a hunger when she looked at him, as they stood together for a long moment, blue eyes gazing into green.

"I'm afraid there's no going back Alana. I wouldn't even know how to send you back even if you wanted to go." Archer said expecting her chagrin or fear.

"Archer, I don't wish to go back." She said very clearly stepping a bit closer, brazenness crossing her pretty face.

He had to pull his mind back from his revelry and his wandering eyes from resting on the swell of her creamy white breasts dusted in freckles. He intertwined his fingers with hers and gently pulled her even closer.

"Come then. I'll take you to meet my family." His voice was deep and husky with desire. Archer grinned widely, giving her his most winning smile, and turned to lead the way.

Alana began to follow but pulled him up short and stepped back very close to him, her presence caressing his senses.

"Will you take me to your fairy castle and make love to me forever then?" Alana asked, a mischievous lilt in her sing-song accented voice.

Archer looked at her, hesitating before answering. He was aching with desire and overjoyed at the sudden turn the conversation had taken. He had been inwardly asking himself how long he would have to wait to lay with her.

"Aye," he closed the hairs-breadth distance between them, pulling her close his chest touched her breasts, and his voice grew husky and low. Sneaking an arm around her waist he said, "I'll make love to you and often." Bending forward he stole a kiss, "but first I'll have to explain you to my father!"

Archer tilted his head back and laughed loud and long. The sound echoed out over the Sacred Lake and disappeared into the sunlit sky.

Epilogue

Ulrik and Tessa sat at the top of the mountain in their favorite spot, watching the sun setting as they usually did many a spring and summer night. Down the mountain in the big house, Emmer was watching Luna their newest daughter and they had a rare moment to sit in peaceful companionship. The fading sun painted their faces with a warm golden glow as it slowly set behind the distant mountains. A gentle breeze caressed the treetops, and a bird twilled its end-of-the-day song.

Ulrik and Tessa discussed the newest addition to their family.

"I'm very happy and relieved for Archer, finding Alana like that."

Tessa sighed and rested her head back on Ulrik's shoulder. He wrapped his arms around her as she continued. "It amazes me that Dr. Tennbaum's time and dimension machine still seems to be working. The lake once again provided."

"Yes, I am glad he has someone *finally*. Now I do not have to worry about him running away to the Solemeyha to steal a wife and bring us more trouble."

Ulrik grumbled but with a slight smile on his face. He turned his head and nuzzled Tessa's sweet-smelling hair.

"Alana is a sweet girl. You know she was only fifty when she died. She had an empty, lonely life, very much like my previous life. I am so glad Archer will bring her the happiness she missed before."

It was still odd to be speaking of things like time and dimension travel and going from old to young as if it were commonplace. She doubted she would ever get used to the idea.

Ulrik contemplated silently while he stroked her arm with one large hand, the other hand he slipped down the front of

Tessa's dress and caressed her soft breast. He was too distracted to do more than mumble an answer.

"I think soon we'll have another baby gracing our lives the way they constantly go at each other!" Tessa laughed as she arched into his hand. "You know I caught them making love against the barn?"

"And in the cellar," Ulrik placed a kiss on her temple, "and at the lake," he kissed her cheek, "and one time bent over the kitchen table when they thought no one was around."

He kissed his way down to her neck.

"I do not think there is any place he has not mounted the girl. I cannot get a good day's work out of him anymore."

Ulrik continued kissing Tessa and massaging her breasts. Tessa laughed again and Ulrik chuckled. She turned into him.

"Just like we used to be. Archer is lusty like his father once was."

Ulrik stopped his kissing suddenly and looked up, "Was?"

He smiled mischievously and reached up to further untie the laces of her dress. Ulrik made love to Tessa on top of the mountain as the sun slowly set. In perfect unison, their passion joined them completely and thoroughly once again. Afterward, Ulrik collapsed next to Tessa breathing hard. He pulled her into his embrace.

"By Odin! That just gets better and better."

"Yes!" Tessa laughed trying to catch her breath.

As the sun continued its slow descent behind the horizon, Tessa's head rested upon Ulrik's shoulder and her hand caressed his handsome face. She had come far from the lonely twentieth-century, eighty-five-year-old woman she had been. Life was finally fulfilling because of Ulrik. Smiling broadly, she leaned over, kissed him, and whispered.

"Just wait, the second time will be even better...*My Ulrik!*"

The End

Dear Reader:

Thank you for reading *ULRIK*. I sincerely hope you enjoyed reading it as much as I have writing it.

If you liked what you've read, please remember to leave me a review. As an independent author, your support and reviews allow me to publish more books and inspires me to keep writing!

For other books I've written, please check out my Kingdom of Jior epic fantasy series:

Of Demon Kind - Book One
Redemption of the Fallen - Book Two
Heirs of Jior - Book Three
Iron and the Arrow - Book Four
The Last Ny-Failen – Book Five

I also have another stand-alone historical romance you will enjoy. A Cut Twice as Deep is a Viking tale of two sisters.

You can find out more about me and all of my books at:

https://www.wendylanderson.com

Very Sincerely,

Wendy L. Anderson

www.ingramcontent.com/pod-product-compliance
Lightning Source LLC
Chambersburg PA
CBHW060529260626
47161CB00003B/820